'Melissa Jones's subject – the collapse of an outwardly successful family after the death of a baby – is compelling, and her writing is clear and intense. Her characters tell the story in their own words, through diaries and letters, and are each convincing and complex ... The pace becomes tense and claustrophobic, like a thriller, as the truth behind [the death] rises to the surface ... You put the novel down feeling thoroughly chilled, and aware of a strong new author' *The Times*

'A chilling and sinister first novel of psychological suspense ... taut, dramatic writing'

'A stark account of a dys
come to terms with the dea
charts the collapse of the f
as they try to deal with the
style used allows Jones to show off her characters in all their complexity ... as the story races to its chilling and unexpected conclusion' *Stirling Observer*

'A bleak, near-brilliant first novel ... the work here is meticulous: bleakness is embraced and transmuted into drama by a writer at the top of her craft' *Kirkus*

'A dark and compelling tale of disintegrating family life. In one sense a story of love triumphant ... in another, of evil and revenge' Frances Fyfield

Melissa Jones was born in London and educated at Westminster and Oxford. She worked in film and television before writing her first novel, *Cold in Earth*, which she is now adapting for the BBC.

By the same author

Sick at Heart

Melissa Jones

COLD IN EARTH

ORION

An Orion Paperback
First published in Great Britain by Orion in 1998
This paperback edition published in 1999 by
Orion Books Ltd,
Orion House, 5 Upper St Martin's Lane
London WC2H 9EA

A CIP catalogue record for this book
is available from the British Library

ISBN 0 75282 604 2

Typeset by Deltatype Ltd, Birkenhead, Merseyside
Printed and bound in Great Britain by
Clays Ltd, St Ives plc

Grateful acknowledgement is made for permission
to quote from the following:
The Four Quartets by T.S. Eliot, © Faber & Faber Ltd;
'They Can't Take That Away From Me',
music and lyrics by George and Ira Gershwin
© 1937 Chappell & Co. Inc., USA
Warner Chappell Music Ltd, London
Reproduced by permission of IMP Ltd.

For N. A. S.

Cold in the earth and the deep snow piled above thee!
Far, far removed, cold in the dreary grave!
... No other sun has lightened up my heaven
No other Star has ever shone for me:
All my life's bliss from thy dear life was given –
All my life's bliss is in the grave with thee.

Emily Brontë

Zoë's Diary

April 16th

My baby – Beth – has just died. Well – that's not quite true. It only feels true. It feels as if it's been one long day since she died – which was Friday, about lunch time I think, and now it's Tuesday. I've been told to write – to keep a diary, because I can't speak to anyone. That is not on purpose, not a punishment or anything, there's just been nothing to say – not since the first shock of finding her lying there not breathing. I'm meant to be writing it all down properly, but it's hard, confusing, like ploughing stony ground. The priest was very upset because she wasn't christened – my husband's Catholic – maybe that was why I thought of that silly analogy. I haven't been reading the bible or anything like that.

I'm at my desk, in my study. I love the desk, it was my grandmother's – ugly old-fashioned mahogany with bow legs. I've got an ancient yellow silk lamp on it too, nothing like what Michael wants to design for me. I'm looking through the bay window at the garden, three tall poplars at the end. The grass is very green, it's a sunny afternoon. I think it's about three o'clock. This room is only sunny in the morning – the front of the house gets the afternoon light.

The papers on the desk are the same, they are all in the same position as they were before. I have sat here every day looking at the garden, but I haven't opened anything or moved anything, and now I'm writing steadily, meaninglessly.

I always thought that cot death was a Nineties' euphemism for neglect or if the mother had killed her baby – quietly suffocating her, and no one could prove anything and then everyone was sorry for the mother. Mothers like that always seem to be older – thankful to have conceived – or young and stupid and poor. I'm forty-six and I'm not poor and Beth was a mistake. I called her Elizabeth because it is a regal, grand and superior name – I've always admired Elizabeth I – and it's also commonplace, English. She could be Lizzie or Eliza and also Beth which I like because it is so simple. Mariana is her second name, just in case she'd turned out to be a romantic, like her father. It was all worked out because we knew what sex she was going to be – just as we knew with the boys – it's easier and you can get organised in advance. With my job you need to be organised – the household has to click along without me – so I don't worry when I'm not there. Even though Michael's very good, I still feel it's me who organises it and him who carries it out. And it's all worked out so well, everything has always worked out so well. Why am I talking like this? As if I'm giving an interview? It's so stupid.

I can hear noises in the hall – the bell ringing and footsteps and voices. Michael is probably opening the door to another bouquet of flowers, the card will have words like tragic news and heartfelt sympathy. There are flowers everywhere, all the vases are full and they're in buckets and saucepans in the

2

conservatory. I won't have any of them in here. My mother wants to come and stay and cook meals – forgetting that Michael's been cooking for us for fourteen years. He's a creature of habit and clinging to his routine, looking after the boys, being here. I sit with them all at mealtimes and try to eat a little, and for the rest of the time he leaves me by myself. I don't think he wants to, but there's no comfort to be found. I don't want to look into his eyes. Eyes are the windows of the soul. (One of the curses of a public-school education is that you can summon quotes for every occasion.)

They've cancelled this week's taping of the show – which isn't disastrous – but I'm determined to go back next week. The line-up is excellent – it's the beginning of the season now and it would be the end of my career if I were to stop. It's unthinkable. If her birth wasn't going to disrupt my life I won't let her death do it. I can't believe I just wrote such a callous thing about little Beth. I suppose that's what makes me a survivor. Beth rhymes with Death. I've given birth to death. Like Sin in Milton – she gives birth to Death. It's much more glamorously vile though, that poem, than this death, as if Milton knew Spielberg would one day want to make a movie out of *Paradise Lost*.

She was such a good little thing, with her tiny pink ears, mewing like a kitten. She smiled a lot. (She was too new to smile properly – it was just wind – but at least I'll have some memory of what her smile might have been like.) She was very sweet-natured. I liked her more than the boys when they were babies – I found it harder to tear myself away from her when I had to go to meetings. I thought about her more than about anything else. And then she died – I don't think she was sickly, she didn't refuse to live or anything, she was overtaken by death, overwhelmed by it, surprised by it – I know that. She was so healthy. But I won't write any more about that.

The doctor came and saw me and gave me a prescription for Prozac and sleeping pills. I didn't like seeing her because she was there all the way through my pregnancy and we used to laugh together. She's quite a fan of the programme too. She knew I wouldn't use the prescription – I'm sleeping a little. Enough, anyway. I don't see why the death of my daughter should be annihilated by prescription. It would be wrong. My silence frightens them. If they're to allow me back to work, I must speak. I must talk to them. And I must try to write about her death.

Wednesday, April 17th

Last night while we were undressing Michael started talking to me about the funeral. I think it such a ridiculous idea that I couldn't believe he could seriously want to discuss it with me. How could anyone make a ceremony out of the death of a baby girl? He said what else could we do – bury her in the back garden like a pet? I said, couldn't they just take her away like they do the waste from operations. He didn't lose his temper with me but I knew he was angry. He tried to put his arms around me but before he could get very far one of the boys called for him so he went.

I'd always wanted a big bathroom so we used the spare room behind our bedroom on the first floor – you can go into it from our room through double doors and then out through the nursery at the back of the house into the children's room.

4

Their bedroom and playroom are connected by a small bathroom, so if you like, you can go round the first floor in a circle. There's a window seat on the landing at the front. At the back of the landing is the nursery, the baby's room. I think I said that. It's very light – the landing, and I always imagine myself sitting and reading in the window seat, but of course I never do. People would be able to see me, and it would be silly. But I keep a vase there, full of flowers. Upstairs, it's more attic-y, with the nanny's quarters and laundry, an empty room called Michael's study, and above these, a loft. Downstairs it's very big. To the right of the front door, our sitting room, which runs the depth of the house, leading onto a conservatory; to the left the small sitting room with the television in it, leading into the kitchen, and behind that my study. The kitchen is a bit squashed, the people before used my study for the kitchen – the heart of the house. But I knew it was perfect for my office. Twice a week – through my maternity leave – a girl called Sophie comes and does some secretarial work for me – but I'm good at that on my own. I've described our house and its inhabitants, I don't know why. It sounds like a suburban housewife's dream – it is. But I have two lives, and somehow the office and the studio have always seemed more real than this big sunny house. Michael's made it work really, designing the lighting, battling me to get rid of my chintzes and heirlooms. He calls our hybrid 'soft modern'. I think my bit's the soft, which is deceptive. He's the one who is kind and good. There's also Seymour the tabby cat. He's my cat, but he tolerates the children.

Anyway, Michael went to the boys' room and I pretended to be asleep when he came back. At breakfast I told him they could have a funeral, but not to expect me to be there. No one said anything. On Monday, while they're at the funeral, I'm going to call the office and say I'll be back on Wednesday, which will be quite neat, only twelve days after her death. Now I'm going to write about finding her.

Monday, April 22nd

The weekend has been difficult because I've had to try and start talking, and not just sitting in here all day. I find faces a blur, and I can't concentrate on them enough to bring them into focus, so I find myself talking to people while looking at a point somewhere over their shoulders – like we do at work sometimes to match camera angles or when we're trying not to get the giggles. Michael is very steady about it. He 'shows his love' – as my American counterparts would say – by not questioning, going about his business in his usual measured way. I don't know if he's afraid to confront me – I'm not sure. Paul is the hardest – he's the eldest – just fourteen. He has my dark blue eyes, and a similar small-featured face, but there the resemblance ends – I'm said to have a searching look, direct (it's how I get results); his is inquiring too, but so pained, so ever balanced on his own precarious knife-edge. I think his sensitivity is meant to make me feel protective and maternal, but instead he's always irritated me. I love him, but he's always irritated me. He knows that, so he rarely asks me for anything out loud – but it's inside him, his need for me, and he watches me when he thinks I don't know. That was before – now I'm afraid of him, and even more unwilling. I know he's suffering – I know he wants me to put my arms around him, but I couldn't. I've never liked hugging and cuddling. I avoid him now more than ever. I know he feels responsible because he and Andrew were up in their part of the house – I can't remember why – at the time she must have started struggling for breath. They were only a few feet away. I was downstairs working.

They're at the funeral now. The reception is going to be here – I can hear the caterers bustling about – subdued. There will be champagne. I love champagne but I really think it wholly inappropriate.

Seymour has just pushed the door open and is coming in with his tail aloft like a banner. He's ignoring me. He will come to watch by the window soon – it's about his time – morning and still sunny. Sometimes he licks himself in the squares of sunlight on the carpet, and sneezes at the dust you can see in the air. The carpet is green.

I'm in my smart clothes and I've done my face. I wish I could remember why Paul and Andrew were upstairs in their room before lunch – I can't. I knew she'd be waking up and wanting her bottle. (I'm not of the opinion that breast is best – when you have a month's maternity leave and have to appear in the nation's living rooms looking smart so immediately afterwards – large inflated breasts are not the answer. And I didn't want that pull breast-feeding gives you. I'd had that with Paul.) I thought I'd go and check on her before Nanny (Beth's nanny was my nanny too – just here for the birth – she's old now). Her radio sound thing's wired into the kitchen so as not to disturb me in my study, but I guessed Beth would have started snuffling. It was my last week before going back to work, so I was busy, but I wanted to go and pick her up just the same. She was such a dear little thing – and smelled better than any baby I'm ever likely to smell. I went into the kitchen, Nanny was there. No sounds from Beth. I went upstairs and across the landing – the door to the nursery straight ahead of me and usually ajar was nearly closed. Not quite but almost. That didn't alarm me. I was thinking she would need changing. Her cot is right in the middle of the room – like a small throne – the rest of the battered white-painted baby furniture hugging the walls. I'd had the room repainted – yellow – for her arrival. I went past her – sleeping – to the window to pull up the blind and let the sun into the room. I didn't notice anything peculiar about the silence surrounding us. I went back to the cot. She was lying on her back (in our day we were on our fronts, but that's been proven to be dangerous). Her eyes were open, sightlessly staring. Her skin was a horrible colour. I knew she was dead and I started screaming, which is very uncharacteristic as I'm usually controlled. I could hear Nanny come running, and the door to the boys' room opening, Paul standing there, round-eyed, Andrew beside him. I shooed them away, flapping at them with my hands and closing the door on them. Nanny came in as I crossed back to the cot. We both stood and stared down at her. I wanted to pick her up but couldn't bear to. Nanny asked me if it was all right if she closed her eyes. I said yes – she did – and then she led me out of the room. I was shuddering and she put me in the kitchen and gave me a brandy while she called 999. The boys were still upstairs. I did not forget about them but I couldn't move. After a few moments Nanny went upstairs to fetch them. Michael came back about that time (he'd been to the dentist). We all waited for the ambulance in the kitchen. I remember thinking about how much I'd been looking forward to teaching her to ride. If she'd been as fearless as I was she would have loved it.

She was only a month old when she died – an utterly

blameless, entirely worthless existence. Her birth was easy and her time with us peaceful (apart from her short suffocating death) which is why we suffer all the more. I wanted a girl – if I had to be pregnant again, I wished for a girl. Perhaps if I'd wished for more than that – if I'd acknowledged her preciousness, she would not have died. As it is, I think I feel more for little rose-and-white Beth than I ever have for any living thing in my life.

Seymour has rolled over on to his back and is stretching himself to be as long as he can, turning his head to look at me and make sure that I'm amazed. I feel entirely alone. (Except of course for the photographers camped outside in the road.)

Wednesday, 24th

It's very late – past one, I think. Today was my first day back at work and I was almost too exhausted to eat dinner – but once I'd got to bed I found I was lying there on my back with staring eyes – rather like Beth must have done actually – and it was unendurable. So here I am in nightdress and sweat pants (I can't bear dressing gowns) and socks – it's a very cold April. I've got a large glass of whisky. The velvet curtains are drawn, and I've put all the lights on in here. I feel acutely awake, as if I could run a race or clean out all the cupboards. I don't want to wake Michael though, I think he'd be justified in deciding I'd gone mad if he saw me running around the garden in the dark. I will write about today instead, my homecoming – out of which I had expected so much. I feel guilty because I'd hoped it would stop the utter meaninglessness of everything and its hold over me. And why should I deserve that?

It was a big day. In the morning I went to my office in town – extra early – and in a taxi (apparently there are still journalists). No one was in yet – I had the whole floor to myself for two hours. My office is rather conventionally the corner office at the end of a corridor along which smaller offices (floor-to-ceiling glass) are lined. Because I'm lucky enough to executive produce and present the programme we make (as well as having editorial control over others we develop and produce) all my days are too busy ever to think about anything else. But I'm not God. There is my co-producer, Jeffrey – he knows his stuff – and the associate producer and line producer, and then the whole pyramid which comprises any production. And there are the channel's commissioning editors – with whom everything must be agreed and who specialise in whimsy and slow decisions. But enough of that. I've got a big desk, leather chair, glass table for meetings, awards and photographs on the walls – it's very clichéd. I like it though. I really do. We're accused of modelling ourselves on the US in both the show's format and the way I run the company – I take this as a compliment. The 'British Oprah' is a lazy description of both me and the show, though. I started off in television journalism, reporting news, and then I presented a magazine-style early-evening soft news show for a number of years. Every time I did a human interest story or caught a public figure off balance with an overly personal approach the ratings jumped. So did the controversial coverage, letters etc. So Jeffrey and I decided to form a company and launch a new show, and in the three years it's been going I've been very happy. I never thought I would have so much freedom. The show's not voyeuristic – or – I can't find the word, obviously caring, but it fills the gap in public demand. Before it had always been either news or screws – one creditable, the other tabloid, and

I wanted to combine the approach to make something – a new format – altogether different – indestructible. But I digress – carried away by my former *raison d'être*.

Anyway. It was a cold early morning. My desk and table had flowers but there were no teddy bears at least. Cards from people in one pile – important post in the other. Most of the pre-production research had been done before I went away to have Beth – and Jeffrey had been left with setting up the show. The line-up was pretty much confirmed. We'd missed our opening week because of my absence (we tape the day before we go on air), and so my divorcing politician had to drop out. They'd pencilled a replacement guest (we have three in fifty minutes) and all her details were there for me to look at and give final approval.

She's a psychiatrist, but what makes her interesting is that she's beginning to make a name for herself in psychiatric circles by combining received medical wisdom with so called 'new-age' therapies (what an irritatingly inaccurate term 'new-age' is) – among them spiritual healing. She's quite trendy now with celebrities, but I'm more interested in the conflict she's causing within her own profession. We found out that ten years ago she was nearly struck off for 'falling in love' with a patient she was treating. She since married him. Apparently she's wildly expensive – saving up to set up her own 'healing centre' (sounds so much nicer than a psychiatric hospital). She's rather glamorous-looking – good for TV – and from a really poor background. Jeffrey was clever to find her – he must have remembered me mentioning her a while ago. It looked like I could be quite combative with her – it would be good television. I'm also interested that she wants to do the show, though I don't see why I should be surprised. Doctors can be such exhibitionists.

I think that early-morning decision was the only clear point of the day. I sat in my chair and read my correspondence, sometimes concentrating, sometimes blank. Anna, my secretary, came in and she and Jeffrey brought coffee and Danish from across the road and looked very embarrassed. I did a little tour of the offices, with them beside me for support, and then we had a budget/scheduling meeting. I was due to go out to the studios at the old Thames building after lunch – suddenly remembered I'd promised to bring felt tips back for Paul – so I put on my coat and went outside. My office is in Soho Square so I thought I'd go to Berwick Street. It was my first time of being alone alone – no one knew where I was – alone in the first different surrounding since she died. As I crossed the square I noticed a dog scrambling along the tarmac after a ball, scattering pigeons. He was a collie cross – black, very dirty, and he moved quickly, with distinctive joy – but with an awkward, uneven gait. I did a double-take before I realised he only had three legs – one of his forelegs chopped off at the chest – no stump or anything horrible. (I can't look at amputations.) He was so delighted, so maimed – in his own world. He belonged to a young homeless couple – also dirty, but without joy. The whole sight was indescribable – I didn't know if I was horrified or heartened by it. But it made me cry and I'm never emotional about things like that. In London you see sights piled on sights that ought to be impossible to pass – sights far worse than that every day. I think it was the dog's happiness that was so hard to bear.

Jeffrey and I were much later in the studio than I'd planned – meetings in the production office – and so many people wanting 'just five minutes' of my time – all taking so much longer than that, prefacing their business with embarrassed apologies about my 'loss' – as if it were their fault. That made me so tired. And the work made me very tired. I couldn't find an answering spark or echo of the interest that used to consume me. It was horrible – groping along a thought process where I'd used to fly. Jeffrey patted my hand in the car on the way back to town, saying things like 'early days yet' and how well I was doing. I'm very fond of Jeffrey, but he's a terrible phony.

When I got home the boys were in their pyjamas – Paul waiting for the felt tips (which thankfully I had remembered) Andrew placidly showing me a pencil drawing of a boat he had done, which was really surprisingly good. They went to bed and I had some stew with Michael. We didn't talk very much. He seemed very worried and I didn't care particularly. When I went up to my room there were more flowers on my dressing table and bedside table (I'm sick of the sight of them) and a book, laid across my pillow like a sacrifice. It was a hardback and glossy. There was a picture of a rose on the front and the title *Grief: How to Own it and Survive it*. Michael came out of the bathroom, looking at me questioningly and with tired fear. I picked it up and threw it at him across the room. I missed. He didn't say anything and nor did I. It's amazing how we both seem to have lost the desire to use words. He came to bed and fell asleep immediately, while I lay there, and now I'm here – as awake as ever. I don't know how I'm going to get through taping ten shows. Jeffrey kept trying to talk about the possibility of postponing further or reducing the amount of weeks or even using 'guest presenters', which would be certain death for the show, I know it – and I wouldn't let him. My determination to do it must kill this exhaustion or I'll sink. And if I do sink, it will be worse – worse. I'd better take in that prescription for sleeping pills tomorrow. I can't bear this 'stilly watches' terror. Not with everything else.

Saturday, 27th

I haven't had any time to write. The days are amazingly long – longer than usual because I work as if I were learning to read – and at night I'm knocked out with sleeping pills. I look like a drunk in the morning – bloated. I don't dream – or remember if I do. But it's done. The week's over. We taped last night, and now it's Saturday, Saturday morning. I'm sitting up in bed. In front of me the door with china flowered doorknob which leads on to the landing – firmly closed. To the right, the double doors leading to bathroom and nursery (baby's room) and on my left two big deep sash windows, and trees and sky and the sounds in the road, muffled. It's breezy but light – spring with that cold northern feel still in it, overlaid with gentleness and promises. Michael brought me coffee and left me here with Radio 4 and newspapers, and the cat. I've got the same feeling of coming round from being knocked out that I've had since taking these pills – but not that usual feeling of the morning after a show of a soothing completeness (and dare I say it, calm but buoyant self-congratulation). My mind is beginning to race – to identify what I have to work out today – what I have to solve. I can hear the front door bang which must be Abbey going away for the weekend (she has a stolid and devoted boyfriend back home in Basingstoke). I'm listening for something else – not Beth's cry – I must be out of the habit of that by now – something else. It's gone – I've forgotten.

My mind's still racing though. I'll go and have a bath. There's no point in lying here feeling as if my legs have been smashed by a mallet, unable to remember what my mind wants to think about. I'll get up.

It's a bit later. The boys and Michael are in the kitchen getting lunch. I'm still upstairs. I'm dressed and ready but feeling a bit shocked. I want to write what just happened. While I was undressing the phone rang and it was Lillian – the psychiatrist woman who came on the show last night, and I remembered, standing naked by my bed, that I gave her my number last night when we were having drinks after the show and she had said she'd call me because she felt as if I needed her and I had said yes that would be fine. I hate psychiatrists and therapists. At best they're parasitic, at worst fraudulent – it's OK when they confine themselves to the mentally ill, but they so rarely do nowadays – they want access to healthy psyches, so they can paddle, splash and play with all their mights, like children being given real guns instead of toys. (Mixed metaphor – is this diary acquiring literary pretensions?) They all want to write books and parade their egos. But this is foolish. The thing is that the show was boring television. Either Lillian was too clever for me, or I've lost my edge – but no matter how provocative I was, she remained steady. She's a big woman, about twice my size, Jeffrey said, and soft and strong-looking at the same time. Powerfully vulgar dress sense – she wore purple and green and quite a lot of heavy jewellery. She's red-headed, her hair is quite beautiful and long-ish for her age (she must be older than me) and she has an eagle face, an eagle nose, big very piercing green eyes. She held forth rather humourlessly about the need for healing in our shattered century and about female power and patriarchy and all that O-level philosophy

– and every time I interrupted her and talked about doctors disapproving of her, or even her famous clients, she was serene and stalwart and made it look as if I were a hideous resistant Philistine along with the rest of her reactionary profession. When I put the question about her love-life she looked right into the camera (not at me) and said, 'I reserve the right to fall in love with whomever I choose.' I could almost hear the nation cheering. She was really good, and beautiful in her way, and I felt like cheering too. When the lights went down and the audience clapped over the titles she sat and looked at me with all the happy triumph of one satisfied performer to another. I saw her sweat and adrenaline-filled stare rest on me with delight and she laughed. I remember trying to laugh back at her for being so audacious – she had been too convincing somehow. It didn't make any sense, but I ended up laughing with her, just for a little. And I stayed still beside her in the false twilight, looking away from her into the audience. Jeffrey came out on to the floor, bent to kiss me and whispered in my ear, '"The best lack all conviction, while the worst are full of passionate intensity,"' and he chuckled. And I really laughed too. 'See you up there,' he said, and nodding to Lillian, set off on his round of the studio floor. Then the floor manager reminded us we could go, the lights came up, the audience began to file out and we stood up.

'I think you're very admirable,' she said, and smiled. I felt unwillingly disarmed.

'Now we go up to the Green Room, and mill around and have a drink,' I replied, and she followed me, her rather swollen legs in their nylons squashed into inappropriately girlish high-heeled sandals. She tapped along the polished floor behind me, rhythmically, and I knew her eyes were focused on me. Michael came to have a drink and take me

16

home (he doesn't usually come to tapings) and we didn't stay long. There wasn't much jubilation in the air at all. Still, Lillian left before me, approaching me in a large green crushed-velvet cloak – chosen no doubt to bring out the colour of her eyes. She was very solemn as she said goodbye, and that's when I gave her my number – it seemed churlish to refuse her. She makes a living, I thought, much like (or better than) any other successful business-woman – and she believes she helps people and wants to help me. She must have known about little Beth. So I gave her my number to signal truce – no one should court enemies. I knew I'd refuse to see her ever again should she call. And now she just has – surprising me naked in my own bedroom – surrounded by linen sheets and brass bedheads and dark furniture – surprising me with her voice's tone, making me feel like a girl being asked on a first date.

'I think it would be good if you came to my office in Devonshire Place, as soon as you are able.'

'Why?' This I felt to be a feeble defence.

'I think I can help you. I think there is a reason you, who are alone, found me last night.'

'I don't find this *faux* portentous style very edifying,' I said – God knows why, it was unnecessarily rude.

'I know you're frightened and frozen,' she said. (Frightened and frozen – this alliterative phrase made me think of battery chickens, for some reason.) 'I'll be in my office, 37 Devonshire Place, all Monday. I'll wait for you until eight thirty. But you will be seen whenever you arrive. It's important.'

'I have to go,' I said and put the phone down. The weirdest thing is that I really want to go and meet her again, now, and I don't know why. I don't want a therapist whom I can talk to about Beth. I don't need a friend. It's just that she's the first thing that's made me curious since Beth died. Perhaps it is the novelty of feeling I have at last found someone whose will is stronger than my own, I don't know. I don't want to think about it, or analyse it, I just want to find out. And now I feel guilty again – consumingly. Poor Beth has no story – all this is mine – the only thing she seems to have is a name and a grave.

Monday, 29th

It's late again – about two – and I'm in my study with a large whisky and a cigarette. I've longed for one since Beth died, but I felt too guilty. Now I'm smoking it and it's so strong I'm getting a head rush and I feel sick – glorious. Smoking is so wonderfully pointless. I haven't taken any pills. Lillian said that if I smeared lavender oil around my pillow and on my neck and wrists and lay counting my very deep breaths – I would sleep. I'm afraid to try it in case it doesn't work. And I want to be awake to write. I've left the curtains open and the light on the lawn from this room is rather magical. The poplars at the end are moving and the dark garden is secret and limitless. I don't feel afraid or as if I were being watched as I sometimes do at night. Lillian is a very strange woman. I knew I was going to see her this evening – told Michael I'd be late – wore a good jacket, everything – but I didn't call her to let her know. I couldn't. Took a taxi to Devonshire Place, put on lipstick and scent in the back of it like I used to on the way to meetings when I was just starting out, before I became too busy or too confident or both. There was only a bored old porter on the desk when I got there (about seven thirty) and he rang up and told her I was there. He told me how to find the office – the waiting room was huge and timeless – big armchairs against the wall – that umbrella and magazine smell. I was glad to be there in the evening and not have to go through sitting there in day time.

The stair carpet was red. Her office is not very impressive – it's at the back and quite small. There's nothing personal in it – I suppose nothing distracting. No clues. There's a big desk she doesn't sit at – two armchairs pulled close and confidingly together. She came to the door to welcome me without surprise, but she smiled in a very delighted way.

'I'm so glad to see you,' she said. She smiles quite a lot, which is unusual in adults I think. She's very bright and very scented and sort of squashy-looking like a cuddly toy. I asked her if she'd like to go out for a drink or some dinner but she said no she had work to do after I left so why not just offer me her usual hour.

'I'm not a patient,' I said.

'What would be so wrong with being a patient?' she replied, smiling again, and we both sat down on the whispering chairs and I started to cry. She took hold of my hand – squeezed it with a brief and extraordinarily powerful pressure – then handed it back to me. I wiped my eyes a bit, but I wasn't embarrassed. I told her about my job because I knew she would want me to talk about my baby, Beth. I told her all about my family, being the youngest of all those boys – my little sister wasn't born until much later, a mistake like Beth – and growing up in the country and practically 'coming out' and the Women's Institute and their watery jam and how I'd known it was wrong and how ambitious I was and all those things I'd not told anyone for so long because I'd met all the people I needed in my life, already gathered them up – so there wasn't much need for stories. I told her about meeting Michael because I was doing a story about businesses collapsing (his was lighting design) and how sweet and unresentful he'd been – and funny (he's still funny now) and how I was so happy to know him and didn't feel prickly and frightened about being nearly thirty-three and not married. It got dark in the room while I was telling her about marrying him and having the boys and my career going better and better and how I didn't mind not being a very good wife or mother or even friend because Michael didn't mind and we all seemed happy enough. And then little Beth came along, and everything changed with her birth. She made me notice things. She made me cry with joy. She made me peaceful. She made me feel blessed.

'Sometimes children are born as messengers,' said Lillian. She got up and turned the spotlight on on her desk – it didn't do much to penetrate the gloom but the bracket lights on the wall would have been very harsh. I didn't say anything. 'She came to show you –'

'How to be a better person?' This made me angry. 'Who decided she was only a bit player in the drama of my life? Why couldn't she have her own?'

'She did. And it sounds as if it was a beautiful life and you shared it with her absolutely.'

'I can't talk about it any more.'

'Everything happens for a reason,' said Lillian, as I got up and fumbled around for my bag. 'You know, you aren't the same person now she's passed through your body into eternity.'

'Beth is *my* baby – *mine*! She – I don't understand why she had to die – to go away.' I felt so helpless then because the words were so childish; and I sat down again on the chair and cried and cried and cried. She handed me tissues. Then we both stood up, and she hugged me, as strong as a tree and as soft as feathers. It was extraordinary how peaceful I felt –

truly enveloped, even though she was wearing polyester and her scent was too heavy and too sweet. It made me doubt myself. That hasn't happened to me for the longest time. She said she'd wait again for me next week.

'Don't worry, I won't send you a bill,' she said. 'This is not about money.' I thanked her, and came out into the street feeling alert and aware of beauty and mystery and other indefinables – and calm. I feel wide awake and calm now, almost as if I'd taken some kind of drug. Has my cynicism been too strong, my armour too crushing? She is doing me a kindness and I feel as if I've been not only loved, but understood.

Tuesday, 30th

Back at work today. Very tired. Michael called the office, wanting me to tell him all about last night and Lillian. He said he was calling because he hoped I'd be easier to pin down on the phone. It was awful, that he made it so explicit that we aren't talking. He never forces confrontations. He said he was worried about Andrew and Paul but even more worried about me.

'Open that determined little mouth and speak to me,' he said, half joking (my determined little mouth is an old joke between us).

'I don't have anything to say,' I said – not wanting to be cruel or aggressive or anything – how could I tell him about the armchairs and the crying and the dim light and about little Beth not being here any more?

He said, 'I think we should go together to Beth's grave – I think we should talk about how we both feel. I love you and

I miss her and I miss you now –' It was excruciating. I thought I was going to be sick.

'No. I won't talk to you about that,' I said, as if negotiating a contract. 'I don't mean to be cruel, darling, but it's no good asking me to use words about any of this.'

'What about the grave?' he said, fiercely – I thought intentionally fiercely. I lost my temper a bit – my stomach being invaded with heat which rose to my throat. 'You don't even know where it is. I chose the place. There's a magnolia tree – it's flowering, it's a peaceful place. The plaque is ready tomorrow.' I told him I would put the phone down on him. He ignored me. 'There are children's graves on either side of her, there is grass that needs cutting – I'm going with fresh flowers today –' I put the phone down and put my hand in my mouth and bit down on the fleshy part to stop the tears. How dare he tell me about the grave, when he knew I didn't want to know. How dare he force me to think about the grave.

All this happened this morning. It wasn't even twelve. I wanted to call Lillian at her office but I'd only seen her last night – it seemed a bit extreme. I felt violently hungry, and I remember getting up and pacing the length of the office (I'm *not* a pacer) and then standing still at my office window looking down into Soho Square. I wanted my study with the green carpet and Seymour the cat. I wanted to be there – transported – watching the sun on the carpet – gentle – and knowing Beth was sleeping in her cot upstairs and the world was right. I didn't know what to do because I knew that if I left the office it would be an irreversible and major step away. But I couldn't stay there. Now I'm home. Michael is in the garden weeding and planting. We had lunch together in silence and he didn't question me. I hurt him so much today, but like me he has nowhere else to go. I'm in my study now – but the sun's on the other side of the house and the afternoon is empty. There is nothing to do. I think I'd better go and collect the boys from school.

Later

Paul and Andrew go to the same school. Paul does very well and Andrew very badly. Not because he's not bright but because he doesn't care – he's not naughty though, he's good. He's creative, quiet – he's in his own world. They came out together, Andrew lagging behind, Paul overcome by seeing me standing at the school gates, smiling his intense smile that I tried to return, carrying his books tidily. Andrew, following, looking down, up at me swiftly, then down at his feet again.

'Mummy,' said Paul, clasping me around the waist. 'Why are you here?'

'I came home early,' I said. I kissed him and kissed Andrew and we all stood still, embarrassed.

'Where's the car?' said Andrew, breaking away from our little game of frozen statues. He doesn't like to be pinned down anywhere – Andrew – he always has plans on his mind. I made them tea at home and Abbey watched me make a mess of it and tried not to get in the way.

'Not too many biscuits because there's supper soon,' I said. (They don't have supper with us yet, though Paul wants to.) I tried to supervise them, sit them down with their homework, but they didn't want to be supervised so I went back to my study and fell asleep.

Now it's very late again – about two. I'm in Beth's room,

23

sitting on the floor opposite the window with my back against the door leading to the landing. The blind is up and the moonlight is streaming into the room – watery, milky. It is extremely beautiful, rarely beautiful for there to be so much of this bright white light. The cot has been dismantled and folded away in the attic I suppose – the rocking chair I used to feed her on is still there in the corner, but I don't want to sit in it without her. The floor is quite uncomfortable because the carpet is very worn. I've been crying and thinking about her and writing, and crying. To my left is the door to the boys' bedroom. Did they go back into the room after Nanny and I had left it – did they go to the cot and see and retreat as I did? I haven't thought to ask them. I wonder if Michael has. I wish I could lock the door into their room from the inside, keep Beth's room private, but it's impossible. Their bolt broke years ago and there isn't one on the landing door I'm leaning against nor on the one from our bathroom – so it's pointless. Three doors leading to one baby, one cot, one throne, now dismantled. I've opened the chest of drawers and looked at her little things. There were the six white cotton all-in-ones that she spent most of her life in. (She was my all-in-one.) A cardigan with rosebuds on the collar. A little hat. The other clothes were different patterns and materials, they were for when she was three months. I think she only ever wore one of those, the navy and white thin stripy one – for Sunday lunch at Jeffrey's. I didn't touch any of these folded things, but I remembered exactly how they felt. I looked in the cupboard at the tiny dresses hanging up that I was waiting for her to grow into. I was surprised her clothes were still there, I thought Michael or Nanny would have packed them up or thrown them away. The family teddies and new ones from friends are gone, I don't know where they are. I can see their faces anyway, just as if they were still scattered over the chair, propped up neatly on the two shelves and at the back of the chest of drawers. Her mobile is here – lit up by the moon – but not the changing pad with the ducks on it, or the talcum powder or the nappy bin – the details of Beth's life have been destroyed. I don't think I should come in here again, even if I can't lock the room.

Saturday, May 4th

I've only managed the office for a few hours each day this week. The taping of the show was very bad. I sit here in Beth's room when I come home, and I cry. I wonder if this is healthy or unhealthy.

Monday, May 6th

I left the office early today to see Lillian – she had a cancellation and I hurried in an awful, breathless, passionate way. She immediately noticed the change in me. Her tone was urgent.

'What is it?' she said.

'My baby's died,' I replied, feeling as if it had just happened, and I didn't start to cry, the tears just spilled over as they have done for all these days now. I haven't been able to see for tears.

There was silence for a time, then she said, 'I want you to listen to what I have to say,' holding my hand and leading me from the door to the whispering chairs. My tears fell on her freckled hands and the purple amethyst of her ring. 'You are like a vessel filled with grief and tears,' she said. 'They are spilling out of the top of the vessel, and there is no room for anything else. You are holding your baby like a kangaroo holds its young, like a lioness with her cub.' These phrases made me cry more. 'You have to put your baby down now so that she can rest, and you can rest and heal, and so that you can remember the message she came to send you.' She gave me back my hand, moving away from me while I thought about what she had said, pulling the yellow blinds down inside the red velvet curtains. She rang a bell – someone came with workman's tea and Nice biscuits, sugary like childhood, they were left outside the door. We sat in silence for a while, dimly lit, while I surprised myself with my appetite for sugar. 'I want your permission to perform a separation ceremony on you, Zoë, between Zoë and baby Beth.'

'Separation ceremony?' I said, and she leaned towards me and looked at me with her eagle eyes. I don't think anybody has ever looked at me with such concentration before.

'Rite of passage. Ceremony. Call it what you will. You didn't bury your baby. Now it's time.' I thought about the grave, somewhere in its acres of suburban churchyard, and Beth sleeping in her cot.

'No, I wouldn't bury her. Is that wrong?' I said.

'Not if you're content to let her go now.' It was not a command. What she was saying was entirely logical, even though it was so strange.

'What are you going to do? I don't want water or flowers or bibles.'

She smiled. 'No. It's a simple ceremony. The time is right.' There was a kind of joy in her green eyes. I wondered what she saw with them that I couldn't see. 'Are you ready?'

'No, I'm not ready. How could I be ready to separate from my only daughter?' I hadn't known I was going to say that.

'You will always have her. The only thing you will lose is your grief, before it destroys you.' I looked at Lillian's face, and I could neither think nor say anything. 'Beth –'

'Don't say her name. *Don't* say her name again.' Confusion – that was all I felt.

'It doesn't have to be today, but the need is there.' Her voice was soothing. 'Think about what I've said, and you can always come back.' It was a signal for me to leave, but I found that I couldn't move, not for a long while.

Night time

I am on the floor in the bathroom, leaning against the door to her room. My daughter, my daughter, my daughter. I would have died for you to live, I would have died. If my grief is the only thing I have left of you I will keep it and never leave you.

Sunday

I cannot work or eat or sleep. I am frightened. My face stings with tears – my eyes – my throat. All I do is make tears. I am not ashamed to show them, but I am ashamed to want to be rid of them. Vale of tears, Michael's religion calls them. My veil of tears. I keep remembering what Lillian said about the grief destroying me and I am afraid. It is only that Beth is – Beth *is* – Beth *is* to me, not was. I am her mother and she is

27

part of me – her tiny arms and legs and every detail of her perfect form. How could I abandon her to her death? How could I be her mother and do that?

Monday night – May 13th

I went there today because there was no other thing for me to do. Lillian knew I would come. She was not surprised. I've found someone who knows better. That is ironic. Michael would laugh if I told him, but I can't. She didn't say anything to me, and so I said, 'I'm ready,' and she said, 'Good,' and she smiled. 'Put down your bag and take off your shoes.' She was gentle. She pointed to the chair where I was to put them. She made the room dark again, like it was before. Then her tone altered – she became like my favourite gym mistress at school. 'I want you to stand up – anywhere in the room where you feel comfortable and I'll stand opposite.' This was achieved with efficiency, as if there suddenly wasn't enough time. We stood opposite one another without touching, and I felt calmer. 'Close your eyes,' she said. 'I want you to imagine you're in a lovely safe familiar place – it could be home, but it doesn't have to be.' I imagined myself beneath the poplar trees at the end of the garden. The vision was so immediate, I was surprised. I didn't choose. 'It can be night or day.' It was day, summer's day. 'Beth is with you, you are holding her in your arms.' There she was, in the summer garden (although she had never known summer), wrapped in her white shawl, looking up at me with her gentle eyes. 'If she's awake, I want you to rock her to sleep.' I did, and she fell asleep without a struggle. After some time, a time I spent gazing on Beth to my heart's content, she said, 'I want you to look around for a lovely place to put her down, somewhere safe and undisturbed.'

I knew what was coming. She was going to make me leave her there. Somehow this no longer seemed to be a wickedness. Beth was fast asleep and there was a place for her – a short cropped grass hollow surrounded by long grass – like Moses and the bulrushes – and there weren't any wild animals or insects or anything because it was the end of our garden where the lawn meets the wild flowers and the trees. I put Beth down and she stirred a little. 'Now I want you to imagine the ties that connect you to Beth. I want you to see them, make them visible.' I thought they might show as a cat's cradle of wool or string, from all different parts of her body to all different parts of mine, but in fact it was only a single cord – like the umbilical cord, but between her heart and mine, and sort of silken and royal-looking, like a fairytale. 'Now I want you to notice that you have a pair of beautiful scissors in your hand.' I looked down at my hand and there they were, shining, but still sharp and menacing. 'Look with love at Beth, and look with love at the scissors.' I did so, with all my courage. 'Now, I want you to say, "Beth, I love you. For your peace and for mine, I let you go."' I said this in my mind. 'Say the words out loud,' prompted Lillian. Then I said them, but my voice cracked. Beth smiled a little, distantly. 'Now,' said the voice, 'I want you to cut the tie with the scissors – and see how happy little Beth is.' When I cut the purple cord it fell to the ground and then vanished, leaving me looking at Beth as if from a long way away. I didn't feel anything except dreaming.

After that, Lillian told me to return slowly to the room.

When I opened my eyes and saw the red darkness and Lillian's peaceful face I was very tired. She told me to lie down on the sofa under the window and sleep – which I did. I imagine that this is quite usual. Lillian went away. She must have been seeing other people in another room, but when she woke me up I felt peaceful and not tearful. I got to my feet. She hugged me – the swansdown hug again – and then she sent me away. I took a taxi home. I feel much better now. I don't want to go back to Beth's room ever again. I can hardly stay awake to write this, but it seems important to keep a record somehow.

Michael asked me why I was early when I got home, and told me that the office had called. I slept in my study till suppertime – the boys didn't even disturb me.

Sunday morning – May 19th

It's very cold today – wind and hardly any sun. I don't remember so much wind when I was a child. But memory's deceptive I think. It makes the house rattle and the garden's hell. Seymour's in a ball on the armchair beside my desk. I'm in my study surrounded by chaos – different boxes that I'm labelling with felt pen – files and rubbish. Yesterday it was hot – one of those rare spring days with a hot sky and a light breeze and blossom. It was so beautiful when I woke up I wanted to cry. I shot out and was there when the supermarket opened, and bought the most stupendous picnic – early strawberries and champagne for me and Michael and grape juice for the boys and those awful crisps they like and all sorts of goodies as well as ham and salads and pies. I tried to make a Spanish omelette to take cold which was a bit of a disaster but it was fun and we took that too. I remember picnics at cricket matches when I was a child and we always had Spanish omelettes.

We went to Richmond Park, I didn't ask Abbey to come, and I think she was hurt as well as surprised – but I just wanted the boys and Michael. We trudged a long way from the car park to find the perfect spot, with quilts and the cold box and God knows what; they complained, but they knew I was right when we got there. We had a view of water (essential), we were on a hill with a light breeze, and there were no rubbish bins or people – people are lazy and always picnic near a car park if there's no room in the car park itself. Paul was anxious to praise me for bringing them. Michael avoids my eyes now as I used to avoid his – he's inherited my fear – and Andrew, Andrew made a catapult, wove grasses, found a rabbit warren – he dedicated himself to the day, but he didn't want any witnesses. Not like Paul. I don't think Paul feels he's done anything unless he's done it publicly. Michael read the papers when we'd eaten and I read the boys a story. They are much too old and I felt foolish, but I did it anyway. It's easier than conversation. Then I told them I had something important to say, and Andrew said, 'Are you calling a meeting, Mummy?' which made me laugh. He was right, my speech had been prepared – but I didn't have any papers to hand out while I did the preamble, and I didn't know what to do with my hands. Andrew is very perceptive. Michael was lying down, his eyes narrowed at the sun and I pulled him up to sit and listen – I gathered them all around me.

   'I have been giving the situation – our life – a great deal of thought,' I said, 'and I've decided I want to be with you all, all the time. I'm going to wind up the series early or have it guest-presented, and I'm going to hand over the company to Jeffrey for the foreseeable future.'

The children, kneeling in a row in front of me, frowned in a kind of doubly reflected way and Michael said quietly, putting his sunglasses over his nose, 'Zoë, if you do that you'll never work again. Nobody will commission a series ever again from a company which reneges on its contract.'

'I'm not reneging. They have choices. They can either cancel the series, or have it guest-presented. There's nothing unreasonable. I don't want to do it any more, not any more, work like that, perform like that.'

He said, 'I think we should discuss this at home privately.' He looked sweaty and ordinary and uncomfortable. I looked at his hands which are very elegant and tried to remember that he was my husband and I loved him and I mustn't annihilate him as opposition, but remember to be gentle, and it was such a struggle I couldn't speak for a while.

'I thought you'd all be happy to have me home,' I said.

'I'm happy, Mummy,' said Paul, looking as if he were about to cry. Andrew looked at me with his pale grey eyes and I felt he understood it all – the youngest, the most disconcerting person I know. So often I can't understand that child, don't want to try, feel his self-sufficiency is God-given but somehow alien – but then I felt as if we were close, as if he applauded, as if he'd been waiting for such a plan.

'I know it's a U turn in terms of the way our family's been running over the years,' Paul snatched up handfuls of grass and I had to stop myself from snapping at him and telling him not to fidget, 'but it's for the best. I have controlling interest in the company still – that means revenue shares above and beyond the show. It won't be the same salary because Jeffrey will need more – but he's more than capable.'

'You are committing professional suicide,' said Michael, 'everything you've worked for.' With surprise I saw that he was very angry indeed.

'That's your opinion.' We never quarrel in front of the boys. I didn't remind him that I had backed him wholeheartedly when he gave up his job to be with the boys – not that he'd had much to give up. I just gave him my steely blue look and he fell silent, but I think it was more out of kindness than fear. 'And I'm going to ask Abbey to leave,' I said, looking at Paul. 'I'm going to look after you both myself.' I waited for his uncertain smile – his relieved approval – but his eyes closed and tears splashed on his transparent hands. Andrew continued to fix me with his unwavering gaze. 'I didn't mean to ruin everybody's day,' I said. I think we all wanted to say Beth's name. I wanted to tell them that she was at peace now, that I'd laid her down to sleep, but it would have been so impossible. If I'd promised them the joy I felt lay ahead for us all over the summer and how Beth's death was the way to that joy I know it would have hurt them. I have been given the message of her death – our rebirth as a family, and it is for me to communicate this through action, not words. They're not ready, and I'm not strong enough for convincing words. But I think Lillian will help me get where I want to be.

I packed up the picnic quickly like a child who'd been scorned. Now here I am sorting everything out, a cold day, and alone. Michael is making Sunday lunch, but there are no sounds of music or laughter. I don't know where the boys are. I want my boys to really love me, I want to be a real mother. And I'm going to try my hardest from today.

Wednesday night

Jeffrey came to the house himself this afternoon to pick up the boxes. He looked woebegone instead of jubilant. When I asked him why he wasn't happy to be in control at last he said he was afraid for me. I tried to congratulate him on finding a new host and getting the network off his back in two days, but he wouldn't play.

'Something's happened to you, more than Beth – more than Beth's dying.' He looked frightened but brave. Puffed up. 'Tough but fair, that's you. That's always been you. Not wild.'

'Beth is gone now,' I explained. 'Laid to rest. I'm free. I'm free of the past.'

'Don't make me die in a ditch like Enobarbus,' he said, as I showed him to the door.

Lillian and I have agreed I'll clear out the house this week. Michael can do Beth's room – I'm just looking forward to throwing all my business clothes away. I wonder if Oxfam will object to Armani. Cheap joke – but I'm feeling frivolous.

Abbey left today. I gave her two months' money.

Thursday, May 23rd

Andrew really is the most extraordinary child. How could I have ignored so much talent (it's the only word I can really find) – in my own family?

Paul was morose at breakfast this morning, complaining of stomach pains and cramps. Michael said they call it his 'worried tummy' and lying down flat sometimes helps. He spoke lightly, signalling to me not to make a fuss about it but I just couldn't send the boy to school, I didn't have the heart. Michael took Andrew without contradicting me, although I felt he was angry, and I tried to talk to Paul.

'Is it anything special?' I asked. He avoided me by clearing away the breakfast things. He's such a tidy child; it alarms me, but I focused on the back of his neck as he stood at the counter, trying to feel his feelings, like Lillian does with me. His hair is cut very short in best public school tradition so you can see the hollow there where it's stubbly-short.

'I miss Abbey,' he said, after a time, and then I think he started to cry, but he was silent about it. I felt impatient that he should feel troubled by what was only a detail in the scheme of things, and more impatient that I couldn't restrain my irritated reply.

'She'll come and visit,' I said, thankfully knowing a bit better than to start pleading with him to be close to me: if anything business strategy helped me. I told him to change out of his uniform, and I took him to the park. He was very obedient about it. I almost wished he'd slam the door, if he couldn't express delight. He's more interested in books – not even computer games – never moving out of the bedroom, brooding, looking over the garden. That's got to change. I grew up on outdoors, and I believe in it. The park was green. I hate it when it gets too pale and yellow all over, but it was bright with puddles and we walked quite a long way. We watched the horses, the sullen riding-school rides, the few lone horses moving quite nicely. I told him about riding as a child – familiar stories. I suggested he concentrate on learning to ride this summer, and then perhaps we could think about having a pony of our own for the family. It came to me just then, the idea, and it seemed so fresh and exciting I wondered why I hadn't thought of it before. Lillian would be proud to hear I'm listening to life so quickly.

'We could think about it,' said Paul, lifting his head towards me, and slightly to one side, attempting to smile. I knew he wasn't excited about it, but I felt exactly then that Andrew would be. I made him race me across the short grass into the woods, and I found some big logs to walk along to practise his balance. His back is straight but he lowers his head. I set him tasks – jumping on and off the logs in fun, bigger and bigger ones. I think he was afraid he'd hurt himself at first, twist his ankle in a rabbit hole or something, but he was game about it, and he laughed in the end – forgetting, I think. Forgetting, I hope.

While Paul and Michael had lunch I went out to buy *Horse and Hound* and looked at advertisements and prices. I called my mother and told her to put the word about at home that I'm looking for a pony – sensible but quick, and big enough for me to exercise.

Anyway – Andrew. When he came home he came straight into my study and presented me with the most beautiful crayon sketch of a chestnut pony.

'How did you know I was thinking about horses?' I said.

He laughed. 'No reason. I just wanted to draw you one.' I questioned him and it was all complete coincidence. These things happen, but what amazes me is how well he draws and uses colour. It's really quite a dazzling picture. I've stuck it on my study wall with Blu-tac. Who cares about the wallpaper.

I am healing my family
I am healing my family
I am healing my family
My family is whole and complete
My family is whole and complete
My family is whole and complete
My family is whole and complete
My family is whole and complete
I am surrounded by love
I am surrounded by love
I am surrounded by love
I am surrounded by love
I am surrounded by love
I am in the right place at the right time
I am in the right place at the right time
I am in the right place at the right time
I am in the right place at the right time
I am in the right place at the right time
I am a good and loving mother
I am a good and loving mother
I am a good and loving mother
I am a good and loving mother
I am a good and loving mother
I am a good and loving mother
My heart is strong
My heart is strong
My heart is strong
I give and receive love
I give and receive love
I give and receive love
I am safe and secure
I am safe and secure
The universe is unfolding as it should
The universe is unfolding as it should
The universe is unfolding as it should

Lillian is teaching me affirmations. This is how they work: you decide how you want to feel and how you want your life to be. There are no limits to what you can choose, and she says this can also include practical things like money and clothes. (I don't need to worry about those kinds of things though.) Anyway, when you've decided what it is that you want you make statements in present tense that these things are already happening to you. You write them out and then repeat them over and over (like the lines we used to learn at school). You're meant to do it morning and evening and by doing it create a state of being (consciousness I suppose) where these things can happen. She used the analogy of the Platonic chair – it can only come into being if you imagine it in advance. You can make wishes come true, i.e. if you believe you are safe and secure, you will be, etc. She tells me it really works. I only have to look at Lillian to see living proof. So I'll buckle down to it every day. (She said I must buy a special affirmations book, but I haven't done it yet.)

June

I've had a dream – you might call it a waking half-closed eyes vision. I was listening to Beethoven's Pastoral Symphony, the lovely bit they've used in so many ads, in my study. Michael and the boys were out – late morning – I forget where. Late sunny fresh early-summer morning: I had a plate of yellow plums. They were delicious. When I bit into them I wanted to cry – juice running down my chin and I didn't care – smeared it with the back of my hand – the deliciousness, freshness – and the music all so beautiful. That passage has a forward movement to it, a kind of sound that is natural and builds forward (I've just realised that's why they call them movements, which is amazing). Listening, and without thinking about it, I saw green-gold fields – the way I saw the poplar trees when I said goodbye to Beth – a high pasture, wooded hills in the distance, and the bright line of the sea on the horizon, and a horse – it could have been a pony – bright bronze orange gold and galloping full tilt, head up – no rider – just for joy, running for joy like a glorious wild triumphant free thing – running with the music. I have never before seen such a high field by the sea – not anywhere at all like that – but by the bright golden light I felt it might be the West Country, very west though – Devon or Cornwall – where this dazzling creature was racing itself across the grass.

The complete vision lasted a very short time, perhaps only a little longer than the music. It made me cry. The horse was like a distillation of all horses – their spirit, their speed, the power and the glory but also the kindness – and there was the overwhelming feeling that he actually exists. I felt an affinity.

It's odd, my memories of ponies and pony clubbing – then riding club (I even hunted and evented a bit) are much more prosaic than this burnished vision – but they are an echo of it. I was happy then. Yes, my family annoyed me, yes, I wanted to grow up and go to London and do big things (vague and unquantifiable as young hopes are) but I was happy with my horses – tranquil.

I know now how much I've failed the boys by not giving horses to them. They must have a horse – I feel sure it will help to unite us all. The animal in my dream is not unlike the animal on the wall. The animal Andrew gave me. Curiouser and curiouser.

Later

When Michael and the boys came back from school, I made tea for us all and it was quite lovely – rather cosy. Michael and I are now adept at sliding by one another – quite close, but not without connection – I must put in my affirmations that we communicate better. I wouldn't let Paul read at the table.

'You know this pony business,' I said, as casually as I could. 'I think it is a wonderful opportunity for the family. When the holidays come we should really start looking. You know how happy I was riding as a child.'

'You've started looking already, and I don't know how to ride,' said Paul, glancing up at his father.

'You know he doesn't even like PE,' said Michael. I wanted to shake him. Has he ever had imagination, or did I just imagine that he had? How droll.

'That's because PE's boring,' I said. 'Horses are different. Horses are real. They smell good, they lick you with their tongues and when you pat them or touch their ears – it's like every safe feeling you've ever had coming right through your fingers and over your whole body.'

'I know it will be like that,' said Andrew, examining the jam he was spreading on his bread. I wanted to burst out laughing.

'I just want you to trust me on this, Paul. Trust me because I know how good this could be for your confidence. I want you to enjoy life more.' Michael, standing behind Paul, started to clatter around the table clearing away: hurrying

40

things up. 'I just want your blessing to pursue this one,' I think I said.

'Pursue this one? I don't know – you bored ex-executives . . .' said Michael, smiling – as if my dream were a joke. It was actually quite uncharacteristic of him to show even such disguised hostility. Humour is a powerful weapon. Lillian teaches me that.

'I would like to find a pony,' said Andrew, looking up for the first time. 'Definitely.' He knows it has already been agreed between us. I barely acknowledged him, but turned to Paul with my best questioning expression – the one which demands an answer.

'If you want,' he said, or some such irritatingly passive phrase.

'Now – homework,' said Michael, beginning to supervise them, and all three went about their business as if I were a ghost.

Later

When I couldn't sleep tonight I got up and listened to that music again, downstairs on my headphones. I listened to it over and over, but it was different each time. It even seemed to take less time each time. I thought about horses – each one I had known, loved or which had had any impression on me. After long piercing thoughts I went up to the attic and dug about in boxes to find the old photographs Mummy had entrusted to me when she moved from the big house to the cottage after Daddy died. It was quite difficult climbing those steep loft stairs in almost complete darkness, but I didn't have time to find the torch. I brought the boxes down the stairs again and spread them out on the top landing. There were plenty of myself as a child – on horseback – from five or six, blurred colour or sharp black and white which gave me the look of a hundred years ago – a child from history. I thought a lot. I felt very moved. I am being shown the importance of continuity. Being a mother is about passing things on. I am on the brink of so many important discoveries, it's extraordinary. I got cold sitting up there, reflecting. My rooting around must have woken Michael, because when I came tiptoeing back into the bedroom he surprised me by turning on the light at his bedside.

'Aren't you taking your sleeping pills any more?' He was wide awake. I felt as if he had been lying in wait.

'No. They just disguise what I'm meant to be going through.'

He asked me if I were still seeing 'that nutty woman – the one who came on your show back in the days when we were real people with real lives'. He asked if that was the voice he was hearing. Was that the change in me? I told her she'd been teaching me, yes. It's hard to answer such questions barefoot and half dressed in the middle of the night. He was very serious and I felt light-headed – wanting to laugh at the sight of him bolt upright in bed with a T-shirt with a purple cartoon cat on it and a stupid caption, while half wanting to explain about all the exciting things in past and future which were crowding my mind.

'How often does this woman "help" you?'

'Once a week. You know really.'

'Yes. Mondays. Do you still think about Beth?' His voice was quiet, but it was still an accusation.

'Beth rhymes with Death.' (I hadn't meant to say this.) 'What is this, twenty questions?' I didn't want to get into bed with him, so remained marooned in the middle of the room, unsure of where to go. The light on his face made it look very white – and thinner, possibly. Possibly he is thinner.

'Come to bed.' It was silly but all I could bring myself to do was just sit down on the edge of the bed – my side – facing the window and trees, gazing down at the eternity ring I wear on my wedding finger, and twisting it.

'Remember when I gave you that?' he said, leaning over me.

'When Andrew was one.'

'I'd had a design for a lamp patented.' This was very boring. Why is it that married couples tell each other so much they already know and find it comforting? Why do they stop exploring, abandon adventure? I thought all this, then, at that moment. I turned to see his face, very eager, and very tender. 'That must have been the last time I made any money for myself.' His mentioning the money came as a surprise to both of us I think. We never talk about his not making any money.

'I've never said anything about that,' I reminded him.

'You're too sweet. Far too sweet.' I felt shivery, like when you're fourteen and a boy you quite like says he really likes you and you just want to go home. 'Sweetheart – Zoë – what's on your mind?' I couldn't begin to tell him all the things, so I settled for the main thing, the thing he already knew about. I looked into his eyes – looked hard.

'The pony. We have to have the pony.'

'I haven't said no. It's impractical, but not impossible.' (It's not his money, so it isn't even up to him – but I didn't say that. We've always preserved the fiction that he might be the head of the house, at least in terms of the children.) 'But, darling, have you thought any more about going back to work?'

'It's not what the universe intends right now.'

'What's the universe got to do with it?' It was stupid of me to have given him that answer, it could only lead to an interrogation.

'You wouldn't understand.' I have never said that to him before.

'Don't think that – and please don't think it's about the money. Our income is lower, but we'll manage. It's just that you used to love your work so.'

It was strange to be talking to him like that, or at least for him to be talking to me, like a dream remembered. I had a flash vision of lying in bed laughing with him – of us sitting up together reading – then the light going out and settling down with my head on his chest. Perhaps he was thinking about the same things. I got into bed, slowly. He moved away from me, but I felt he wanted to come nearer. I felt crawly about it again. Then I think he said something about not wanting to talk about Beth.

'Why must you do it, then?' I said, the music and the burnished horse and the photographs retreating and Beth's presence – her absence – threatening to return.

'If we had another baby –'

'No.' Vile thought. He wouldn't have dared look at me and say it. Honeyed words for a selfish vile thought. Controlling horrible priggish man. I am right to feel so little for him, to retreat. He is selfish. He is limited. He is small.

'Zoë, I think –' His voice was becoming monotonous, insect-like, horrible.

'No advice.'

'We are no longer together in our hearts.'

'It is not for us to resist the natural changes of the universe. Not for us.' I tried to put it calmly. If only I could teach him – if only he wouldn't stand in my way, opposing and stubborn.

'What's happening to us is not natural.'

'Who decides that?' (Spiteful, but it silenced him for a while.) He took a breath. I wanted to throw all the covers off and run out of the room.

'It would be good if you slept. Perhaps half a pill. It's three in the morning.'

'You take it. I have things on my mind.' I felt sorry for him just for a minute. 'Don't quarrel with me. Leave me. Let me find my own way.'

'No. We won't quarrel,' he said, then turned his light out and turned over.

I wonder whether it has been killed – murdered – by accident or design, I don't know – our marriage I mean. (Lillian would say by design.) Last night, that was a turning point – pulling back and looking at him and feeling my heart harden. A cliché, but that is exactly how it felt.

Sunday night

I told Andrew about my vision of the pony today. He is the only one in the family who understands. I had been saving it up until exactly the right moment. We'd had Sunday lunch and Paul had gone out with Michael (to the grave I think – stupid stupid stupid). I brought him in here and put on the same music, and tried to describe the vision in time to it (which didn't really work). Nearly cried because of how beautiful it was. We sat together on the floor in front of the fireplace (empty) because that is the half-way point between the speakers and you need to be in the right place or the balance is wrong and the balance (the sound's pitch) is wrong. He knows the tune anyway.

He kept asking me to describe the field and we agreed after searching our memories that neither of us had ever been to such a place before. (We went to Devon and Cornwall when the children were quite small, Michael's mother was still alive and she came too, but we went to the beach mainly, once to Tintagel – glorious – but never drove through such emerald patchwork fields.) We think I was right to gauge the field as being in that part of the country because of the characteristic patchwork and also the position of the sun, which in the vision was beginning to set over the sea. Andrew ran upstairs to fetch the new crayon sketch of the pony he's been working on and we studied it. The extraordinary thing is that it matches my vision. My dream only animates it really – puts it into true context. We discussed it and decided that there's no reason why I may not have had a vision of an animal that truly exists. That animal could be our saviour – our winged horse – just waiting for us – our burnished gold horse. Andrew is very excited. He can't wait to feel the power (gentle power) a horse can give you. We listened to the piece of music over and over and talked. What is the purpose of our time on earth if not to realise dreams? ('I will not cease from mental strife, nor will my sword sleep in my hand . . .' etc. etc.) This is what life can give us. We can have as much of the sublime as we are prepared to grasp.

Gloaming – in my study again – it was a true gloaming.

Andrew asked me if he could paint me. (We had sat in exultant silence for a while.) The others were back by then. We had heard but not seen them clattering in the kitchen like tiny domestic Disney creatures going about their evening chores. I haven't even let myself hope Andrew would ask me, but ever since I saw his first sketch I've hoped. A portrait of his mother, for posterity. It is an honour. I said he should do more of the pony first because that is the object of our quest (we like the word quest) and we need images on the wall for inspiration. But I am very flattered. We agreed he'd paint me on the window seat at the front of the landing. (A bit of a joke because of my fantasy about sitting there like some nineteenth-century lady of leisure – the person I could never have been ... But we're going to indulge our imagination and be frivolous.)

> The universe is unfolding as it should
> The universe is unfolding as it should
> I am safe and secure
> I am safe and secure
> I am safe and secure
> My life is better every day
> My life is better every day
> My life is better every day
> My life is better every day

Monday – June

Lillian had a cold today. We laughed about it. All that humankind can accomplish, but it cannot rid itself of the sufferings of a summer cold.

I told her she works too hard.

Whenever I see her I love her more. I told her I loved her and she didn't flinch the way one senses everybody in the world would (except Michael). She just told me she loved me too.

Afternoon sun streamed through her windows today.

We laughed when she sneezed.

She is very interested in my vision. She thinks that the ceremony with Beth has opened up my subconscious and now I am able to receive messages from the universe. She told me to add an affirmation to my daily routine, something like, 'I am open to receive'. I will do my affirmations after this. She's very intuitive about my growing bond with Andrew. Children are closer to the universe than adults she said, because they are closer to the origins of life.

I told her about my scene with Michael. When I told her how angry he made me and how closed he was, she responded with sympathy for him, not even scorn. It's amazing how she can feel so much love for everyone. She thinks I should give him a chance – he may make some discoveries of his own. She understands that right now I can feel nothing for him, but I don't think she thinks it will last for ever. She was rather enigmatic about it. She didn't even mind when I told her how much he seems to hate her – she just looked pensive and sad. I told her it was strange, experiencing life without Michael – without so many of my old props.

'They don't call them growing pains for nothing,' she said, holding me in her look – in those amazing green green eyes.

The laundry's driving me crazy. I don't know how Abbey – or housewives for that matter – coped. (Should it be cope or coped? I can't remember my grammar.) It's a blue day outside and I've spent the morning trying to sort it all out. I've decided to take it all to the laundry with the dry cleaning. Life's too short. They can give it all back to me in a brown cardboard box with a strap around it like my mother used to have when we lived in London when I was very young, and then all I'll do is put it into the drawers. In the middle of all the confusion – me gazing into the garden in between bouts of dividing colours, whites and hand wash and falling over the ironing basket – Jeffrey called. Michael – in his study for once – called me to the phone. (His study is dismal – all white and bare with unpleasant line drawings in aluminium frames.) Jeffrey told me that the channel has cancelled the series, and more frighteningly, all the other shows in development as well. He said that he could pitch these to the other networks but he feels the answer will be no. The ratings on my show have plummeted apparently and the word is that my company doesn't function properly without me running it. This made me so fucking angry I shook. Can't these people see that I wouldn't have put Jeffrey in charge if I didn't think he could do it? And what about the writers? Are they suddenly idiots without me? I said this to Jeffrey but he said I was being naive (rather wearily) and that he'd anticipated it all – I've never heard him sound so cowardly. He further annoyed me by saying he hadn't thought all this would be such a surprise to me – hadn't I seen how unconvincing the new presenter had turned out to be? (As she was chosen by him, I just said, 'Well, she *is* blonde' and left it at that.) I said it as a joke, but he sounded hurt by it, hurt that I hadn't turned the show on – amazed that I hadn't read the papers or *Broadcast News*. I told him I didn't care. Then he asked how I was in the voice he reserves for Beth's death. I told him again that I couldn't care less about any of his doomy news, that I was happy, that I was buying a pony for my sons.

'Zoë, there'll be no money for you now – do you understand that? The company's going under.' He said this in pleading tones. Michael was standing close by, his back to me while this ludicrous conversation was taking place. He turned towards me as I was telling Jeffrey to shut up, and asked for the phone. This surprised me as they're not close and Michael never interferes. But I didn't care. I walked to the attic window and looked out – the garden looks different shot from another angle – it was interesting – I wondered where my camera was. I lifted up the sash and leaned out into the wonderful high soft breeze. It was very weightless – a good feeling. High places are good.

Michael said, 'Yes. I know. Of course I understand, I'm sorry ...' ridiculous non-committal phrases, for quite a long time.

As he put the phone down I shouted, ''Bye, Jeffrey – love you,' to show I had no resentment, did not blame him, and so he could have the opportunity to share at least some of my freedom – joy.

'Zoë, this is very bad news. It means no income for us – do you understand that?' I noticed how tired Michael looked and also that I didn't have any feeling for him – none whatever.

'Why do you and Jeffrey keep asking me if I understand? Of course I understand. I'm not stupid.'

'We'll be broke.' He didn't say this kindly, but furiously – like a threat.

'Why don't you go out and earn us some fucking money then?' I shouted this – burning rage leaping '– instead of cowering up here in this pathetic little room?' He spluttered as if he would answer – but I was too bored with it all, too shaking, too angry. I went back to the laundry room and kicked the ironing basket so it skidded against the door. He really is such a weak man. I look at him and I wonder how I could have loved him – made love to him – listened to what he had to say – taken it seriously. So my company's life is ending. A new life will take its place. Lillian has taught me that. It is all very simple if you open your heart and mind. Andrew would understand. Paul wouldn't. I'm beginning to think that Paul might be a dead loss like his father. How does Michael dare to get angry with me? Why doesn't he do something for once and leave me alone? I've looked after him – all of them – for all these years.

He didn't come down for lunch. I'm in my study by myself – no Seymour – looking at Andrew's picture. How it reminds me of my dream. The pony has no white on him, which is unusual – children tend to draw stars and blazes and socks. Their minds are vulgar in many ways, I think. But this is just a golden chestnut, burnished gold, restrained. Almost as if he knew. How difficult he will be to find.

Later

Michael appears to be growing a beard. Self-protection I imagine. I'm awake in my study again – it's two. I'm not afraid because I realise now that I don't need much sleep and there's so much to do – more than that – experience. Paul's teacher called this afternoon to say she wanted to talk to us about him (Michael was out shopping). I pictured her in the staff room with her biscuits, surrounded by rolled-up umbrellas and newspapers and that awful school smell. I asked her if Paul were in any trouble. She said no, so I said, 'Why don't you mind your own business then?' and put the phone down, which gave me immense pleasure and satisfaction.

Michael was on the phone a lot this afternoon. Looking for work I hope. But at least he's still looking after the children. It's irritating if I have to remember when to pick them up all the time, and to buy lunches and children's teas for them. I don't want to eat dinner with Michael tonight. I'll have it in here, and Andrew can come and visit me in his pyjamas and we'll talk about the pony. I think we should wait until the school holidays to go looking for him – which are only a week or so away I think. There'll be more time then and I think I'll be able to concentrate better. At the minute television is very intrusive. I listen to music in here – I can't read – there's thinking I need to do, and I like looking out at the garden, and sometimes, when Michael's gone and not watching, I lie on the grass on the old quilt and look at the first bees visiting the flowers.

June – Monday

Michael's got a job. That's a novelty – and was announced this morning when he knocked on the door and came in here. An invasion, but I didn't know how to avoid it. He's been asked to design a lighting plan, through an old friend of his who's an architect, for a new theatre in a university in Scotland. Hardly fascinating, but a comprehensive job with a 'proper fee' – he said these words as if they were in italics, but I didn't take his cue to dissolve into tearful praise. I'll be glad of the separation. And of the challenge for Michael. Another way in which her death has helped us all grow. Anyway, it was a bad time for me – he wanted to give me all the details but I was preoccupied – I'm going to see Lillian this afternoon and I was worried about my duck-egg blue angora sweater – it might be too warm in town to wear it, even with linen trousers (summer is still refusing to start) and I wanted her to see me in the colour. I think it's significant. (I've since decided to go ahead and wear it.) After he had left the room I started to cry. I'm not sure why and what it means.

Later

I took the original sketch of the pony to show Lillian this afternoon. She was very impressed, her eyes narrowed as she studied it in the light (she pulled up her yellow blinds specially and took it to the window). It's very peaceful sitting in her room with her, and more and more informal. We overran the hour. (I can't say I object to special treatment.)

It was a reflective session. She asked me about Beth and I told her how happy and at peace the thought of her made me – how she had changed my life exactly as Lillian had predicted. I am no longer a crazed and ambitious person pushing through life as if I were trying to get to the top of a queue. She smiled at me.

'I love that colour you're wearing.'

'I chose it specially,' I said, and she smiled. I felt so happy it was worth all that time deciding. I told her about Michael and the job. She was very philosophical about it. She's pleased, I think. She thinks we will all benefit from his time away. I told her how wondrous it was that I am understanding how gifted Andrew is – that he might be going to become an important man – and how neglectful I have been of him in the past.

'And what about Paul?' she asked, almost tenderly, acknowledging my praise of Andrew, but cutting through it in her insightful way.

'He's still morose, troubled.'

'He's in pain about his sister's death. Have you considered bringing him to see me? I'd love to meet him.'

I'm very excited by Lillian's suggestion – if she could somehow help me to see into Paul – I know I am wrong to find him so impossible – and I almost didn't want to admit to her how angry he makes me – how I forget about him. She was very forgiving. 'So now you want to be perfect as well as beautiful?' she said, and we laughed.

We've organised an appointment for her and Paul for Thursday next week.

July – (2nd day of the holidays)

Haven't had time to write over the last few days – everything going very fast.

Michael busy getting ready for his trip so I took the boys to the theatre (matinée now it's the holidays). It was difficult. I thought nothing too demanding so *Private Lives*. But the comedy too sophisticated even for Andrew, I think. Stalls seats very close together – we weren't at the end of the row because I hadn't booked in advance – it was a spontaneous thing, which is good. They'd put all the audience together in a clump in the middle of the auditorium (typical lazy seat allocation). It was hot. I had planned once the lights went down to move to the empty seats in the aisle, but as they dimmed people kept coming towards us so I couldn't pass them to get out. I did a horrible leap and I scrambled over the back of the seats of the row in front (boys didn't follow). Felt wild and animal. Scraped and bruised my shins. Very silly. Unnerving because it all happened so quickly – the impulse irresistible to get out – claustrophobia, I suppose. Paul was embarrassed. Andrew didn't care. Even more of a crush in the bar so we sat in our seats and ate ice creams. I tried to explain the plot and got uselessly angry when Paul asked questions. Andrew said nothing. Not a good day. But only a day as Lillian would say. Michael had dinner ready for us when we got home but I wasn't hungry. Not hungry.

I want to see Lillian. I'm trying to imagine her voice.

July

Today Michael packing. Paul – silent – helping him. I stayed down here imagining Seymour jumping in and out of the suitcase. Andrew upstairs drawing, I imagine. I wanted to go out for a long walk – preferably by the sea – and barefoot. Only possibility Richmond Park, but I couldn't face the other people in it. I want solitude. I've stayed in here (waiting for Michael to leave I think). Before, I used to pack for him, it was one of those wifely duties that I never felt the need to refuse. Now I don't care – I don't care if he's got enough socks and a jumper in case it's cold and a realistic amount of shirts but just two pairs of trousers and a jacket for client meetings and nail scissors and enough toothpaste. It is hard sometimes to get used to this new freedom from the habit of our marriage.

I feel a craving for really fresh apple juice – in a glass jar with sediment at the bottom that I'll have to shake, and if I drink enough of it there'll be a slight acid crinkle on my tongue – also a milkiness – that milkiness I've never understood and half hated, almost a butteriness, but which has never stopped me from wanting to drink more – cloudy, uncoloured apple juice. There's a delicatessen a drive away that might have it – but I only know for sure where to find it in Soho. No Soho now. (No Soho now, no Soho now, no Soho now – the demons are singing again . . .) Fuck it – I'm going to go and see if I can find some.

Later

On my way back with elderflower cordial (no apple juice) Michael called down to me in the hall in the casual voice he now uses. I was out for ages going to different shops and no apple juice, standing in front of possible substitutes feeling confused, conscious that I looked stupid, unable to stop myself from inwardly debating about whether pear nectar would be too sweet or elderflower cordial not much more than squash and not being able to keep my mind on any of it properly. Anyway, I came when Michael called. Compliance dies hard. Case on bed – Paul guarding it solemnly – Michael holding his sponge bag.

'Paul would like me to ask you something for him.'

'What's the matter, Paul – afraid of me?' Another attempt

to coax him which failed. But he wasn't afraid to look me in the eye even though he didn't speak. I found myself wanting to psyche him out and I stared back at him fiercely.

'Darling –' Michael broke my concentration. 'Paul feels – are you sure you don't want to ask her yourself?' Paul shook his head.

'I'm bored with this,' I said, feeling so angry again, wanting to cry I felt so angry. I almost walked out on the dreary domestic scene.

'Zoë, just a second – we need a bit of time with you. Paul feels he would like to be a proper help to you while I'm away – take responsibility. He'd like to shop and cook, be domestic.'

'Of course, darling,' I think I said, turning away to the window. Michael – so thoughtful – was trying to give Paul a purpose (however mundane) and had come up with a cute little idea. He's probably given him an apron as a goodbye present. When neither spoke, I realised more was called for. 'You're a super little cook – what a help you'll be.' I tried to sound sincere, but I was irritated. I'm irritated writing about it now.

'Also, he'd like to sleep in my study while I'm gone – keep the room warm so to speak.'

'What's wrong with your own room?' I said, turning on him. I know it was wrong to attack him but I felt him to be so sly forcing me into this ludicrous negotiation, demanding to be treated like an actor with his first starring part discussing his dressing-room requirements in the presence of his agent. There's both cowardliness and his own form of stubbornness in that child. It is not straightforward intransigence like mine. Lillian calls it 'passive aggressive' (though she's not fond of labels) and says it's because he's insecure.

She's too sweet about Paul to call him downright sly, but the fact remains that demands made through Michael are far harder to refuse. For an instant I felt threatened, almost as if – if I'd refused – he'd have taken the children with him or sent them to my mother's and then I'd be deprived of Andrew and I need him.

'Of course you can sleep there if you like,' I managed to say.

'Andrew will be happier too I expect,' said Michael cheerily. 'He's getting to the age where he'd appreciate a room to himself.'

'Andrew doesn't make demands,' I said, again unable to keep my temper and seeing Paul red and almost tearful. He's my curse, that child. I exited on that line – it was as good as any I was likely to invent. After a murmured reassurance of his son, conducted as I went down the stairs, Michael followed me down to the kitchen (where I was gulping elderflower cordial) and ambushed me.

'Zoë – you will take good care of them and of yourself too of course – promise me?'

'Why are you even asking me this?' (I felt like a fight by then.)

'You'd be the first to admit you've been preoccupied recently. It hasn't been easy for Paul.' (What a kind and tactful reply.)

'Spare me the launch into psycho-babble.' (That was unfair, inaccurate, and enjoyable.)

'It's a very difficult time for us all. We're all affected. Paul's attached himself to me. You know how highly strung he is – it's important to try to make him feel –'

'Make him feel what? As if I'm his mother and I love him? Oh, I forgot, I am his mother and I do love him.' He didn't

say anything, so I went on, 'I do find scenes so very boring.'
I could tell I'd made him angry at last.

'I am no longer sure I believe that you do love him, or any of us. Not since Beth.' What was horrible about this was not the anger but the fact that it was the first time I've believed anything he's said for a very very long time.

'Aah. Cue, moment of truth,' I said.

'I'm sorry, Zoë, I lost my temper.'

'Boring boring boring,' I goaded.

'Please, pretend you like them – pretend that it matters.'

'You misunderstand me,' I said, and I was wonderfully cold.

'Don't be angry with me Zoë.'

'I'm not angry now. But I might be angry soon. Anger is good. Anger is honest. Anger releases. Anger cleanses. Anger defines self. Anger defines boundaries.' (I had to tell him this.) 'Yes. I promise to look after them.' I meant it and he knew that.

'Be gentle and good.' (He always says this.)

'Yes, yes.' I had to almost walk into him to get out of the room.

I'm tired now. I've tried to write it down the way it happened but I feel as if I'm writing and remembering through a fever, an old-fashioned raging fever of the blood.

July

I found Seymour on Paul's bed this morning (we moved it into Michael's study before he left) – a new place for him. The room has the same light as my study so that's probably why, but I told him he was a fickle cat nonetheless. He was washing and didn't care to communicate. The room is very tidy. There's his bed (which he actually makes), his glass of water on the bedside table (I almost expected to see false teeth in it he's such an old man) and the book shelf (he's brought it up with him too) – alphabeticised of course.

Andrew's got a whole suite of rooms now. Their playroom looks more and more like an artist's studio. I don't think Paul will use it any more. Andrew's done many more pictures of the chestnut pony – some sketch studies as if from life, others watercolours. They're wonderful. I sat with them a long time – in the shadows – (although I'm not meant to have seen them yet) wisteria covers that window. Now we're a week into the holidays and Michael's gone, Andrew and I are going to see two ponies tomorrow which we think might match his drawings – animate our vision. They're not in Cornwall, but who knows. He's been on the phone a lot – he's in charge of answering the advertisements – he has a list of questions written in rather lovely black ink, and he ticks them off meticulously. I couldn't concentrate for that long. He's emphatic that no bay or grey or brown ponies are to be investigated, which makes me laugh. The pony is Andrew's quest really, I'm just protecting it. (I wish I'd had his kind of freedom as a child.) Andrew also deals with my mother and sister who call most frequently. I know there'd be a row if I talked to them, so he takes charge. When he's not here I have to listen to their long hesitant messages on the machine. Sometimes I put my fingers in my ears to block out their voices. I don't talk to anybody who calls these days – it's all so trivial. I don't think Paul even wants to come with us tomorrow, so I'll probably leave him here – Seymour can babysit him.

With Michael gone at last the whole house seems to have breathed a sigh of relief. All the doors are open and I wander from room to room opening windows and letting in light.

I took Paul to meet Lillian today. It was strange dropping him off in the red-carpeted hall and not hurrying up the stairs to hug her – strange not even seeing her. Paul didn't want to be taken to her door or to have his hand held. He said he'd go by himself. He's always said that. We should put that on his tombstone.

When I came out into Devonshire Place I had no plans – just knew I had to amuse myself somehow for an hour. It was odd walking down those steps without my usual accompanying exhilaration – incomplete. I hadn't seen Lillian and wasn't going to. It always amazes me how many people there are on the streets of the West End on an ordinary weekday, looking as if they have money enough to shop, but by no means all rich wives – young people. Young men. I suddenly remembered laughing about it with Michael when we first met, and for some reason were having lunch at Debenhams' café. (He was obviously trying to impress me.) He put forward the theory that these were all people just popping out of their offices for half an hour coinciding with others doing the same, and that that was where they all came from. This made me laugh helplessly (I was very much in love) and yet it was not a theory that I could ultimately accept. We had given up in the end and amused ourselves by holding hands I think.

There they all were again today though – hurrying and

purposeful – and there was I, alone with an excited summer heartbeat. I walked for quite a long time – I had energy I wanted to burn – along the back of Oxford Street then across it into Soho and through Soho, hoping I wouldn't meet anyone I know, into Regent Street. London's become like the Third World. I was accosted by beggars and it made me quite angry where I used to feel guilty and sad. The city is brutalising. I wanted to shove them all out of my way. It was all right on Regent Street though – and all of a sudden I found myself window shopping and then going into shops, pulling armfuls of clothes from the rails, hurrying into the changing rooms and tearing off my old clothes, longing to put new ones over my head and walk in them up and down in front of the long mirrors admiring myself. This is new – I found I could decide without hesitation which clothes were right and buy them with total clarity (purpose). I've always seen buying clothes as a chore – in my last life it was part of the job and sometimes I enjoyed it but mainly I was preoccupied with calculating when I'd wear things and how often, what the value of each garment might be, what the purpose of each purchase was. (Purpose of purchase, purchase of purpose – here I go again – now the sounds are repeating themselves to the tune of 'Moses Supposes' in *Singin' in the Rain*, which isn't even my favourite film and I'm thinking about the apostrophe in singin', and how ridiculous it is and Gene Kelly's short arms – and I don't want to be thinking all these things I want to be explaining about the clothes. It's important.) These purchases had no purpose other than to give me pleasure. That was what was new. That is what I want to write down. I bought so many dresses – with short skirts – a silk print one with cherries on it – and I have tight trousers (I've lost an awful lot of weight) and a shirt dress and three pairs of shoes and two hats. Two hats – I can't believe it. I can't remember the rest – I haven't unpacked them yet – but I was so happy, so happy in those shops.

The ridiculous thing was that I completely forgot about Paul only being with Lillian for an hour and that he'd promised me solemnly to wait in the waiting room with his grown-up book (which he'd remembered to bring, poor darling). It was nearly lunch time and I'd said I'd pick him up at eleven. I took a taxi with my boxes, thinking about the tissue paper inside them, feeling so gloriously 1930s and supremely happy even though I'd forgotten, which is probably bad of me. (Lillian reminds me not to expect too much of myself, especially at this time of growth and change, but even now my upbringing bites deep.)

Paul was very kind and forgiving of me. Perhaps he hadn't expected me to be on time. He was very solemn on the way home and refused to discuss what he and Lillian had said, even when I got angry, which I suppose is good because it means they're building therapeutic trust and I shouldn't interfere. She'll tell me all about it next week, I'm sure. When we got home he went up to his father's study carrying a resigned Seymour, and I showed Andrew my clothes, and he invited me officially into his studio (the playroom) and we talked about the pony. He loves my theory that we've been inspired and that it actually exists. We talked about predestination for a long time. He hasn't read the books I've read – obviously – but he's so quick about picking things up.

Hot evening. Lovely. Played with Andrew in the garden under the sprinkler. He was the chestnut pony (as yet unnamed) and I was his trusty stable companion (Sunset – bright bay mare with black points and glossy tea cup hooves ...) At last it's summer. Proper summer. I made weak lemonade (due to the lack of lemons, Paul can't think of everything) and we had a scanty picnic on the grass near the poplars at the end of the lawn. Sun seeping into our bodies and hearts and minds – renewing us. We sat near the hollow I had imagined for Beth, and that made me feel even more uplifted. Paul wouldn't come outside. I saw him watching from the window of Michael's study for a while. He's so pale his face shines like a light. When I waved he disappeared – probably back to his books or whatever it is he occupies himself with. Andrew and Paul don't seem to speak to one another in front of me though I'm sure they chat like anything when I'm gone.

Anyway, after lunch – close to tea-time, I don't know, I've stopped wearing my watch – Paul came out to say that the doorbell was ringing. I think I snapped at him – he is fourteen after all, why couldn't he open the door. Anyway, it was Abbey, the boys' ex-nanny (I can't remember if she was still here when I started writing this). It was really most extraordinary: (a) I hadn't invited her, (b) I hadn't expected to see her ever again, and (c) I haven't seen anyone at all for such ages, so it was odd. She looked strange. I think she's put on weight and she stood in the doorway without explaining herself. She never did have much conversation (I think it's a class thing). Paul, next to me, stood as still as a little statue and then flung himself into her arms, which I found mildly irritating. She was very unembarrassed then, like a fat rock.

'Do come in,' I think I said.

In the garden she said, 'I thought I'd drop by – I miss the boys.' Andrew was resolutely ignoring her and had returned to the far end of the garden, so I couldn't really say that they'd missed her too. We sat on the terrace. 'I tried calling,' she said, 'but the machine was always on.' I didn't say that that usually encourages callers to leave a message. I didn't want to be unnecessarily rude.

'I'm having a holiday from the telephone,' I said. I knew then that I really didn't want her there. Having to explain myself has never been my strong point – but Paul, holding on to a part of her body or clothing at all times, was obviously so delighted to see her that I couldn't say anything. I felt he might shock us all if I did by making an uncharacteristic scene.

I went and made tea, leaving them together. She had produced the appalling iced biscuits she used to buy them from her bag – they were melting but I got a plate for those too. After a few questions – she's unemployed and about to go on holiday with her boyfriend, I told her about the pony and Michael's absence – we gave up talking and I moved the sprinkler to another part of the garden and pretended to do some weeding while she and Paul sat on the bench and I heard indistinct words tumbling out of his mouth. I felt myself getting angry and troubled and wanting to make her go away and leave us alone. This phrase repeated in my head a lot, and it had a tune too. As if in answer, Andrew, who had been sketching the delightful scene from under the poplars, suddenly ran full tilt down the lawn, arms outstretched like an avenging angel towards Abbey and Paul and said loudly, 'My mother wants you to leave now. You are an ex-employee, not a friend.' Abbey blushed terribly, and I dropped what I was doing and came over to apologise – I don't know what got into him – but somehow the group became me and Andrew standing on the grass above a silent Paul and Abbey sitting with their iced gingerbread men (or whatever they were), the low sun slanting into Abbey's eyes.

'Andrew should not have been so rude. Say you're sorry, Andrew,' I said.

'I'm sorry.' To his credit he smiled very sweetly at Abbey and then at Paul.

'Children are so unpredictable,' I said, but hot and blushing at the attempt to control my feelings. Fat cow get off my bench was what I wanted to say.

She eventually scrambled to her feet, blushing. 'Please don't apologise,' she said, 'but I must be going. I've got to catch a train.' I didn't offer to give her a lift to the station.

'We'll see you to the door, won't we, boys?' I said, and we marched through the house in formation, Abbey and Paul followed by me and Andrew. When we got into the hall Paul ran straight up the stairs without word or look. Abbey stood staring after him.

'He's a bit thin,' she suggested without looking at me, which was rude but that was all. I bit my tongue and tried to resist shoving her. I didn't even need to frighten her by looking her in the eye (something I've always been brilliant at). I think I might have laughed.

'Thank you for coming to see us, and have a lovely holiday,' I said.

'When's Daddy coming back?' she asked Andrew, quickly. He didn't reply, but just said goodbye politely, giving her a suggestion of a kiss as she bent down to him. When she had gone – her feet crunching on the gravel – I couldn't understand why I'd been so disturbed.

Wednesday

I had a gorgeous day 'pony shopping' as Andrew calls it with my delightful son today. I'm very tired but not sleepy. I'm in bed with hot chocolate and the blinds up – moonlight and dark leaf patterns moving on my bed. No Michael – it's wonderful. Seymour was here but he's gone out for a gambol under the full moon. Either that or he's defected to Paul's bed again. The moon is full I think. I've just been out on to the landing to check.

English summer is perfect when it wants to be. Everything was so alive and dancing today – very gay. I felt an uplifting sense of adventure. My spirits rose. How else can I put it? 'Up, up and away!', etc., etc. Andrew map-read – he's very good at it – and he had to be: we saw THREE different chestnut ponies in different parts of the country. The first in a yard on the edge of the Cotswolds – a show pony but it jumps – the girl's outgrown her and is moving on to horses. It's a (family) competition yard, slightly intimidating because I haven't been properly horsy for so long, and as Andrew can't ride yet I had to try out the ponies myself. The woman (I forget her name) suggested that we might need a less experienced pony. The point is that she didn't seem to understand that I'll be riding and exercising the pony while Andrew learns, and I know he'll be a natural – at competition standard in no time – and that we don't want to be stuck with some graceless creature without ability, courage or speed. Anyway, I rode the mare in a very nice outdoor arena. But I felt no affinity with her. We were very civil to the woman, but somehow I didn't feel that she had the right attitude to us. I can't say exactly why or what it was that made me so wary. (Lillian will know – or put it down to accurate intuition.)

We had lunch in a pub by a stream which was rather full of tourists, but we didn't care. Andrew sketched the swan which is their principle attraction – un-yellowed like the ones in St James's Park – and we talked quite a bit about divinity and the spirits of animals. I quoted him Yeats's *Leda and the Swan* – what I could remember of it – and he loved it.

The next pony was further into Gloucestershire in a rather untidy field (a sea of mud in winter I imagine). A gelding – thankfully – with four white socks (not so good). Rather amenable, towards the end of the best years of its life I would say. A farmer's daughter's pony – she was nowhere to be seen, probably off at college, or pregnant by some idiot in a squalid cottage somewhere. The farmer was clumsy. Our minds were on other things. We made our excuses after the animal was trotted up: I couldn't see the point of trying it out. As we drove away I had to conquer unbearable sadness about the animals who aren't wanted, who aren't stars, who are too old, or spoiled, or ruined by people. Andrew couldn't understand it, but there were nearly tears.

The last animal was the one we had the highest hopes for. For one he was the youngest (eight) and we'd been assured he was whole-coloured, and a spirited ride. No one had lied. We were moved by him. He's owned by a friend of a friend of my mother's so there were cups of tea on painted china instead of tack-room mugs, and cake for Andrew. (He ate three pieces.) We were treated with respect and Andrew was very polite to this lady in return, but I could see his mind was away from the whole enterprise and I felt as if I were in a room with his ghost. The lady was lovely, horsy without being snobbish in a concealed-emotional way. But the pony bucked. I can't go against everything I've been taught and seriously consider buying a bucker. We put the pony back in his stable and Andrew talked to him and untacked him in an endearing way (I can't remember his name) and we felt wistful in our hearts. But we had to say no, and we did it there and then instead of later, on the phone, like cowards.

Not back until after seven. Paul had cooked us supper as promised. Michael called. Thankfully I was in the bath but Paul talked to him. He's back on Monday. I don't want to see him.

Monday

I didn't want to be at home when Michael came back, but I knew he'd be upset if he found out I go out and leave them by themselves so I stayed here in the study, writing, with Andrew on the floor by the window sketching me. Paul upstairs. Evening summer fire in grate for comfort. A dew on the grass outside. I wanted to hide when I heard his footsteps in the hall. Andrew put his drawing aside, hiding it beneath a blotter. I could hear rustling paper as I stood up. I think we both said, 'Hello, darling,' but did not embrace. I have to watch out for him because he will try to impose and intrude. His beard's really a beard now. He asked us a lot of questions – first being where is Paul. I explained that he liked being left alone, upstairs, but he didn't pay very much attention to that – he's become very dictatorial. He seemed to take up a lot of space in the room.

'Is there supper?' he asked. I told him there was food but nothing cooked.

'We eat when we want to, when Paul doesn't cook,' I said, Andrew's eyes on my face. 'It gives us more freedom.'

'I'll make something,' he said, ignoring my statement, and he went out of the room, his footsteps echoing in the hall – lights coming on all over the ground floor (I don't bother so much – only in the room I'm in) and he called for Paul, over and over again, loudly. 'He likes to be left alone,' I said, to myself, and Andrew looked up at me and smiled, resuming his drawing.

The returning lord and master summoned us to roast chicken and rice (no vegetables to be found, he said). It was delicious. I was glad of it. Michael tried to talk to Paul, who was very silent. He's been in this phase for weeks so it would take a miracle to get him to respond, but such was Michael's ego (I've never seen him as macho as this) that he thought he could change all that. Andrew was quiet too. We didn't ask him, but he gave us news – news from Scotland – stories and jokes. Apparently it is all fine, the theatre is happy with what he is trying to do. He has to go back in a week or so, thankfully.

I didn't want to share my bed with him – but a solution presented itself. While Michael was in the bathroom and I was sitting up in bed pretending to read, Paul appeared in the doorway, holding on to the handle.

'I have to talk to you, Mummy,' he said, but did not advance into the room. I've never encouraged the children to be physically intimate with us.

'Can't you sleep?'

'I have slept and I've had a terrible dream.' For a second I was terrified that he was going to mention Beth's name, but he didn't. In fact the poor child would not even tell me what the dream was. 'I'm afraid that it will never be morning,' he eventually said, 'that the sun is not going to rise and it will be dark for ever and ever.'

'You're being silly,' I said, rather pleased that he was having such an imaginative fear. (I must remember to tell Lillian about it.) 'And it's not the case. Everyone knows it's going to be morning.'

'That's because it has always been morning before. But that doesn't prove it will be again.' The light of conviction shone in his eyes and silenced me. I was just about to lose my temper and tell him that fourteen was much too old for nightmares, when Michael came out of the bathroom in his towelling dressing gown and a cloud of steam.

'Tell Daddy,' I said. Paul repeated everything he'd said to me in the same hypnotised way. He was obviously distraught.

Michael went over to the child and took him by the hand.

'You're going to sleep with Mummy, tonight,' he said. I tried to signal over Paul's head that this was the last thing I wanted, but Michael was quite oblivious, and I couldn't reject the child openly. 'It's a big bed,' said Michael. 'You needn't bump into each other. Now you know that Mummy is here, and she loves you more than anything else in the whole world.' He tucked Paul in, talking constantly about foolishness and the bright day dawning tomorrow and being safe with Mummy in his 'Daddy' voice, which made me want to recoil. (I probably did.) Michael went to fetch Seymour from Paul's bed, who though baffled was not as contrary as he could have been, and settled down right on Paul's chest and stomach in a heavy comforting way. I turned over and pretended the child wasn't there. Michael went off to make him hot milk with brandy in it, and after drinking it obediently and a muttered goodnight, he was asleep long before I was. Michael slept in Paul's bed in his study. I hope he's comfortable enough to want to stay there.

Wednesday

I don't know what it is with Michael. He appears to have completely lost it.

He shouted at me today – in the conservatory – he shouted at me about the children and how disturbed they were and how it was all my fault. I couldn't believe it. He was in a murderous kind of rage. I'm trying to remember what his accusations were and I can't but I do remember the phrase 'retreat from reality', which he kept repeating like a charm. It was like a politician's favourite soundbite – rousing yet meaningless, threatening and exciting all at the same time. I stood and thought about this phrase as his voice and footsteps crashed and clattered around me. He'd closed all the windows and doors so we were trapped in there and it was a hot hot morning (he said he didn't want the children to hear, but I think he was simply being deliberately bullying). Andrew was in the long grass near Beth and Paul was upstairs. I'm sure they both knew exactly what was going on.

'You've changed,' I said. 'You used to be such a gentle man.' That was my overall feeling – wonder and detachment. (I didn't want to get angry and break the glass.) He dropped his voice and murmured to me about Beth's death disturbing me and I said, 'No no no. It's made me happy,' and he turned away from me and began to cry.

'What has happened to you?' he said between sobs. He was being such a drama queen and I felt really sick.

'I'm happy,' I said again. 'It's you who is lost.'

'You're still seeing that woman, aren't you?' he asked, and I nodded, dreading an attack, but he just breathed heavily as if he'd come to the end of a race and had no strength left to quarrel. I didn't tell him about Paul seeing Lillian but I explained he was working through his pain in his own way, and that Andrew has such gifts, and how the boys are growing and changing.

'No one should be forced to be normal,' I said, and then, when he didn't stop crying, 'If you don't like us why don't you leave us? Why don't you go and have an affair? That just might do it for you.' (By then I was angry and hadn't intended to say that cruel thing.) It was necessary though, because he has become so horrible. I think he was crying because he was so angry – he's become so angry and mean and closed.

'There's no money in our account,' was the only thing he said.

'I must have spent it then,' I replied, finding lovely anger, being lifted on a wave of it. He told me he wouldn't be paid for the job he's doing now for another month. I told him not to bore me.

'You can't buy a pony. We can't pay for it and we can't afford to keep it in London.'

'Try and stop me,' I said, feeling the wave carrying me, unfurling and green. (On reflection, why do marital rows always end in money? I'm on course, he's floundering, so he's trying to punish me, and it has to be with money. Perhaps that is what we all worship most, after all.)

'You must stop giving yourself to Andrew like this,' he then said.

'Jealous of your own son?'

'Paul needs you.'

'If you make any more demands on me or tell me how to live, how to relate to my own children, I'll take them and leave you one day and you'll never see us again – you'll never even know where we are.'

As I said these words I immediately knew that such an escape was both possible and inevitable. To Michael it was a threat which made him see how much I've changed, how far I've travelled from him and what I would do to escape if I need to. But it had to be done. He has to be disarmed. I won't have him interfering with us. He was silent for a while and then he called me a bitch. That was horrible because he has never said a word like that to me before and I've never heard him say it about anyone. Then he said, 'I won't let you win,' and made rather a clumsy exit.

'Still waters run deep,' I called after him, but the truth is he'd frightened me and I began to cry. I called Lillian, but even her private line was engaged and switched to her secretary (who is neither friendly nor efficient) so I'm not sure she'll even get my message. I feel quite bitter now. I didn't expect Beth's death to make Michael so cruel.

Thursday

Paul came into bed with me again last night. I put up a row of pillows to divide his side from mine.

Friday

Paul must have told Michael that he was seeing Lillian because he came storming in while I was doing my face this morning and demanded to know 'what I thought I was doing'. I told him Lillian was a genius. He tried to smash my bottle of scent. I think he's really gone mad. Paul was in my room (still asleep I think) – I was getting ready for a pony expedition, Andrew waiting in the hall. He woke up when the clattering started (I was commendably strong during the struggle) and cried out to Michael, 'Don't hurt Mummy,' over and over again. Thankfully that distracted Michael and he went out of the bathroom and over to the bed to talk to the child, calming down, murmuring and apologising.

I don't know what to do now though. If he's going to become violent I really will have to leave. I want Lillian's advice but she still hasn't called me back and my next appointment isn't till Monday. I don't want to abandon my refuge – my study, my garden, my home. I can't bear the thought of going to Mummy's – there isn't even enough room at the cottage, and it would be against everything I've worked for.

Monday

Felt very confused before I saw Lillian today. Couldn't think straight. I never thought the day would come when Michael would threaten me – when I would be afraid. True – he's been calm enough today, leaving me be, in and out of his study. He took the boys somewhere. I just couldn't think straight. I felt so alone.

She wore blue today. She'd had her hair done. When I first sat down on the whispering chairs I couldn't speak, even though she said, 'Tell me, tell me,' in that encouraging bright way she has – as if it were a midnight feast in the dorm in some story-book boarding school and we were about to giggle about pranks. I had to look at her amethyst ring (that steadies me), the net curtains in the breeze, the tired wallpaper (particularly the bit peeling near the skirting) and study her wise face – look at her make up and see if it is the same as last time . . . Stupid, I know. But I had to make extra sure my Fairy Godmother was really real and there today.

When I told her about Michael's rage she surprised me by breaking into laughter, a big tinkling laugh which became deeper and deeper in true merriment and joy.

'He has had a jolt!' she said. 'What a fuss he's making.' She wiped her eyes with her handkerchief and I felt my heart begin to lift. 'You know what it's like disciplining children?' she said. 'When they first realise they are not the centre of the universe and the world outside has a different agenda? He's going through that phase.' After giving me a good minute to take this in, she said, 'What do I always say?'

'There's no change without change.'

'Exactly. He's been away. He wanted to come back and find everything the same: his wife paralysed by grief, an automaton of suppressed feeling, his children obedient and polite. Don't forget, they've always been more his children than yours.'

'Yes.'

'Now he's finding that you're exploring new avenues within yourself every day, that the children are grieving, Paul emotional, Andrew expressing his creativity, and he's terrified. Men always express fear through rage. Now he wants you to believe it's your fault. That would make him feel much better. Are you going to satisfy him by believing that?'

'No.' As I said no it all became so clear – like the click of a seatbelt into its holder. What was wrong became clear. I know now that I must be (will be) undeterred. The way forward is still open.

She doesn't think he'll act on any of his threats. He's a good and decent man at heart. I must remember that and forgive him and try not to let him provoke me.

He's going away again tomorrow anyway. The time away will give him a chance to take it all in. I wish he'd come with me to Lillian, we could accomplish so much. But I know there's no sense in even trying with him. We also agreed that there's no need for Paul to keep sleeping in my bed. He's using this place-changing bed-hopping as a way of avoiding his feelings, and it's also Michael's way of exercising control. So I must reject him, but as gently as I can.

Saturday

I think Michael's been through my desk (looking for Lillian's number?). It's not that it's all upside down – it's just that everything feels just so slightly disturbed.

Tuesday – 3 a.m.

Michael gone again – thank God. I am lying in bed – Paul sleeping beside me still. Tomorrow I'm going to have to tell him it's got to stop. I think there are some women who aren't intended to marry and have children, and I'm definitely one of them. I look at Andrew and I think, What a marvellous child, but in a distant way, as if he grew up with someone else (on reflection he did grow up with someone else – Michael) and was then given to me fully fledged as a walking talking dream companion. I marvel at him, at his imagination, his good manners, his natural feeling for silences, his self-possession, his intelligence – his drawing talent. I feel connected to him, but not as if I were his mother, I feel connected in a spiritual way, a twin-soul way, a like-meets-like way, almost the way I felt when I found Lillian, that's how it has felt, to discover that my son is such a treasure. But I don't feel protective towards him particularly (I admire that he never seems to require it of me) – I feel wonder towards him. It's just as well he doesn't need my protection. Look at the way I failed Beth – and the way I continually fail Paul.

The difference, though, is that I don't really care about failing Paul. He doesn't interest me. As a baby Paul was another chore, another thing to fit into my day. Michael loved him, Michael was a father to him. I was a milk machine. I didn't want to admit how little I felt about Paul, and the weariness in the idea after he was born that I'd have to have another baby to complete the family, and fulfil my side of the unspoken bargain between myself and Michael. The tediousness of Paul – his eyes fixed on me, one hand reaching for the hem of my skirt – toddling after me, other hand in his mouth, eyes wide with entreaty. I remember calling for Michael to come, or Marie (she was the first in a long line of au pairs). I must tell that child today that I don't want him in my bed for one more night. Not one more night. He's sleeping beside me now, quite peacefully. From now on he can sleep in his own bed.

Took Paul to Lillian for his second visit. I wish I'd had the chance to see her, but he went up alone again.

At least I was on time to collect him today. He looked taller than I'd expected, standing on the Devonshire Place steps. His fringe needs cutting. I felt as if I had not seen him for a long time. When he saw me he smiled and I was taken aback. I never feel the urge to smile when I see him.

'Hurry – I'm on a meter,' I think I said.

In the car he said, 'Mummy, I think you are very brave, and I love you.'

'What makes you say that? Has Lillian been telling you to open up?' I couldn't stop my voice from coarsening and I couldn't look at him.

'I say it because it's true. You are a very brave mother.'

'Thank you,' I said, as graciously I could.

'I don't forget that you gave up your career to be with us.'

'Yes, that's true,' I said, 'I did,' wondering why I had, what my reasoning had been, wondering why my life seems darker and narrower and less clear to me every day. Now with the dark around me I'm trying not to wonder.

'Mummy, I loved Beth, and I miss her.'

'What has she given you? A truth drug?' I replied. 'You know that we don't talk about Beth. It's all over, and she's at peace now.'

'But we are not at peace.'

I pulled the car over to the side of the road – they hooted and shouted behind me.

'Look at me, Paul. I have taken you to see Lillian because you are having nightmares, you are in distress, you are unable to relate to your brother, or to me, or to Daddy, you cannot concentrate on your school work. Whatever you feel about the family, about your sister, I want you to tell Lillian, that is what she is there for. Just don't tell me.' Almost as soon as I started making this speech, Paul turned his head away, and gazed out of the window – it looked as if he were contemplating the open mouth of a particularly insalubrious newsagent's. I carried on venting my irritation at the back of his head, which has remained the most endearing thing about him. I knew that, ten to one, one of his slow tears was making its crooked way down his cheek. 'Darling, I'm sorry. I didn't mean to snap. I'm glad you're talking about things – how you feel – with Lillian. Really. She can help us.'

'I just wanted to tell you I thought you were brave,' he said in a choked but determined voice. 'I don't like Lillian. I'm going to see her because you want me to go. This has nothing to do with her.'

'You idiotic child,' I said. 'Do you *know* how stupid you are?' He began to cry properly this time, turned away from me, his curled-up fist in his mouth. 'I'm sorry,' I said again, tired, irritated.

I rang Lillian when we got home.

'Tell her I want to talk to her about my son,' I told the fucking secretary. I still don't know whether she got the message, whether she'll call or if I have to wait till Monday.

Friday – July

Woke miserably early this morning (not unusually) listening to the dawn chorus and Paul's child breathing. Hungry, my stomach rumbling. (Food is difficult. I feel empty-sick most of the time – then sudden stabs of hunger and strong thirst and I have to eat very quickly – starchy sugary things or fruit, not meat really and I have to eat very quickly before I start to feel sick again.)

Lying here I've been thinking about breathing. Not Paul's breathing, Beth's breathing, I don't know why. I never think about Beth. I don't need to think about her any more, it's not what matters. But Paul was just breathing on and on and sometimes making little sucking noises – a bit like babies do – or a tut tut tut of teeth knocking one against another – he's lying very still now – he's a tidy sleeper. I hate him so much I want to shake him awake – I want to shake him as if he were a fruit machine that has taken my change – I don't know why I'm thinking of fruit machines lying here useless as a cripple, now I see fruit and fruit juice and feel my hunger leap up again like anger – it's a salty face-stained tumult because I want my thoughts to stop so I can rest and not be hating Paul so much – so completely. I'm trying to think of things he's said to me – or done – any things that might make him feel worthwhile to me – but I can't think what they are. I'm trawling the past for memories – any memory at all of Paul and I sharing a look or a word or a silence which would make up for the years he's irritated me, the hours and days and years he has made me guilty and embarrassed and wretched in the way only a mother who dislikes her own child can feel. Birds in dawn chorus no harmony. I can see it all in colours and lights – the past – then Paul's eyes looking at me, following me, that child shadowing my bright days and new discoveries. Paul missing Beth – as if he had that right, as if he dare bore me with it.

All I've just written was so horrible. I've got out of bed and pulled up the blind – unremarkable summer dawn. Light on the other side of the house if there's any light yet at all. Dreary. I didn't try to be quiet, going to the bathroom, running water over my wrists – trying to feel cool – as if it were a new day and not just a continuation of the old one.

Back in bed. Restless. I haven't been trying to lie still, just sat up and reached out for this book and began to re-read it, looking for Lillian, just a feeling of her (I won't see her today). Morning, unhappy dawn, and dawn all over the city, the whole country – people getting up who have somewhere to go.

I just put the book down and sat up higher in bed, back of my hand over my eyes, when Paul stirred and turned over towards me. When I moved my hand away, his eyes were open and fixed on my face. They were frightening – alive but dark and dead eyes. He said, 'Mummy, are you all right?' and I said, 'I will be when you stop sleeping in here with me.' As I said it I had an irresistible vision of putting a knife blade into his eyes. He shrank back and flinched with pain, as if I had, but he only said, 'I'm sorry, Mummy,' and got out of bed quietly as if not to disturb a baby, put on his dressing gown and went out of the room.

I feel so bad about it. How could I have let him know – after all this striving to achieve something – how could I have let him know how I feel?

Now. Now this is despair.

August white day. It's always been my worst month.
Nothing ever happens in August (unless you're sixteen).
Even when it's windy it's still: nothing happening – nothing
arriving on the breeze. Michael is back – up in his study. Me
downstairs in mine. Andrew is drawing in the playroom,
Paul reading in his room. After lunch I lay on the grass
(which needs cutting) on the quilt. Had to go inside, though,
not an enjoyable heat – sweaty – no direction. Have had two
baths and one shower since I got up today. Seymour has
disappeared, probably under a bush somewhere. For some
reason I thought about the office, how those stupid portable
fans are usually on – last year we got a quote for air-
conditioning and were hovering on the brink (too expensive).
Jeffrey must be still laying people off, winding things up.
Until now I've been happy and felt cleaned out, but now I
feel heavy and encumbered – not pain like *pain*, just
heaviness. Nothing.

Later

I really needed to see Lillian by the time this evening came,
but I was late because I couldn't decide what to wear (kept
changing my clothes).
   'I feel full of poisons,' I said. 'All in my guts. Perhaps I'm
riddled with cancers and don't even know I haven't long to
live.' Of course it was a deliberately provocative thing to say.
Lillian was wearing a turquoise dress patterned with peacock
feathers which had purple and indigo centres to them (she's
the only person I've ever met who can carry off such vulgar
colours) and she had on white tights (I've always wondered
who actually bought these) and her strappy sandally shoes (a

different version of the black shiny ones she wore when we first met). She probably buys her clothes and shoes in three different colours like politicians' wives or queens of industry. Her heavy curtains are open now it's summer evenings we share but the half net curtains were still drawn, fluttering against the open window and dark tinged where they hit the sill. I thought that was bad – it is Devonshire Place after all. She looked as if her face had been sweating and she'd blotted it with one of those coarse green-paper towels you find in institutions and then put on more powder. I'm almost sure that was what she'd done before I had come in.

'Sorry for yourself? Is it suddenly so hard?' she challenged.

'I feel as if I'm losing my way.' She didn't answer this. It's part of her technique. She was acknowledging that I was seeking reassurance, playing a game which required her to coax and humour while I stamped my foot. By her silence she was indicating that she didn't have time for such games.

'How's Michael? Has he threatened you since he's been back?'

'No.'

'I thought it would pass. Are you still afraid?'

'Not of him.' She didn't ask me what I was afraid of because she didn't want me to change the subject and invent. She wanted to know about Michael. 'He doesn't want me to leave him. So he's keeping still, waiting for it to blow over.'

'What to blow over?'

'I don't know. Me. The new me – you and me's me.'

'Aah.' She smiled. Right answer. 'Are you feeling ready to blow over?'

'No. But things are changing. I used to feel very busy inside, quick. The world was different, faster and more beautiful than before, than ever before. She died – we met –

and it was good. It had a meaning. Now I feel tired, heavy, no direction.'

'A contemplative place to be after all your exertions.'

'I wish I saw you more. Outside here.' I hadn't expected to say that. Her eyes flickered with something (pleasure?) but before I could look she got up to answer the knock on the door which meant the tray of tea had arrived. She had to cross behind me and the space in front of me was achingly empty and ugly without her in it.

'One day, perhaps – later,' she said in reply. 'There's still a lot of work to be done in this room.'

'I don't know what to do now.'

'"Teach us to care and not to care, teach us to sit still."'

'I didn't know you knew T. S. Eliot.'

She smiled again. To the tea-pot she dedicated her divine smile. 'Stay still with Michael, and don't close yourself to him. Don't be afraid of his rage – or his love. Is Andrew still creative, busy, himself?'

'Yes.'

'Have you found the horse?'

'Pony. We haven't looked for a while.'

'Why not?'

'It seems less important. Andrew is still drawing him.'

'Don't allow yourself to be deprived of your dreams. Don't forget them because it's August and you're hot and tired.'

'How's Paul doing with you?'

'Oh, I love little Paul – he's beautiful!' This came out in a spontaneous outburst of almost childlike joy, as if he were her own new-born baby and he had suddenly been placed in her arms. Her capacity for the enjoyment of life, of those sent to her (as she describes it) never ceases to amaze me.

'What is he saying to you?'

'I think that is between myself and Paul, don't you?' she said, as if the delicate matter of coming between a mother and her son was just another piece of etiquette I had forgotten in a momentary lapse of concentration. Her voice, though, was low and gentle. It pacified me.

'I just thought you might be able to tell me how serious it was – what exactly you feel might be the matter with him.' I didn't dare tell her how cruel I had been in defence of my bed.

'His soul has been suffocating. Together we are loosening his bonds.' She was pouring the tea. I admired her rings. But I felt (for a fraction of time) as if she were administering a punishment.

'I'm sorry. I'm just worried. I don't love him enough and I'm cruel to him and I don't want him to suffer because of me.'

'People don't suffer because of other people. They suffer through allowing themselves to let others make them suffer.'

'Am I part of what troubles Paul?'

'Why don't you ask him that yourself?' I began to cry – water in the shiny surface of the orange tea. She put down her cup, took mine out of my hand and clasped it, standing above me, bending down and touching my head with her other hand. It was tranquillity and love. If I had wanted to pull her down beside me and cry on to her breast it would not have shocked or displeased her, but it was not necessary because the nearness of her and just the touch of her hands were enough. 'It is not all going to be clear at once. How long have you been coming to see me?'

'Nearly four months.' I already felt less tightness, as if I might be ready to laugh through my tears. After all, it really is a very short time in which to redirect the course of a life. Quietly handing me tissues, she went back to her chair, studying me lovingly while I wiped my eyes and blew – picking up my tea, and drinking it with new appetite.

As I left, she told me she's going away on holiday so next week both Paul's and my appointments are cancelled. I wish I'd known earlier. Now I'm lying on my bed remembering all the things I'd wanted to ask her about, especially whether she gets my messages when I call and if she does why she doesn't call me back. I keep forgetting that.

Perhaps it doesn't matter. Perhaps it's a sign about self-sufficiency, discipline.

Everything feels remarkably the same. I must not be defeated. I must summon my strength.

August

I am not feeling very good at all now.

I am a very bad woman and a very bad mother. I know this. Michael was right to be afraid about leaving the children with me. One has died under my care already. Baby Beth died and that was my fault. A mother knows. When she started struggling for breath that day, that moment when I was getting restless here in my study and hungry for lunch, I should have known. A true mother would have known. I might have been yawning or stretching the moment she struggled for breath up there, and they panic, cot-death babies die in panic, paralysed and choked with fright. Not very far for me to run up the stairs if I had sensed it, and find her, and massage her little chest and hold her in my hands. She might have lived – or even died in my arms. If she had died in my arms perhaps there would have been less suffering.

No. That is stupid. Opening and closing her little unfocused eyes, gasping like a fish, me – frantic – it would not have been better. But still I should have known. I should have been less selfish – had the cot in our room at night and in my study by day. She was too small and defenceless to be alone in a room so far away. It could have been prevented.

To fail her and now fail Paul. My cruelty to Paul has been measureless. I don't know why I've been so wild – I don't know. Now I am here and so ashamed I don't want to be seen by any eyes – no eyes at all.

I wrote that this morning and have been so tired I've slept all afternoon. Ghastly waking in twilight and not knowing what time it is, and with this weight on my chest – heavier than Beth's body would have been.

I cannot make it up to the boys. But if I leave them together, at least I cannot contaminate them. Still sleepy. Frightened by discovering Seymour on the back of the sofa I've been sleeping on, staring at me hungrily then scratching the velvet.

Not a sound from upstairs. What are those boys doing? (Michael away again.)

Went upstairs to have a bath. Dead weight on my chest invisible in water, but I still feel it. Rested on bed. Paul knocked and came in, fixing his eyes on me. I was so ashamed. He asked me if I was all right and told me it was six o'clock. I explained that I was tired. He asked if I would have supper with them – he is cooking – if I would come down. I said I would and managed not to cry. He is simply a son who loves his mother and is worried for her. He does not hate me.

Silent supper. Deadly summer darkness. Electric lights hurting my eyes though Paul lit candles (God knows where he found them). A very good version of one of Michael's stews. Clever boy. Andrew seemed miles away. He told me he was still working on the drawings. This while Paul putting plates in dishwasher. For brothers they are very guarded with each other. I am so tired I will put light out now, only ten o'clock.

August

Have been lying in embryo position all morning. Radio 4. Rainy outside. It is Sunday. Paul told me he has put chicken in, but is going out to visit Beth's grave. This has made me cry. Andrew will not go. Paul will take some time without his father to drive him. The bus is slow. Perhaps I should make myself get up and take him in the car. I don't have to look – I can wait in the car. It's the least I can do.

Of course I didn't stay in the car, idiot that I am. Four months after her death, my first appearance at the grave. Paul knows the way well because he goes once a week with Michael when he's here. You have to walk through what seems like a mile of graves to get to the children's corner, a kitsch name for the infants' burial plot. Her grave is extremely small – there's a shiny plaque – and Paul took away the flowers from last week, and added the ones he'd picked from the garden (stocks and campanula) and we stood with our heads bowed in the rain (typical graveside weather I assume). I felt so exhausted I knelt down on the grass and put my hand on the plaque. There was her name and her date of birth and death, and then it said, 'Remember me', which is better than 'sadly missed'. Michael has taste. I felt giddy. Paul helped me up and was very kind and solicitous. I came back to bed after lunch.

Monday – August

Took most of my strength to get up and go to see Lillian today and in the end it was a wasted effort. There was a message which the porter/doorman person gave me. She'd phoned to say she was detained at another clinic and would I wait. I did, for over an hour, but no Lilly. I came home and crawled upstairs. Paul brought supper on a tray – later Andrew came in with a finished picture. What a beautiful vision. What a complete waste of time. (I didn't tell him this.) He says he's starting on my portrait now. He seemed very happy. He doesn't understand that everything has changed. None of these things matter. I'm so exhausted I can't write any more. Wouldn't it be good if I were dying?

Thursday – August

Two things happened today. Michael called – I did not speak to him. Andrew dealt with it all, explaining I had flu and was too weak, everything was fine, Paul still a wonderful housekeeper, etc. etc.

Second, it was Paul's day to go to Lillian and he asked me if I would cancel and not take him.

'Is it not helping?' I asked.

'No.'

'Why do you think that is?' As his mother, I should ask the question without bias.

'I don't like her. I don't trust her.' He is a very truthful child, which is good.

'Why don't you like her?'

He looked at me for a flicker of one of his penetrating glances and said, 'I think she's a bit mad, Mummy.' I wanted to laugh – I knew the whole thing was absurd – this great doctor being called mad by such a little boy.

'Why?'

'She thinks Beth's death is good, when everyone knows it is bad. The worst thing that could ever have happened.'

'The worst thing that could ever have happened.' I repeated the phrase after him, and it seemed to just about sum it up. 'Why do you go to the grave every Sunday?'

'To be near Beth and to say I'm sorry. I always say sorry to her.'

'Why? What are you sorry for?'

'Sorry for being still alive.'

'But that's not right, Paul. You must not say that. You must not think this. Daddy and I don't think it.'

'You and Daddy loved her more than you could ever love me. She was very good and pure, not like me.'

'Paul, you're a very good boy.'

'No.' I didn't know how to go on. Too shocked to reassure him, I suppose. (Too incapable, more like.) I tried to hug and kiss him. I couldn't tell him I loved him because I have no feelings, but I tried to do right by him – tried to reassure him.

'You're a very good boy,' I said again.

'I know you don't really think that.'

'I do.' He made me move over to the other side of the bed, and he smoothed the sheets and did the pillows for me. Then he tucked me in. Only a few minutes between his shutting the door and the black heaven of unconsciousness.

Michael's Journal

September 26th

Felix Bracewell, my solicitor, brother-in-law, and I hope and
pray my very dear friend, has asked me to provide a written
account of the last few months, for purposes of my trial.

I will be on trial for murder, for murdering my family. It is
very strange, writing that, but rather than confusing me I
hope it will make me see more clearly. What I'm about to
write should not – will not – be muddled. I am determined.
Felix does not know when the trial is going to be but it could
be as long as a year away. We do know it will be very
expensive and there will be a lot of publicity because of Zoë.
Also infanticide is a big public issue at the moment. Papers
have offered me money for my story, and I would be lying if
I said I had not been tempted. It would help with the legal
fees, and for me to give Zoë's mother money for the boys,
but it would be wrong. More pragmatically, Felix says it
would make me appear dishonest. So I've put the house on
the market instead, and here I am in prison: I will not be
entitled to bail because I am considered a danger to my sons.
I actually find it quite a comfort to be here. It's the discipline,
the alien quality, the distrust, suspicion, stupid aggression,
but above all, routine that comforts me. I feel separate. If I

were in the world I'd cry all day long, and visit the graves, and drink too much and embarrass and exhaust my friends. Here it is not that I am safe from the wickedness of the world, but rather from my own wickedness, from the particular and specific evil which engulfed our family from the day of Beth's death – April 12th, to my arrest, September 18th I think it was. At least I hope and pray that that is the case, that evil respects prison bars and only dogs an active man.

I miss Seymour the cat. He has gone with Paul and Andrew to my mother-in-law, Beatrice's, in Berkshire.

I'm Catholic. Right and wrong, rules, hell-fire: they've always been real to me. Both my parents are dead. They were good people, mostly: they were poor and lived their lives according to the rules for the poor and did not complain. They thanked God though when I escaped them and their class, without seeing how ironic that was. I escaped, not so much through my profession, and the money I made at first, but through my marriage to Zoë. They could hardly speak to Zoë but they were so proud she was their daughter-in-law. I don't think Zoë ever understood that. They wanted the boys to be brought up as Catholics but Zoë was an atheist so they contented themselves with our agreement: to give them Instruction, to make them aware, but not force them. It was a strange compromise – being given inviolate values and then told you could choose whether to believe them. Like most compromises it didn't really work and it inevitably meant that I practised less. Zoë said none of that mattered because I was a good man and would make our sons good by example. She used to tease me and say that I even made *her* better. She felt so guilty about her success, her go-for-it temperament, her wonderful bossy nature. In that way she was more Catholic than I am, full of guilt and struggle. I was so proud of everything she did, everything she was, and she was the kindest, sweetest, bravest. She was always so extraordinarily strong, driven almost, and because of that I believed she was not fragile, which was a misjudgement. I think single-minded people are more vulnerable because of their fixed ideas.

She went mad. There's no kinder way of saying it, and I don't approve of psychological terms. Zoë went mad with grief. Madness made her hard, without dimensions, like somebody acting a part. I was powerless to help her, and to stop it. It made me furious which I'm ashamed to admit. It made me furious, but it did not make me murderous. That is the case I have to argue and that Felix has to prove: that our family is innocent of everything except the fact that evil made itself manifest in our midst and that we were powerless to withstand it.

Extremely unfashionable – evil.

Enough preamble. On April 12th, our baby – Elizabeth – died. It was a cot death, she was a month old, and it was a tragedy. I think Zoë suffered most because of her guilt. She was never a very maternal person, and we hadn't planned Beth. During her pregnancy she moaned and carried on about it: she was uncomfortable, she was fed up, she was too old to be having another baby, etc. And she was at the height of her career. It meant maternity leave right in the crucial pre-production period for the fourth series of her show. She felt guilty for not wanting Beth but I knew she *wanted* her if that makes any sense. Hard to explain the distinction. When she was born we were both besotted. I think the boys were amazed by how soppy we were about her. When she died I think Zoë saw it as a punishment for all her selfishness – as simple as that. She didn't ever say that, but it's what I felt was in her heart. She wouldn't talk about it. All the practicalities were dealt with by me. The doctor was kind, the inquest was brief, I chose the burial plot – I managed it all.

Zoë wouldn't speak, but what happened was worse than silences. She wouldn't look up and see any of us. If she were with us, she refused to *be* in the room with us – it was just her body. I didn't understand fully that this, the manner of her withdrawal from us, was what put us all in such peril. I just suffered because I felt she distrusted me, which was terrifying. I had never felt it before. I was very selfish and forgot to remember that I didn't really count.

Then she took up with this crazed monomaniac psychiatrist: one of the new breed who think we are all suffering from a disease called life which only abdication of will and wit and surrender of both these to them and only them will cure. It's the kind of thing you would credit Zoë with seeing through in a maximum of ten seconds but I know now she was in the wrong place at the wrong time the night they met. It was an appointment with evil, and there was I mildly looking on, shepherding her away at the end of the show after smiling at the woman and shaking her jewelled hand. Lillian had – has – rare concentration: the way she looked at Zoë and looked at me . . . She dismissed me: I may have been 'in pain' but I was certainly not 'in need' and she could sense the difference swiftly and with no difficulty. But Zoë, who was electric and glittering with a beautiful kind of suffering, must have appeared a perfect prize. Zoë behaved as if bits of her body were bandaged and seeping blood, she moved awkwardly like a knight who had been wounded in battle but would not stop fighting. Her face was taut, her little firm mouth set and her eyes dared you to look into them, to address what was inside them instead of the made-up exterior and the immaculate Armani silhouette.

And of course – Zoë was famous. I should never have forgotten that.

I know that at the beginning Zoë felt that if she could just keep working, doing what she could, she would get through Beth's death. And she might have done, and I would have been there, patient, and completely on her side. But Lillian didn't want Zoë to survive. She wanted to destroy her and make her again, re-make her as she, Lillian, imagined her. I don't think anyone had dared tell Lillian for a long time, I would think, that there were limits to her power, that the Creator fashions a person and that it is blasphemy to interfere. God is really rather *de trop*. You can empty a room by mentioning His name. Now we have fancy witch doctors like her. Perhaps Lillian believed that after she had destroyed Zoë's world view, a new and better one would emerge. I wonder how many people she has destroyed who could not re-form and who went as mad as Zoë. Of course there are plenty of mad people walking about still. Zoë had the misfortune to die. On reflection I think perhaps that that is more my misfortune. How could I wish any of this on her, that she were still here?

They think I killed her, (a) because I knew she was mad, had possibly murdered Beth, and was now a danger to Andrew and Paul, or (b) simply because I was angry with her because

I knew she had killed Beth. A doctor cannot always tell the difference between cot death and suffocation. Sometimes the blood vessels in the eye are affected by suffocation, but this is not always the case. There's also (c) that I killed Beth and then Zoë because Zoë found out about my murdering Beth. They've charged me with both murders and I think they will work out the details later. Mercy killing, crime of passion, or even lunacy, it is all the same thing to them. All these theories are the inventions of stupid people. Their ideas are false. I don't think that when Oscar Wilde wrote that each man kills the thing he loves he meant it to be taken literally. We live in an excessively literal age. Beth's death was an accident. Zoë's death – that remains a mystery. She was found face down, smothered and choked. Accident or murder, the post-mortem cannot distinguish. The physical evidence is inconclusive. I think that's the phrase. Because Beth was also smothered it stands to reason: not two accidents, two murders. I write this calmly. I am amazed at how calmly I write. All I can say is that I would not kill her but no one believes in such coincidences, so I am a prime suspect. They can't think of anyone else, and neither can I.

It may sound odd to you, Felix, but I must admit that in these strange days I have asked myself whether I could have been capable of killing Zoë. As you know, there have been murder cases where the perpetrator buries the memory of his crime even from himself, goes into a trance or delirium or sleepwalker's state. The trouble is that there is no answering such a question. My conscious mind will always deny it. I can only say to you from the depths of my soul that I loved Zoë and could never harm her. I prayed for whatever it was that afflicted her to die, I'll say that freely – but never her sweet self. I repeat to you what you already know. All these circles. I hope this is all clear. Felix, as you read this, fear not, I will go back and give details. But I'm tired now.

September 27th

In the post today came a short note from Andrew inside a card made from one of his drawings – beautifully, I might add – also a copy of the estate agent's details for our house.

I don't know which one disturbed me most.

Because the house is in a 'premier road' and a 'sought after' location, there are three colour photographs: of the outside of the house, of the garden, and of the double reception room. The outside is smart, to use a Zoë's mother word, and ugly, and well cared for: a herringbone path, gravel, a low wall, a tree. The drawing room is sparse, we were never in it very much really, especially at the end. But the garden, that view is taken from Zoë's study, practically from her beloved desk through the bay window and up the lawn to the trees. One of her favourite sights in all the world, and the photograph has a feeling of collusion, of being in Zoë's secret world – now gone – and I'm probably inventing all this out of longing. The grass definitely needs cutting, which does not look good – I know there's no one living there now, but the agents should have sorted it out. After all two per cent of an eight-hundred-thousand-pound house ought to just about cover it.

I love that house.

I wanted to be in that house until I died. The deaths I imagined, mine and Zoë's, mourned by our grandchildren, those deaths will never happen. Instead there are grotesque deaths, untimely I think is the word. I can't blame the house for being the site of those deaths. I've suddenly had a thought: will it fetch more or less because of its ghosts? Knowing the world, probably more.

I remember, when we bought it, Zoë thought it a terrible chore. We were just married, she was in the middle of wowing the nation with her early-evening news show and had just renegotiated her contract. It was before she and Jeffrey had the idea of 'putting on their own show' but it was at the time of her first taste of fame – and of love. I know that sounds corny and awful, but it was true. I know she felt that she had more than she'd ever hoped for. She told me she had become almost resigned to her loneliness when she met me. We were both so surprised, as if people didn't fall in love and get married every day. We were very happy, but she was incredibly busy so I did the house hunting. I wanted something big we could renovate and fill with children. Being a lighting designer I wanted to wire each space appropriately. Zoë accuses – accused – me of being a modernist and wanting to turn the house into a monstrous igloo but we compromised, simplifying a lot of things, but keeping the heirlooms. I supervised it all, spending my new wife's money (my own business went bust before we were even married) and she lectured me about not feeling guilty that I wasn't the conventional breadwinner. That was the deal. She made the money, I made the home. And when we brought Paul home, under a year after the wedding, my cup overflowed.

September 29th

Felix, some thoughts following our meeting. It was quite an occasion for me. Being here makes me forget the outside, you running the press gauntlet to get in. I expect the attention will fade after a few weeks. Don't blush while you read this, Felix, but I like you more than ever. Even though we married into the same family, we've never really found time to know each other. You're very simple and direct, you remind me of Zoë in the way your mind works, but you're much softer. Why did we never talk properly before now?

I'm grateful for the books you brought me. I get so bored with Radio 4. They won't stop going on about the Second World War, either that or politics, and the presenters are so repetitive and self-indulgent. Yes, I suppose I'm angry about being cooped up. And I want to see my sons. I wish Beatrice would bring them but I can understand why she doesn't.

Felix, you mentioned specific incidents with corroborative evidence. While I have plenty of the first I'm really not at all sure about the second. There were so few witnesses to our lives after Beth's death, and then I was away and Zoë was completely alone with the boys. I don't want to involve them at this stage, but I am pretty sure that Zoë kept a diary. It must be still at the house, in her desk amongst her papers, unless the police have it. I never read it, I wouldn't pry, but she shut herself up for hours writing and I'm sure there must be a lot of detail. Also it will tell us a great deal about her state of mind. I'll call you about it as soon as I can – I feel an idiot for not thinking of it before. Of course it could hinder our case more than help it.

I'm trying to think hard from the beginning. This witness thing is frightening me.

Beth's death – thought to be between ten and one on that morning. Nanny, Zoë, Paul and Andrew were all in the house. I was at the dentist's from about half past twelve to half past one. I could have killed her before I went out of course. Everyone was in different rooms. I was in my study, which is on the floor above the nursery, although I don't expect Nanny and the boys can absolutely verify that fact. If only time of death could be proven to be while I was actually at the dentist and that is impossible I think.

I can't believe I've just written that last sentence about my own daughter.

The next incident I suppose was the meeting with Lillian. I'm sure Jeffrey will vouch for the immediate and powerful effect she had on Zoë. Felix, I'm going to ask you to approach her and ask if she can give any testimony about Zoë's psychological state (I'm sure you've thought of this). I'm equally sure she'll try to refuse. But if we can establish how unbalanced Zoë was – I realise as I write this that it's probably pointless. Lillian would be the last person to call Zoë unbalanced. But I digress. At least their first meeting was a corroborated incident. There were a lot of people there that night, most of whom were concerned and protective about Zoë and less than impressed by Lillian's obvious showmanship. She took advantage of Zoë's weak state, attacking and attacking, and all her much advertised sensitivity was obviously reserved for herself. It was like watching a snake charmer being charmed by the snake. Anyway, I can provide a good list of witnesses. And thank God for Jeffrey. He was on the other end of the phone the day Zoë was too crazy to understand she'd bankrupted us. That was a terrible day. Where does this lead us exactly? Jeffrey will say I was very controlled, which would be a good thing for me. As far as I know the boys are the only witnesses to my rage at Zoë towards the end. And they won't testify. If it comes out through another source, I don't know how we will show I was justified. I'm just trying to think, to make sure. Abbey had left. We didn't see anybody as far as I remember. I'm getting confused.

This is looking like a very short defence.

Perhaps the prosecution will rake over my past and find character witnesses. I will write more later.

October 6th

I dreamt about Paul last night. I'm not sure exactly what I dreamt. I stupidly thought I'd remember and so didn't write it down, but the feeling has been with me all day. How lonely he is and has always been. It's strange about the boys – I knew them so well, was with them all the time, and what was between us was strong, but you had to keep an eye on Paul, keep him occupied and motivated or he wouldn't stay cheerful. He has nightmares. You have to give him simple tasks when he worries. Cooking is good; there's both order and creativity in cooking and he was proud when he helped me. As I write this I know I'm deceiving myself. He has been lonely all his life, and I helpless. I have been a friend, but always outside his soul's walls. I don't think he likes Andrew and I don't know whether that is because he envies him his self-sufficiency, I'm guessing. It's not something I've wanted to think about but I've always found Andrew so easy, he can occupy himself for hours, painting, reading, sometimes at the bottom of the garden with his imaginary friends – he doesn't like other children much. I can't say I blamed him. I was a bit like that as a child. And because of Zoë I think the boys were more sophisticated than their contemporaries. We were proud of that of course, which was our vanity.

That's the thing about Paul – whenever you start to talk or write about him you end up skipping to Andrew or Zoë. There isn't much to Paul, except pain. He has no talent, and he feels very little joy. His sensitivity has been a gaping wound in the family so we've all avoided it. I've always thought that if I made everything around him as normal as possible it would help him haul himself over all those obstacles towards that great prize, becoming an adult. I think Paul loved Beth. He held her quite a lot, gave her her bottle sometimes. It was Andrew who hardly noticed her.

October 8th

Dreamt again about Zoë's death, her funeral. Painful impressions, no action, nothing tangible.

When a child dies, the public thinks that that death is its property, its grief. If I were to be kind, I would say that no one can bear the idea of an unfulfilled life, and the death of the young and innocent becomes a symbol of the world's injustices, etc. etc. The spectacle of a celebrity's funeral, however, is a disgusting thing. Because of Beth's death, people were overcome with a kind of hysterical sympathy when Zoë died. Also, because she was famous, the crowd mourned them both, so Beth seemed to be being buried all over again. There were photographers and there were TV cameras outside the church. Zoë's mother, with stretched white skin, wearing a veil which seemed Gothic and overwrought to me, was surrounded by a horde of these people. I remember her saying to one, 'Who do you think I am, Jackie Kennedy?' I would have laughed but she was too far away to hear me anyway.

The actual service was held at the same church as Beth's, so there were crowds outside, and then people in the street as we got into the cars to go to the cemetery. Police kept people away from the actual burial plot. They were all outside the wrought iron gates so at the graveside there was just Zoë's mother and myself, Paul, Andrew, Zoë's brothers and their wives (you and Laura, of course) and there was Abbey and Jeffrey and old Nanny, which moved me.

Just as Father Owen, who had christened the boys, was beginning his reading at the grave, I saw a figure walking towards us up the paths and across the wet grass. It had rained the night before I think, but was a beautifully sunny morning. It is a big cemetery and that part of it is just on the brow of a hill flanked by a row of trees – there are also new trees being planted so that there will be an impression of woodland copses sheltering the graves, an effort to make it all less stark. It won't look as they've planned it for years yet of course. There we were at the top of the slope – not really a hill – and at the gates you could see the policemen and the crowd, some with flowers and photographs of Beth (God knows where these had come from), and divided from these by a hundred yards or so were a few people with placards and slogans: 'What really happened to Zoë and Baby Beth?'

One, I think, used the biblical quotation about the slaughter of the innocent. It was the first public expression of the idea of 'foul play'. This huddle of demonstrators – that's what the police called them – could not be taken away handcuffed in vans as they should have been because it was a peaceful protest, that is what the head policeman said. So there we were, scattered around the graveside looking down at this strange mêlée of people and then up into the sky and down into the grave trying to concentrate, and I remember noticing what a beautiful September day it was and feeling tears. I was hoping that Father Owen would finish the whole thing quickly. Zoë's mother, at my side, was trembling, and I was afraid she would collapse. She kept leaning forward as if she were about to jump into the grave after Zoë, and sometimes I steadied her with my hand, and she didn't object, or notice, I imagine. I am not convinced she knew exactly what was happening. She did not look at me or speak to me.

Up the hill came this figure, walking slowly, partly hidden by a huge bouquet of deep red roses, and I thought, Why have they let that person past? Why have they let this stranger make such a dramatic entrance at our service? when I realised it was Lillian. Against the background hum of Father Owen's intoning, Paul, next to me, made a sound of recognition which I can only describe as fear. Neither of us moved. Lillian could not come right up to us – it would have been too disruptive as we were on the far side of the grave. So she just stood next to Nanny and those mourners with their backs to the crowd. Then she looked across the grave at Andrew, and smiled. That smile: Felix, I don't know how to tell you how blasphemous – brazen – wicked – that smile was. It was almost like the secret smile a woman gives her lover, intended to pass unnoticed in a public place, intended to include just those two in its universe of ease and understanding. Lillian did not look at me or anyone else, then bowed her head in semblance of humility.

I am ashamed of how wild that smile made me.

I remember anger and weeping taking me over, my fingers clenched, warm sun on my neck, the sound of Father Owen's voice, the sight of the colours behind my eyes and then the look of the open grave and the coffin being lowered and the clods of earth being thrown. I remember opening my eyes to see Andrew looking up sideways at Lillian, slanting and curious. Then Lillian, contemplative, head bowed; the family walking away from the grave, straggling and leaning on one another in the sunshine. Only the Father, the children, Lillian and myself remained. Andrew made as if to move away, to walk around the grave to greet Lillian. Lillian, looking up now, was watching us both with her eagle eyes. As Andrew moved, I gripped his elbow hard, saying, I don't think at much louder than a whisper, 'No – you don't go to her – no.' He weakened, then stiffened, then struggled. All this was very slight. Not even a scene. Not even a scuffle. After leaving the proper portentous pause, Lillian said loudly, uninhibited, to the air, 'It is all right, Andrew. Obey your father.' Her voice was loud, so loud that Father Owen looked at her for the first time, and he too lost composure and froze like a startled rabbit. It might have been funny but it made me very angry that he should be disconcerted, and I felt choked, but nonetheless started shouting at her, 'Get away from him – from here – from us,' and Lillian didn't move a muscle, her coppery hair like a horrible flame, her eyes challenging. I understood then, but not consciously, that I was making her happy, that she was in her element, standing by Zoë's grave, defying me. Andrew struggled again, so I moved and stood behind him and held on to both his elbows.

'You are a wicked curse on our family – go!' I knew that I should not be holding on to my son like that or be shouting over my wife's grave – none of these surreal things should be happening – but I could not stop. It was just so disgusting that the person I hated more than any other – who has been responsible for so much that is unimaginable – should make such an appearance at Zoë's grave, and try to charm her son, a child she has never before seen, away from his father. It still makes me sick with anger. Father Owen, recovering himself, ordered me to let my son go, and of course I did. Then he came over and spoke to us both, leaning down to where I was kneeling on the grass, Paul's hand on my shoulder, ashamed, without being able to pray or even think, and I can't remember what he said, but he comforted me, and I got to my feet. When I looked up, I saw Lillian walking away down the slope, alone.

That was how it happened at the funeral and of course – besides yourself – there are witnesses to my manhandling Andrew. I hope you can understand why I did that. Ask Nanny to be a witness. Ask Nanny and Father Owen.

October 12th

Felix, thank you for your letter in reply to the last pages I sent you. In answer to your query, let me confirm that I have kept photocopies of everything I have written and sent to you, for my own reference.

You ask why I am so convinced that Lillian is a wicked woman, and whether I feel she may have had any influence on Zoë's death. Whatever the circumstances, of course I understand that there is no evidence that you could find which would prove Lillian wicked. If we look at the facts, they are only that she began to counsel Zoë after Beth's death. Her attempts at comfort were a failure and did not in any way arrest the onset of Zoë's madness. Looking back I'm not sure anyone could have accomplished that. Perhaps Father Owen could have helped her. He's not very holy though, Father Owen, not particularly impressive or devout. He is kind. In any event, it is indisputable that Lillian failed Zoë. We have no evidence to show that Lillian encouraged Zoë to neglect Paul, although she did encourage her to believe Andrew was a genius, which I think disturbed him. I'm talking in circles. I'm sorry. Lillian's notes may tell us more – but of course we don't know if she's ever been professional enough to keep notes. Time will tell. Empirically, the only thing Lillian can be accused of is incompetence.

But I know better. I know she is a cannibal who feeds on suffering and who consciously or unconsciously seeks to promote and accelerate suffering and the dependence of the sufferer on her. She provides brief relief – a short-lived balm – then propels the sufferer back into the world to try to live according to her peculiar teachings, about which I know nothing except that they are unholy. She lies and distorts and contorts the world for her own sake, to save herself from her own crippling loneliness of spirit. That is where she is wicked. How melodramatic I sound. Forgive me.

October 16th

Felix, you comment in your last letter that I am sounding increasingly convinced we will lose this case and that our defence is weak. I can't lie to you and disagree. Perhaps I *am* becoming reckless about my own safety. But please believe this has nothing to do with a lack of faith in you. I spend so much time remembering, seeing how blind I was – being consumed by hate, trying to overcome that hate. I am exhausted by it. Father Owen visits me, which is some relief. There seems to be so much more to the rights and wrongs of our tragedy than our feeble court case, which does not even begin to address – what's the current slang – the real 'issues'. And I know this record is not as cool and factual as I thought it would be. I am sorry. I leave it to you to sift out what you need.

Still, your idea of a day together brain-storming this is a good one. I'd be grateful for company for a whole day. If you can persuade the prison to allow you to bring a picnic as you suggest I would be really touched. That is a sweet thought of your Laura's – please thank her.

November 3rd

Felix, I apologise for the delay in writing to you following your visit, but as you know, I have been ill and too weak to write. No, no one seems to know why I have had this fever, but it's been very debilitating. Perhaps quasi-nineteenth-century hygiene – or lack of it – may have something to do with it.

It feels like a long time since I saw you, but I must thank you for your conscientious efforts on my behalf the day we spent together. I do quite understand that to demonise Lillian, in your phrase, is not going to help our case. I understand that she is not on trial. Further, we will never know what she did/said to Zoë. I know you are right in saying it does me no good to brood about her so much. You are not the only one who advises this. I won't push it any further and will leave you to decide whether we should ask her to appear for the defence. After all she loved Zoë and perhaps understands it was a tragedy just as we do. Perhaps you're right and she doesn't blame me. Doubtless you'll let me know her position in due course when you have managed to get an appointment to see her.

On another point, it's very disheartening that you have not been able to find Zoë's diary. If I'm right and she was writing one, it could bring us so much nearer to how she was then, so much that is dark to us could become clear.

I'm glad your approaches to Jeffrey and Abbey have been so positively received. I agree, Nanny is too old and frail and we should not involve her in the trial but I'm pleased you are going to see her. Send her my regards if the right moment comes. I will think about your advice about the boys. Yes, they are crucial witnesses and their omission might well damage our case. But they are also only fourteen and eleven years old, and they have lost their mother and sister in a matter of months. I am not sure any father could be selfish enough to insist they appear.

November 6th

    Dear Felix,

I have a favour to ask you. I've just received a very upsetting letter from Andrew. He sounds lonely and writes as if he's miserable at Beatrice's. I have had no idea that she has done nothing about finding them a school. I haven't been thinking for them – it has never even crossed my mind that the boys might not be feeling entirely safe and sound, or at least as safe and sound as they could be. I know that Beatrice would rather behave as if I am dead than in prison, and it would aggravate the situation greatly if I tried to write to her or call – though of course I'll write to Andrew straight away. Could you possibly go and visit them? I feel powerless in here and the only other person I can think of is Jeffrey: it's just that there's something silly about Jeffrey – plus he's never really been interested in the boys – and now that he has such financial problems and is trying so hard to dig himself out of the ditch Zoë dumped him in I think I'd better leave well alone. If you can tell me the lie of the land I'll be clearer on what to do – if there's anything I can do for them.

    Yours,
    Michael

November 8th – Friday
(Private Journal – not to be sent to Felix)

Felix away for a long weekend so my frantic letter useless. I think he told me he was going but I forgot. I don't know if it's just that I haven't got over my fever – or being locked away here – but I'm feeling dizzy and afraid in my body, all through my body, not just heart or stomach or that sudden weakening of lower back or tension in the neck I used to get when I was working and always felt running scared.

It's late and I'm in my bunk bed in my cell and I'm trying not to be, trying to be in the boys' room at Beatrice's, tucking them in, telling them everything's all right. I can't imagine the room, though. I can see the house, long and low, overlooking those 'dreary fields' as Zoë used to call them, and the room with the rose silk lamp shades. The house is full of such terrible lamps, and the smell of furniture polish, lavender and another unidentifiable kind of dried-tea smell, the one that pervades such country houses. Perhaps it's generations of exhausted pot-pourri. I can see it all in physical detail, Beatrice's Jack Russells swarming over the beds, but I can't imagine comforting Andrew. He has never needed comforting. Even in the few moments of pain or distress I've seen him experience he's been self-possessed, resilient. I've never had to explain anything to him in what Paul calls my Daddy voice. Why should I be surprised that his peace of mind has been shattered now? I still am. Those few lines of entreaty make me feel impotent and weak. If there were cruelty and evil in even our home, perhaps there is no home which is free of them and safe. Oh God, I pray that Felix goes there as soon as he can and finds out what is wrong with my boys.

November 9th

Waiting here on this lost weekend – this long Saturday afternoon which will become a longer Sunday – I feel a peculiar free-floating sensation. Present is days and hours, but not real time, not life. Life was Zoë, and then the boys. Life really began for me when I met Zoë. I grew up adoring those old Fred Astaire movies. Zoë said it meant I was a traitor to my class. There was no need to expand on this, I understood exactly what she meant. When we first met I used to sing to her, in bed mostly, my favourite song of his:

> The way you wear your hat
> The way you sip your tea
> The memory of all that –
> No, no, they can't take that away from me ...

'Nobody's trying to,' she would say, and laugh. Then there was the coda:

> We may never never meet again
> On the bumpy road to love
> Still I'll always always
> Keep the memory of –

Then more:

> The way your smile just beams
> The way you sing off key
> The way you haunt my dreams
> No, no, they can't take that away from me,
> No – they can't take that away from me.

In deference to my enchantment with this song we danced to it on our wedding day. From as far back as I can remember I always wanted, half expected even, grown-up life to be like those films: the black shining lake of a dance floor, women in diaphanous dresses with tight glittering shoulder straps over milky arms, powdered faces, gleaming ironed hair, answering in short, staccato sentences to men's equally staccato questions, 'Dance?', 'Drink?', 'Cigarette?' Then finally, 'Marry me' – a statement, not a question. I think those films must have been the inevitable precursor to many lives' disillusion, but at that time the dreams seemed unique to me, growing up in my grubby house in its rural prison, going to the movies by myself. This probably all sounds pathetic. But those gleaming people in those gleaming places gave me another dream, large white shining spaces, and they made me want to create a beautifully lit world. That was the general idea. I studied art and furniture design and bought endless copies of *Interiors* magazine as a youth and dreamer of dreams. My bed was narrow, rather like the one I'm in now, and the family house I left behind a floral swirling cheap nightmare, but I saw clearly, though utterly fantastically, my vocation.

I worked in a lighting shop in Soho when I first came to London. Drew my own designs in the evenings. I liked clean lines, adjustable form, concentrated uses, I still do. I didn't like all the black and chrome that was fashionable then, what became the Eighties' look, it was too harsh. The shop supplied various architects and interior designers – there was a rush of them – at trade prices, and there was an amazing explosion of building and refurbishment: it was a narcissistic Boom Town. That was the beginning of a London where the secretaries and shop girls you met at parties wore black and shoulder pads and red lipstick, and gave euphemistic names for their jobs, I can't even remember them now. We all drank disgusting cocktails as if they were the real thing. I had a girlfriend – Helen – she was a nurse, and a Catholic, both of which pleased my mother. I would not ask her to marry me, which distressed them both, but I remained inflexible about that one thing. Helen was good to me when my father died around that time.

My friend at the shop – Matt – liked my ideas, and he was

deputy manager so he had more experience than I had. He was really champing at the bit, 'tired of being kept down', as he used to say. We used to go to the pub and he'd complain and I'd be staunch and quiet, and eventually we hatched the idea to start out on our own. I would never have had the courage without him. Matt was another 'working-class lad', as Zoë would later call him, her snobbery laced with humour – also rivalry – I don't think she was happy about how much I loved Matt, in the early days. Matt was badly educated, he was a chauvinist, a big drinker, big talker. He had charm, which Zoë said she was unable to appreciate; but I certainly did. He was warm. He was a good friend when Helen left me for someone else, just after we'd started the business. He took me out drinking every night for a week – beer and whisky chasers, until I couldn't stand up, and I cried out of self-pity rather than grief, and there he was, cheerful and stocky. He went out and made us a lot of deals. One in particular tied us into providing one developer with all his requirements, it was over eighty per cent of our output. We nearly quarrelled over that. It gave us our livelihood far beyond the first year, but it didn't include any allowance for my new designs. Matt used to get chippy if I spent too much time at the drawing board anyway and I got fed up if he didn't give enough time to trying to sell my original work. One or two he managed, but nothing major. So I was the arty one, he was the businessman and we lived together in those days, renting a flat in the East End near our warehouse studio.

It turned out that Matt's business sense wasn't as 'watertight' – one of his phrases – as he'd always promised. He made the mistake of putting all our eggs in one basket and when our main client went bust it meant massive losses, fast losses. We watched our business going down the drain and we couldn't do anything to stop it. Enter Zoë. It was Matt's idea. He volunteered us for the TV story from a researcher's ad in the trade paper. He felt we might be able to turn our fortunes around just from the publicity, particularly if we could persuade Zoë to feature one of my new designs, which happily she loved and gave good camera time, pronouncing it 'elegant and beautiful'. She also bought an uplighter and a pair of my wall lights – they ended up as our bedside lights and are still there in our house. She even came right out and said to Matt that if he'd built the business on my talent, rather than flogging standard designs like anyone else, people would be beating our door down, I wouldn't be able to design fast enough. I think she enjoyed rubbing it in. She was fearless, Zoë. A bit like those Thirties and Forties film stars, I suppose.

My first sight of Zoë was of the top of her head. I'd leaned out of the studio window to check her out because the video entryphone had broken and we needed to make sure it was her and not some creditor. She wore a black wool greatcoat, almost a man's style, and black rubber-soled shoes, which I could see even from so great a height were extremely ugly. Her sound and cameraman were with her. She was smoking a cigarette, and she dropped it into the gutter before coming into the building. The cameraman held the door open for her and she nodded to him. It was a grey autumn day. All I could really see was that she had shiny mid-brown hair.

Zoë is not tall, but she was fierce enough to drive any protective instincts out of a man – at least at first. I loved her for how gutsy she was, and how charming, putting us at ease by laughing at my jokes – she didn't insult Matt until after she'd finished filming – and thanking us over and over for having them as if it were some desirable social occasion rather than carrion picking over our livelihood's carcass. Zoë dignified television journalism, human interest stories, because her approach was unique. Yes we were gossip-TV, but we were also real and human to her. The thing about Zoë also was that she was big-hearted, she actually cared about the people she reported about. She was restrained, though, which was a sign of how genuine she was. She called about a week later and asked if I'd like to go and have a look at the rough cut of our piece, and we had dinner afterwards and laughed a lot, even though I was terrified. It didn't take long for me to recognise her as my twin – through the terror – a cliché, but in our case absolutely accurate. She understood that I didn't care about success, that I didn't want it for myself. She never asked me for it. She knew I just wanted a home and her and space to dream in my head a little bit.

Forgive me my rambles, Felix. Laura has probably told you most of this, though as she and Zoë were never close she may not have done. I don't think Zoë ever had a confidant apart from me, she was my best friend. But you can never be sure, particularly with sisters.

Sunday – November 10th (Remembrance Sunday)

I must stop reminiscing about how we met, and how good it was, and go on to the time when I came home to her – for the last time – from Scotland, and saw her and pitied her, but nonetheless screamed abuse at her and threats.

I came home, I think it was early afternoon, the end of

August. Two days before she died, I think. Paul answered the door. He was even more grave and unchildlike than ever, and he didn't smile at me, but he put his arms around my neck and let me hug him. The hall was dark because all the curtains were drawn at every window I could see on the ground floor. I asked him why that was, and he said that Zoë had insisted, because she said it was a house of death.

'We are in mourning,' he said. I felt angry because it was not trying, and because it was so bad for the boys. But I didn't open the curtains, my instinct, because I did not want to contradict his mother directly in front of Paul. I asked him where Andrew was and he said in the playroom, but the door was locked. The rooms and even the kitchen were tidy, as if uninhabited.

He told me that Zoë was lying down upstairs, which I knew – had guessed – almost immediately.

'I'm worried because she's hardly eating now.' He told me he had been cooking, making sure she ate three times a day. He had been taking her trays – and this had been going on since I'd gone away on Monday. It was Sunday afternoon. At first she had been quiet, and sometimes smiled, and spoke to him, and ate her food, and said thank you, but since yesterday she had started to moan and talk to herself – nonsense – and she was distressed, and could not eat.

Our bedroom smelled fetid – it is the only word – when I went upstairs to see her. I knocked, but she did not reply. It was dark, blinds and curtains were drawn, and the sheets smelled, and it was horrible, and I stood there thinking I was in a nightmare but it was all my fault because I should not have gone away. It was stupid and irresponsible and blind of me. She lay curled up, a mound under the covers. I spoke to her – I can't remember what – as I approached the bed. She wasn't asleep but she was not awake. I took her shoulder and shook her gently, and she sat up in bed – eyes wide open. She was wearing her pyjamas. Her lips were dry and cracked and her hair lank, almost matted, and she looked at me in a frightening way as if I had come from a long way away and was a stranger.

'I've come home,' I think I said. 'Zoë, are you all right?'

'Beth's died –' she said. 'But it was an accident – I had nothing to do with it. You believe me, don't you? I was downstairs in my study.' The words were muttered as if she gave voice to only a few of those whirling around her brain.

'I know that, Zoë.'

'You didn't love Beth.'

'That's not true.'

I got her a glass of water from the bathroom. She took a few sips from the glass, wiped her mouth with her sleeve and said, 'Nasty,' as if she were five years old.

'It isn't very fresh.'

I won't go into all the details of how I coaxed her into a hot bath and a clean sweat suit, her baby-blue one, and how I changed the sheets and made her sit up in bed. Paul helped me. We opened the curtains and put the blinds up enough for a little bit of light to show on the carpet and we made her have some soup, Cheddar and brown bread, half an apple and a cup of tea. She co-operated with everything like an obliging nineteenth-century lunatic. She let Paul brush her hair.

All this time Andrew did not emerge from his 'studio' as Paul now called it. I was too busy. I called the doctor, Sarah Longden, and she said she could come at about seven. (We had had her home number since Beth.) I would have cried if I hadn't been in shock. I felt so worried about Paul and kept asking why he hadn't told me all this on the telephone when I'd called and he said because there would have been nothing I could do.

I sat with Zoë until the doctor came, but left the room while she was examined. I think I had a stiff whisky and paced up and down on the landing outside her room as if she were having a baby. The doctor said something about delayed shock, and that she felt it had triggered severe depression, even dementia. I think I was quite sharp and said that would be obvious to anyone. She didn't register or respond to my show of temper, but said she would refer Zoë to a psychiatrist as a matter of urgency.

'He'll have to come to the house,' I think I said – and because of Zoë being Zoë, miracle of miracles, she said she'd see what she could do.

Paul and I made supper together, and I tried to interest him in the television, tales of Glasgow, anything to take his mind off his mother. Andrew finally came downstairs at about eight thirty. He greeted me, but did not really seem to take in how ill Zoë was – he was in his own world. I tried to look upon it as a natural defence mechanism against the unfolding Gothic nightmare of our domestic life, but his lack of distress worried me even more than Paul's obvious fear and unhappiness. If I had not been so determined to make everything seem normal – as it had always been – I would have questioned him I think, but I didn't. He ate well, Paul badly, and I as well as I could. I made them watch television with me before bed – comedy – and tucked them in and fussed over them with all my strength. I checked on Zoë before going to sleep in Abbey's room. She was asleep.

The psychiatrist came the next morning. He looked like an academic or businessman who had no interest in people and what goes on in their minds. He had a moustache and he was bald with liver spots on the top of his head and I did not warm to him, while realising that that couldn't really matter. 'You don't have to like a plumber to see that he can fix your drain,' was the phrase – my father's – which, for some inexplicable reason, went through my head.

Dr Pettigrew, for that was his name, said that Zoë was in a deep depression, which could be treated with drugs – medication is the term – but that he would like her to be admitted to hospital where she could be placed under observation. I said that I really didn't want to do that. I just knew it would be wrong, that if she could be cared for at home I would be happier. I told him I was planning to send the boys to their grandmother in the country until Zoë recovered. They had been exposed to too much already. The doctor was remarkably pliable. After muttering something about the expense of treating her at home, he seemed to give in. I wonder now, over and over, why it should have been that I so instinctively refused to consider the idea of Zoë being put into hospital. Everybody has a horror of such places – I was unable to put mine aside and look at it dispassionately. I just saw white coats and corridors and trays of evil-smelling food and I could look no further. I wanted Zoë to stay in the nest I'd created for her.

If I hadn't made that unconsidered decision, Zoë could be alive now. They would have looked after her properly. I remember him writing out a prescription for sleeping pills, which surprised me: she'd told him she was having trouble sleeping, while from what I could see she was rarely awake. I didn't think about the implications of that either, I just went straight out to the chemist and got the pills – Temazepam, I think, I'm not sure.

When I brought in her tray of lunch she seemed much more herself – present.

'Well, Michael – what is it?' She said this in her work voice, which I don't think I've ever been more pleased to hear.

'You're ill, Zoë – you're – Beth's death –'

'Disturbed?' she said. 'Nutty?' and she smiled her firm, ironic, beautiful smile at me, looking straight into my heart.

'They don't know. They want you to go into hospital so they can observe you – but I said no, I wanted you to stay at home.'

'With my children.' She said this in an unsettling, triumphant, childlike voice.

'That's what I wanted to talk to you about. Things have been very distressing in our family for some time ...'

'Fudge, fudge, fudge,' she said, impatient. 'Cut to the chase.'

'I've thought hard about this and I think the boys should go to your mother's until you're better.'

'No one is taking those children out of this house!' She sat bolt upright to say this, and the words made me thrill, but thrill with rage.

'Don't you dare dictate,' I said.

She got out of bed and I saw her white legs trembling. She gesticulated, pointing and waving at me like a silent screen star.

'How do I know you didn't murder Beth and aren't just waiting for the opportunity to hurt Andrew and Paul?' Neither of us said this, but I felt as if she had, I felt as if she thought me a danger to her and her children.

'You wouldn't dare take the children.'

'You are not in a position to lay down the law. You're ill. When you're better you'll be glad I made the decision I'm making now.'

'No. I'll kill you if you take my children.' She dropped her voice and went on, confidingly, 'Beth sleeping. A mother knows.' She said this about three or four times, as if to another person close by – someone she trusted and loved.

'Beth get back into bed. Now.' I hadn't meant to call her Beth, I don't know why I did it.

'See! A mother knows!' she exclaimed excitedly, and began to pace up and down at the foot of the bed, biting her nails. 'A mother knows.' When I took her by the elbow and led her back to bed she did not struggle with me, nor did I feel her comply.

'You are staying here and nurses will come to look after you.'

'The boys –'

'If you argue with me about the boys I'll send you to hospital.' That was my threat, babyish and unkind.

'Evil – bad man. A mother knows,' she replied, twisting in the bed as if in pain. 'Hell-fire,' she explained.

'All right, Zoë. No one will leave the house. We'll all stay here.' I don't know why I gave in to her – she didn't, couldn't, force me to. But I pitied her, and did not want to divide her from her children.

I sat with her a little after that: it would have been ridiculous to storm out. She was so obviously not herself. By that I do not mean to use a polite euphemism: madness destroys self. One mad person is ultimately very like another. I remember thinking that Zoë was becoming remarkably like Lady Macbeth (she had forced me to go to the theatre with her a lot, when we were first courting, and we'd seen the play together). Thinking that led me to the conclusion, as if playing a game with myself which was nothing to do with real life, that Lady Macbeth went mad out of guilt, because she had killed Duncan – coldly she had planned it. For the first, but not the last time, I hope you can understand that, Felix, I began to wonder whether my Zoë had in fact killed her own baby. Not planned it, of course, but just like a reflex action of her subconscious. Rather than being outraged by my own wickedness, I began to pursue this idea in my memory – all while I chopped onion and began to soften it for spaghetti sauce. Even while I read the familiar recipe and went through the accustomed motions, even then, my mind raced over the days before and after Beth's death, and I counted the points to support my theory. She did not want Beth. She only did not have an abortion because I am Catholic. She was more interested in her career than having children. She seemed to love Beth when she came, but she refused to disrupt her routine for her – never breast-feeding, planning to go back to work at the earliest opportunity. Every action she performed denied Beth's life. And when she died, there was no human, gentle, recognisable grief from Zoë. She wouldn't go to the funeral, she wouldn't talk about it – all she wanted was to go back to work and then to see Lillian, a stranger who would provide absolution. As I laid the table and moved Seymour from one of the chairs, fished clean napkins out of the ironing basket – heaped as high as a hill – and chopped the cucumber for the salad, I remember thinking that, rather than adding to the horror, it would make everything so much simpler if Zoë had killed our baby. I suppose that sounds unbelievable to you, Felix, but I just felt that if she had had post-natal craziness, resentment, anger about Beth, and she had suffocated her with one of the tiny animals which we had put beside her in the cot, had then been sent mad trying to hide it and blaming me, we might be saved. A guilty secret would have been simple. We could have purged it and then there would have been forgiveness. There was already forgiveness.

When I look back on it I see – I see how close to the edge I must have been myself, to think that if Zoë had killed our daughter it would be a welcome solution. I'm not sure now if I actually believed my own story – my fancy – but I certainly came close to believing it. It is a notion which might even be argued in court, Felix, but I'll leave that to you. I loved her so much that such an idea, if possible, only made me love her more. Nothing would ever, has ever, will ever, prevent me from loving Zoë.

At dinner the boys looked on my attempts at explaining the situation in silence. I told them that a nurse would probably come the next afternoon – which would have been Tuesday – but that Mummy would stay at home. Andrew seemed particularly anxious that she should not be moved. I told the boys that there had been an idea to send them away to stay with their grandmother, but that Zoë had asked especially that they stay. Better that we all keep together, however difficult life was. They would have to be patient and pray for their dear mother's return to health. Paul fixed his eyes on me the whole time I was speaking, while Andrew looked down at his plate, as was his habit.

'Paul tells me you've been working hard on your drawings,' I said to him, prompted by an instinct that I had been letting myself neglect him.

'Yes.'

'Would you like to show me?'

'Not today.'

'You're full of secrets, all of a sudden, aren't you?' I said, trying to sound comforting, but I was irritated. The strain was so overwhelming and to add to it was the worry about Andrew and how withdrawn he was.

'Daddy, we have to buy flea powder for Seymour,' said Paul. 'He's scratching such a lot.'

'We'll have to spray the house too. He hasn't been treated all summer, has he?'

'No,' said Paul, as if the admission was a cruel act of betrayal. Zoë would not have given a thought to Seymour's fleas.

'It doesn't matter. Don't worry, we'll get to work on those fleas,' I said. No response. 'I won't be going away again, boys. You understand that, don't you? It was wrong of me to leave you here alone to care for your mother, and I'm sorry. Do you understand? Can you forgive me?'

I think that question put an unbearable strain on Paul, and he said nothing, but Andrew said, 'Yes, Daddy,' and smiled.

The day after that, of course, was the day she died.

Paul did her breakfast. I'd asked him to tell me what she said to him – in case it was significant, if we could wring a meaning out of it. He said her eyes were focused on him – she wasn't as badly off as she had been when I came home. She seemed glad to see him. Andrew locked himself in his 'studio' immediately after breakfast, and did not come out or show an interest in anything. The only thing which happened that morning was that the phone rang and it was Lillian. She said she was worried because Zoë had missed two appointments and hadn't called to explain or cancel formally. She asked to speak to Zoë. I told her that she couldn't come to the phone. She asked me if Zoë was all right. I said that she was perfectly fine. I couldn't let her know that Zoë was so ill, in case she tried to interfere.

'You're keeping her prisoner, aren't you?' she said. I think I said nothing but just put the telephone down, which was very weak. That call was mid-morning. Paul came into my study and said, 'That was the crazy doctor lady, wasn't it?' I didn't ask him how he knew this – whether he'd been listening at the door.

'What do you know about her?'

'Mummy took me to see her.'

'Yes. Of course. I had forgotten.' I asked him how many times he'd been to see her and he told me about three or four, during the time that I was away. He said that she tried to talk to him about his mother and about Beth – but the last time she hadn't been concerned about him. When I asked him what he meant by that he said that she had spent the hour talking to him about her own life, her past, when she'd lived in South America for many years, as a doctor to the poor.

'She told me she had a son who I reminded her of. I don't know what happened to him. I suppose he's grown up now.'

'What else did she tell you?'

'Things I promised never to tell anyone in my whole life, ever.'

'Why would you keep a promise made to her?'

'For Mummy. Mummy loves her.'

While we were having this conversation, and I was grilling him about this mysterious session, Zoë was dying. Well, that is my estimate of time of death. It could have been either before or after when I was by myself in my study and the boys were by themselves in their rooms. It was the second time in five months that this had happened: we had all been occupied in separate rooms while one of us was dying, one of us destroyed with no reason or motive. We were all meant to love and protect each other, that is what makes a family a family.

Paul checked on her – opened the door and thought she was sleeping, so we didn't bother with taking her lunch. That was the first time we hadn't bothered, which was odd in itself. That she was dead – had died – was not apparent until I took the nurse up to meet her at about three o'clock in the afternoon. She was going to come in every day, eight thirty to five thirty – she was a psychiatric nurse, surprisingly nice – and I took her up to introduce her to Zoë, Paul following us up the stairs, not wanting to be left out of anything.

We knocked on the door. No reply. We tiptoed in – thankfully Paul stayed outside. Zoë was lying face down, the way she sometimes did when she couldn't get to sleep and all else failed. We talked about it once I remember, wondering whether it worked because it reminded the subconscious of babyhood. We were all on our fronts in those days. The nurse touched her and couldn't wake her – I was hovering by the door – she took her pulse – no pulse. It was too dark in the room to see her blue face and cold lips. I think the nurse said something like, 'Mr Warren, there's something wrong,' and asked me to come inside and close the door against Paul. She opened the curtains, and pulled up the blinds, and there, with autumn sun streaming over the bedclothes, was Zoë's body. Zoë had gone. I think I howled – that is what the nurse will say if she's a witness. I howled and shrieked and sobbed as loudly as any wild animal. The nurse was remarkable. She called an ambulance from the phone by the bed. She closed Zoë's eyes. She made me sit down, went to the door and told Paul to get the brandy from the drinks' cupboard downstairs. I was beside myself even after the drink. While she took Paul aside and told him that his mother had died, I went to the bathroom cupboard for nail scissors and cut a lock from Zoë's hair. I still have it. It was very bad of me not to tell Paul myself. We didn't tell Andrew. We genuinely forgot about him until after the ambulance had come to take her body away. The family doctor came – she was in great distress herself too, I think – and then the three of us, the three who were left, sat on the sofa in Zoë's study – intruding on her so shortly after her death – and hugged one another and shook and wept. The doctor and nurse stayed in the house. They were afraid to leave us by ourselves I think. I called Zoë's mother and she said she should come and it was agreed that she would. I called Jeffrey – I don't know why – he just muttered something incoherent about having tried to get hold of Zoë for weeks, and gasped for breath. I could hear Zoë saying, 'Well, what did you expect? Jeffrey's always been awfully wet.'

As I write all this now I see Zoë sitting up in bed and smiling at me, so close to the end of her life – at that moment she was herself again and we understood each other. 'The way your smile just beams . . .' sings Fred Astaire in some part of my brain. There were reporters and photographers outside the house again that evening. We had a 'police presence' to protect us. Zoë's mother called all the brothers and you and Laura when she arrived. We had an Indian takeaway. Andrew cried a lot, and I was relieved, grateful that he could.

I prayed. Paul, his face like a stone, trying to join in beside me, but no sounds coming out of his mouth. I loved the boys very fiercely that night. Our children. Our surviving children.

I think it was the very next day that the police came and asked me for a statement. They also took separate statements from the boys. Two days went by waiting for the post-mortem result, but they did not arrest me for the murder until about two weeks later. It was after the funeral. Thank God they let us bury her. I didn't realise then that the police were talking to neighbours who had said they'd overheard constant rows – you've since told me that, Felix – that our relationship was obviously 'strained' and that Zoë was unhappy and had become reclusive. They also found out that she'd been seeing Lillian, and that Lillian, without accusing me directly, had said that our marriage was 'troubled' and that Zoë had spoken of my making threats to her on more than one occasion. The detectives tried to piece together our whole lives, and they must have been clever to find out about Lillian. Zoë was not referred to her by our GP so perhaps they discovered after asking a lot of questions of her former employees – I really don't know.

Sunday is beginning to close now. I have written much more coherently about Zoë's last days than I would ever have thought possible, partly I think because I don't really comprehend or understand that I've lost her, that she's dead and will not come back, come home any more. I think I understand far less – if this makes any sense at all – that Zoë is gone, that I'll never see her again, than that I've been arrested for her murder. Since we lost our darling baby, Beth, the world has been upside down. I ceased to be me and Zoë ceased to be Zoë. We became maddened and perverse and no good could come of anything we did, either for ourselves or for others. Our actions and words just contributed to the evil and badness.

Zoë would say I was sounding 'medieval again' – that's how she teased me about my Catholicism, 'superstition, no more, no less', or if I ever referred to dogma or talked about the existence of good and evil. She said she didn't believe in good and evil, which was partly an explanation for why she never thought of herself as good, but she was. She was a good person. So that's why, however horrified, shocked, over-whelmed, emotional about my trial I am, it is not the worst. Even if I am convicted of Zoë's murder it is not the worst. The worst is losing Zoë, knowing I had her and she was my wife and now she is dead and gone. I must sound like a self-pitying wretch when really I know I should be lucky that I was ever given more than that original half day of her time. I should have remained a story of a failure she covered before moving on.

I must sleep now because this must all sound crazy.

Sunday – late

Can't sleep. The last part of what I've just written was – I realise now – the beginning of my excuse for one of the things I did about Zoë that I'm ashamed of. I know you have to know everything, Felix, if you are to prepare my defence, but it's humiliating to have to admit, especially as you are a member of the family. I have to go back now, to July, I don't know the exact date but it was right after I went away to

Scotland, my first homecoming. I'd come back to London, just for a week – I remember it was a hot summer day, which I always hate. I haven't the metabolism for summer. I've never understood why people long for it so. Coming home, I remember how deeply shocked I was by Zoë, by everything to do with her and the boys. She was beyond reason, all communication. I remember shouting at her one morning in the conservatory – I think I more or less trapped her in there. She paced a lot. She could not sit still during that time – as if she were possessed. She wouldn't look me in the eye – I remember that too – it was so uncharacteristic.

I was very selfish, letting loose and shouting at her. It did no good and only frightened us both. I think I was more afraid than anything else – afraid of her. Worse, I knew that I was too afraid of what was happening to do anything about it. I should have called my friend Nick in Glasgow and said I couldn't go back, that my wife was having a nervous breakdown – but I kept thinking about the money and if I let Nick down he wouldn't pay me, and worse, word would get out and I wouldn't be able to get work again. I couldn't bear what was happening to Zoë, taking her over, but I was a coward.

After shouting at her pointlessly, alarming the boys, I went straight over to her office to see Jeffrey. I'd given him no warning – thankfully he was at the studio and so he missed out on seeing me out of my wits with panic and rage. His secretary, Kate – thin-lipped and unhappy I've always thought – gave me what I wanted anyway: Lillian's Devonshire Place address. At the time I knew I wasn't going to do anything normal like call and try to make an appointment with her. I don't think she'd have seen me anyway. There I was, sweating in that hot office, and then standing on the pavement in Soho Square, holding the address on a yellow Post-it in my hand, watching the pigeons fly up in thick ugly clouds, the tables and chairs on the dirty pavements pretending to be like Paris, people sitting at them like fools. Without consciously deciding anything I began walking as quickly as I could in the direction of Devonshire Place, breathing in the sickening fumes on the stinking air. Whenever I'm in Oxford Street I get seized with an apocalyptic vision of lifting the entire street with its tarmac, buildings, cars and buses, and peeling it away from the earth's surface as if it were a plaster. That street symbolises to me all our evils, suffocating the innocent earth, inflicting hideousness upon it. I didn't stay long there and cut across behind it through Mortimer Street and left into Cavendish Square, walking parallel to the backs of the department stores. Remembered having lunch in Debenhams with Zoë when we first met and felt innocent as children. It was a horrible walk, I was out of control, I didn't know what I was going to do when I got there.

The receptionist – untidy – told me that Lillian was seeing patients all day, and was not available without an appointment. I did not waste time trying to persuade her or by saying it was an emergency. I could have waited outside all day – on the pavement, until evening when she left to go home, like they do in movies – *noir* movies. But it was unnecessary. Somehow I felt Lillian wouldn't refuse to see me when she knew I was there. I sat in the waiting room and waited. No one tried to stop me. It was dark, cool, stuffy. Everyone trying not to make a sound or noticeable gesture, playing the invisible game. I think I sweated even more, in animal streams. I don't think I cared. Perhaps I was only then discovering my capacity for hate is as great as it is for love – at least when it comes to Zoë. I was the betrayed husband preparing to make an amazing scene.

After nearly an hour of waiting – getting colder as my clothes dried on my skin – Lillian came down the red-carpeted stairs. She was with a woman who had obviously been crying, and who was leaning trustingly and with great affection on her arm, turning her head into Lillian's shoulder. They said goodbye at the foot of the stairs, Lillian squeezing her hand and smiling and telling her to take good care. The woman did not want to go, but she did as she was told.

In the few seconds between the woman's departure and Lillian's moving into the doorway of the waiting room – her next cue – I saw her adjust her dress a little, pulling it down under its plastic belt, her head drooping. Then she straightened and took a breath, lifted her head, appearing to grow at least six inches, and moved forward into the doorway, her green eyes scanning the room for her next victim. She saw me very quickly – very quickly indeed – and our eyes met and she blushed, which I wouldn't have expected. I got up and hurried towards her – clumsy. Her face became harder, quite fierce.

'I have to talk to you,' I said. 'Now.'

I had thought that she would refuse, threaten me, or look embarrassed in front of all those people, but she stood firm and tall and answered calmly, 'Of course, let me just explain to Philippa that this won't take long.' She spoke unusually loudly for such a place – without intimacy – as if she were on stage. Everyone looked up and listened obligingly. I could tell she loved people to look up and listen to her voice. I was not anxious to share the spotlight, so I waited at the foot of the stairs while she made her excuses. Together and in silence we went up the stairs to her lair.

People who have manufactured their personalities always have bland rooms. They do not know enough about who they are pretending to be to let it show in their surroundings. That's how you can tell they are fakes, and that's how it was with Lillian. Not a picture on the wall, not an object in sight. She sat behind her reproduction mahogany desk, and I sat on the chair, upholstered in red, in front of it. Dark curtains open but windows smothered in net curtains – a small fan disturbed the air.

'Is this about Zoë? I hope there's nothing wrong?' She began with an air of deep self-satisfaction. She did not really believe that anything was wrong with Zoë: she was just warming up, hoping to disconcert me and make me feel foolish.

'I think you know that Zoë is very sick,' I said. 'She's sick in the head. Worse every day. I hold you responsible. I want you to know that I know you are a charlatan and a fraud and an irresponsible, greedy, disgusting woman, and I am going to speak to my solicitor about bringing charges of criminal negligence against you.'

'Zoë doesn't pay me, so I don't think you'd have a case,' said Lillian. What shocked me was that she did not bother to exert herself by looking insulted. She calculated the reality and struck back fast, knowing that I was powerless and she was powerful and she was going to come right out and say so. 'Zoë comes to see me as a friend and spiritual adviser. It's not about money. It's not even about medicine. It's woman healing woman, I merely help the natural process along.'

'She's sick. She can't make decisions. She trusts no one. She's afraid. She's retreated into her own world.'

'Sometimes people have to "retreat", as you put it, into themselves, so they can discover who they really are – not somebody's wife, or somebody's mother, but themselves. Zoë's soul, her womanhood, is under siege right now. Can you not see that your antagonising is only making it worse?'

'The person you describe is not Zoë. Zoë's always known exactly who she is, why she's done things. These details are irrelevant – she's not some little woman in need of self-help and the god of feminism, she's strong. She *was* strong but she blames herself for the death of our baby – that's what's making her crazy, that's what she's got to get over.'

All the time I was speeding through these words, while these pleas disguised as explanations were coming out of my mouth, I felt a deeper and deeper horror about what I was doing. I should not be discussing such details, such private matters about Zoë's soul and mind with this high Priestess of Evil, glittering and cruel.

She left a dramatic pause before her very deliberate reply. 'I hear what you are saying. I just don't think you are necessarily the right person to decide on Zoë's treatment at this time.'

'You don't care about Zoë. You just care about conquering her. You are wicked.' I think this sounded petulant and childish.

'Mr Warren, I don't think threatening me is going to get either of us anywhere.' She said this slowly but I saw her eyes widening and she showed her red tongue when she spoke.

'You want me to threaten you,' I thought aloud. I should have kept this discovery to myself.

'You are more than unreasonable. I did not have to see

you – remember that. I hoped I could help you also to heal. But I see now that you would rather hate me. I think this interview should come to an end.'

'You are a bad woman. I'm going to get you.'

'I wait with bated breath,' she replied, smiling her snake-smile at me. 'Believe me. In the meantime, I want you to know that I forgive you.' In the maddening heat of the room I became closer to becoming violent than I'd ever before come. I wanted to beat her with my fists and kick her soft flabby body and spit on her, but instead I began to cry and hot tears fell on my cheeks. 'Take good care of yourself,' she said, moving to the door and opening it.

The passage and the stairs and the journey home remain a blur.

Felix, I know I acted wrongly and foolishly – but you have to understand how terrible an enemy Lillian is. I know that you want to persuade me that it isn't true, that my enemy's within, not without, but she is cunning, and quick, and she identifies weakness and she goes for it. I don't know why she is the way she is – but it was only for Zoë's sake that I went so wild. What I should have done after that was stay at home and care for her. Instead I arranged to have her watched.

I admit that this was another mad thing to do. I was frantic by then. I needed to know what she was doing. I thought that eyes being on her would keep her safe. I'd better tell you about how and when – for your notes. I did it by getting back in touch with Matt. He'd moved to Bristol with his second wife, and had quite a good recruitment business going up there. At the time Zoë said he was always better off relying on other people's talent, and it was a good thing for him that he'd understood that. We'd lost touch – as a class traitor I couldn't very well invite him to dinner. Zoë and I made a joke of it but that was the exact truth. And as I told you, they never got on. By then I remembered him affectionately only as a stage in my life, I didn't miss him. I got in touch with Matt because he had contacts everywhere and had thrived on a succession of dodgy deals made with mates of mates, no questions asked and a night in the pub. He was strangely incurious about why I should want to get in touch with a private detective, but he obliged me with the name of a firm – a one-man band as he called it – who'd worked for a friend of his in London a while back.

I had to organise it all before I went away, and it was a rush. I met the man in a pub in Battersea – his suggestion. He looked like a bookie or a grubby bureaucrat, uncertain age, polyester shirt, cheap shoes. I told him about Zoë, not that I thought she was being unfaithful or anything like that, just that she'd been going through a rough time and I had to be away on business for the next few weeks, she was alone in the house all day with the boys and I was worried for her. He said something about being more of a guardian angel than a spy, and I agreed, wondering how many times he'd said that to a husband and how many times he'd heard an explanation like mine and whether or not he believed me, and whether he cared about the truth. I decided that he probably didn't – believe me or care – but that it didn't matter, and indeed was probably safer that way. We agreed that he would watch outside the house in a car parked up the road. If she went anywhere in the car he would follow her. He would fax me a report every third day. No photographs would be taken. His name was Don Goldsmith – I can give you his address – and he shook my hand.

It was another crazy and inexplicable thing I did that summer. Perhaps I was losing my mind too. The idea of Don, as I sat and gazed out of the window of the train on the way back to Glasgow, made me feel both comforted and ashamed. Don would not intervene, he would not curtail her freedom, but he was like a chaperone, he was an extension of my eye being kept on her and on the boys.

He followed her to see Lillian.

He accompanied her on a shopping spree – clothes.

He was there when she took Paul to see Lillian.

He clocked up mileage with her and Andrew on pony trips.

I think he became fond of Zoë. He was very expensive. I dispensed with his services before she began to visit Beth's grave and later take to her bed. Her pattern seemed to hold fairly steady and I knew it was only another fortnight or so until I came home. I've come to understand now that he was there more for me than for her: he gave me the illusion of standing by her when in fact I was doing nothing of the kind. There were no surprises in Don's reports. There was monotony. I believed that the worst was over.

Monday, November 11th (Private Journal)

Felix called me first thing about the boys. He is going to drive down and see them tonight after work and come and see me tomorrow afternoon to discuss the visit. He's going to take Laura with him.

Jeffrey came to see me today, about tea-time. He brought me some *Interiors* magazines. I found it too touching, imagining him going to the newsagent's and buying them and hoping they would cheer me up. He's lost weight. Zoë always worried he'd have a heart attack – he's always liked a good lunch and a drink and a cigar, and taken no known form of exercise. There's something adolescent about him, as if he's modelled himself on those Hollywood moguls of fifty years ago and won't let the idea out of his head. He'd had his beard trimmed. He's starting up a new company – he wants to make comedies and quiz shows, working from a talent base that's as exclusive as he can make it.

'A producer's nothing without talent,' he said. His accountant had filed for bankruptcy, which he said was a good thing because it released him to start again. He hadn't had to sell the house because it's in his wife Stella's name. The girls – his umbrella name for wife and children – are well, growing up, boyfriends, he was trying to be tolerant. I think he wished he hadn't mentioned girls as both mine are dead and gone.

'I can't begin to tell you how sorry I am that on top of everything you should be here,' he said. But he seemed confident that your defence, Felix, will get me off. 'You must be frantic about the children – I wondered how you'd feel about us going down and taking them out for the day one weekend.' I said I would be grateful and it was kind and of course. 'You must be worried sick because of Paul being so highly strung.' I nodded because I couldn't really talk about it. 'I can't believe I'm going to be a witness at your trial – it's so surreal.'

'Make a good mini-series though, wouldn't it?' I said. I thought he was going to cry.

'I just can't believe old Zoë's gone – you know. She was too much of a fighter. I never thought for a moment she wouldn't survive all this.'

'We can't expect life to make sense,' I think I said. 'It's not up to us to understand.'

'Don't start that fucking God stuff, for God's sake,' he said, and we laughed a bit and Jeffrey trembled.

'You'd better go,' I said. 'This is too upsetting for you.' I thanked him, because it was good of him to come, good of him to put himself through such an ordeal and actually talk about what was on his mind instead of treating Zoë's death as an embarrassment. It did me good – not the words he said, but the sight of him with his spotted tie and his handkerchief sticking out of his jacket and his raincoat and his umbrella. I went to sleep after he'd gone, waking up to remember I hadn't sent my love to his girls.

Wednesday (Private Journal)

At last word from Felix about the boys. He was too busy to come yesterday afternoon. I'm pasting in the handwritten letter he sent instead:

Boys in good shape considering – it is Beatrice who is really shaky and Laura blaming herself that we have not called and been down to see her more often. Grief and nervous exhaustion. I don't feel she's come to terms in any way with all that's happened and just isn't coping with looking after the children. Paul seems to be coping, though distressed. Andrew unresponsive. Kicking ourselves for not thinking of it sooner, but would like to have them come to live with us. Our cottage being renovated and Laura there by herself a lot during the week – as you know I'm in the flat in London much of the time. Think about it and I'll visit soonest.

Love,

Felix

At first I was angry that he hadn't found time to come and see me himself but I'm relieved that the boys more or less OK. I've never thought of them going to Felix and Laura's either – it seems I haven't thought of anything since the day Zoë died – but it makes perfect sense. She's great with children, teaches Montessori at kindergarten in Marlow. I think there's an older school attached to it that they could go to. It's ideal, but it's asking a great deal. I think I'm going to ask him to bring the children to visit. I know that in one way it will upset them, it will upset me too, but I think I should talk to them about what happens next. I don't want them to feel as if they've turned into parcels which are just doing the rounds. I know that Felix and Laura will do their best to really provide security for them. It's a good idea. But I wish I were out and back with them – very badly – right at this moment.

Thursday, November 14th (Private Journal)

Felix and Laura brought the boys today. I suppose I should write a bit about them before going into it. They've been married about four years, I think. She's twenty-seven or eight, more than fifteen years younger than Zoë. She was a late mistake like Beth. In their family it was the three boys, then Zoë, then Laura, who was very spoiled as a child by all of them. She and Zoë never got on. Laura is fine, but she's a bit of a goody-goody. She's fair, but with hazel eyes – doesn't look at all like Zoë in features, although there's a family resemblance. She's got a narrow face with a high forehead and bloodless lips, transparent skin, sometimes you see green veins. Felix says she's like a Lippi Madonna: she has rather hooded eyes, pale lashes. She can look stunning and she can look awful, but she's never looked healthy. She's the only one of Zoë's family who could possibly be described as delicate, but there's nothing specific wrong with her. She doesn't behave as though she's sickly, ever, though. She's very good with children, instinctive. She's a conformist: she went to all those terrible upper middle class coming-out parties, balls – cattle markets, as Zoë called them. She rode a lot, was very horsy, but didn't have Zoë's nerve. Part of the plan in moving down to the country I think is for Laura to have a horse again. She's very much a wife to Felix, defers, goes to all the law functions with him, encourages him to think very highly of himself. That's the tactful way of putting it. He adores her, they're deeply in love, and that has to be good for the boys. Zoë always said Felix was too good for Laura, had twice her personality, but that's a bit unfair. She's fine. She's all right. I've never described Felix. He's dark, stocky, a bit hairy, febrile. He slicks his hair back in that slightly gangstery public school banker way. Exceptionally intelligent, idealistic in the right way. He's magnetic to be with. A dazzling talker. Zoë always said she thought he'd go all the way, knighthood, everything. I think she's right.

Both boys needed a haircut. That's about all I thought of when they came in. They were all washed and scrubbed though, clean as clean could be. Laura wore her hair up in a high pony-tail, which made her look girlish, no make-up but she was wearing scent, a flower one, which was lovely – I noticed it particularly because I haven't smelled scent for such a long time. Felix in suit and stripy shirt. What's the matter with me? I'm writing as if I'm so overcome with people's clothes that I can't see any further – but I think it was something like that, at least to begin with. I felt like a poor relation all of a sudden, being visited by the nice law-abiding successful part of the family who hadn't come from some unidentifiable country slum. I had this weird feeling of anonymity, as if my children didn't really belong to me any more and never would again, as if I'd borrowed them from Felix and Laura rather than it being the other way around. All this was just a feeling, not as conscious as it is now.

After initial greetings there was a silence as if I'd been called in front of the headmaster for some unmentionable breach of the rules and I had to make some account of myself. For the first time it occurred to me that the boys might imagine that I had killed their mother. This had honestly never occurred to me before. The boys sat and the adults stood behind them as if posing for a family photograph.

'How's it going, boys?' I asked, meeting Paul's pained eyes, in whose hollows seemed to be concentrated a world of cruelty and fear. Andrew looked at me but with a blankness and emptiness I found even more terrible. They were both very pale. 'How's your grandmother?'

'She's OK,' said Andrew, though we all knew that wasn't so. I realised I'd forgotten how to talk to them, so I just stared at them instead. Felix began some splurge, interspersed with Laura's encouraging interjections about how we had all been thinking about what might be best for the boys, etc., etc. Andrew said that our idea sounded good. Paul asked me when I'd be coming out. I said that no one knew.

'I know it must be awful to see me here,' I said, 'but I'm still Daddy – I'm still thinking of you all the time, trying to do what's best. I wanted to see you so that you would understand that and not think I'd gone away and left you.'

'Last time you came home you said you wouldn't go away again,' said Paul.

'None of us could have known what was going to happen to your mother, or that your father would be blamed,' said Laura.

'Laura's right,' I said. 'I didn't want to leave you, but there it is. Felix is going to try his best to get me out, and he and Laura are going to take the best care of you.'

'You haven't seen the cottage yet, but it's great,' she said. 'You can both sleep in the attic, and there's a big garden.'

'Like the one at home?' asked Paul.

'Nearly as nice,' said Laura. 'I'm going to get some ducks. You can help me look after them.'

'That means Seymour can't come,' said Paul. 'He hates it at Granny's because of the dogs.'

'I'd forgotten. How silly of me. Of course Seymour must come and Felix and I will get ducks later, when you're back with Daddy. What I'm really hoping for is a horse.' Andrew lifted his head when Laura said this – she noticed but did not try to draw him out. She's obviously not dumb.

'So that's settled,' said my voice.

'Good,' said Felix.

'You can come and see me if you like, but not if you don't want to,' I said. 'I know it can't be fun, seeing me here.'

'I'd like to come and see you, Daddy,' said Paul. Other things were said, phrases, platitudes. I made sure that I got up to go before they did – I didn't want to see the backs of their heads.

Last night I dreamt that the private detective and I had to go to the house and check through the rooms, which we did. All the furniture had gone. It was a cold grey day and I was very cold in the dream. There was that grim December light – it looked dark but the sky was light, and the colours of the leaves under my feet on the garden path were bright and lurid, as if they had sucked up all the light there was into themselves. The house was cold and rattly and seemed very big – the rooms were not in the same order. When we went into Beth's room her cot was there, and the mobile above it. I was frightened of the cot, but it was empty. No ghosts. In our bedroom, Zoë and the baby were lying together on the bed, the baby on her back in the crook of Zoë's arm. I thought they were alive and I had found them again, but they were dead. I was wrong. The private detective and I stood beside the bed and looked at them, and I think we spoke about something but I can't remember what it was.

Horrible dream. When I woke it was with me and it felt true. The day is sunny and bright, but I feel as though I am in the cold world of the dream. I had a letter today from Paul:

Dear Daddy,
I am so relieved I saw you yesterday. Now I don't have to imagine where you are, which is far worse than remembering the real thing. I think Mummy would be pleased we are going to stay with Felix and Laura. I like Laura very much, and I think Andrew does too, so you mustn't worry. I think of Mummy all the time, and I know you do too. I hope to come and see you again soon, dearest Daddy.
  Love from your son,
  Paul

Paul's letter – trying to make me feel better.

I worry that Felix must be shocked by the latest pages I sent him. It does not feel reassuring that he has not discussed them with me yet. Must remember his life does not revolve around mine and that there are other cases and other clients. Feeling very low.

November 21st (Private Journal)

A letter from Felix:

Good to see you with the boys. Concerning the case, must admit that content of your last letter detrimental.

That you made Temazepam available to Zoë in her last days makes it easy to conclude that you wanted her weak and drugged so you could suffocate her.

Also from the fact that you made no effort to feed her on the day she died could be again construed that you wanted to weaken her.

Worse, that you refused to have her admitted to hospital shows you denying her right and proper care. It does not look good and I must put it plainly.

Threatening your wife's psychiatrist and having her followed are also not actions to which a jury will respond well.

I am concerned that all this may tempt the prosecution to try to prove Malice Aforethought. You must think again about having the boys – Paul at least – testify on your behalf.

They can say how solid an upbringing they have had and how good a father you have been.

Please note that this catalogue of judgements is not mine, merely conjecture on behalf of the jury. Also, remember that the physical evidence is inconclusive on both counts. I am going to defend you as a troubled man, but by no means a murderer. Jeffrey will be a character witness I hope, and I'll call Laura, whose angel face could conquer anyone's heart.

Best regards,
Felix

I suppose I should be glad that Felix is being so honest, but I suspect he just couldn't face telling me all this to my face. I can't blame him, and I'm not surprised. His is the only intelligent interpretation of the facts.

December 1st (Private Journal)

More than a week has passed since I last wrote, I have been idle and feel emptied out. Feel is the wrong word. I have not felt, but I have thought, and remembered. It has snowed. I can't remember the last time I have watched snow fall. In my life before – outside – snow meant that the boys were excited and did not want to be taken to school, begging to stay at home and make a snowman and have snow fights, days when Seymour sat at the window and became mesmerised before settling down to sleep, days when Zoë swore about the traffic and having to change her shoes, how she'd never get a taxi in town – or on taping nights, how the audience would stay at home rather than risk wet feet and stinging hands: never true, the English love braving weather. I sit and watch the snow fall from my window. It falls in a stately way, unhurried but for the occasional flurry, either with great purpose or with no purpose at all – I am not sure which. I have been numb and I have been low. I go over and over the boys' visit in my mind, my own awkwardness and their unhappiness, and all the ways I could have tried to comfort them and did not – like some flailing snowbound figure.

December 5th (Private Journal)

I had a letter from Laura this morning, which I paste in below.

Dear Michael,
Forgive me for not having written sooner, but we have been busy settling the boys in at the cottage. They have been very good and helpful. I've been thinking about what might make them feel at home and wonder how you would feel about our bringing their beds, books and furniture from London, for the attic. It's being painted now – yellow with green paintwork. There is a large window at the end, almost floor to ceiling, and the eaves are very low, so you have to stoop if you walk to the sides of the room. I'm having the floorboards stripped, and I think it would be fun if they were painted yellow too, but that's for the children to decide. There's a stepladder which you lower to get up there, although I'm having what they call paddle steps built which will be far more convenient. The attic runs the length of the cottage, some thirty feet or so – enough room for Andrew to put up his easel at one end if he decides he would like to.

It is all chaos now – children sleeping in Felix's study – builders everywhere – it's a relief that I only teach in the mornings. The boys come with me – they are my little shadows until the new term starts. They sit in the corner, Paul reads, Andrew watches the children. I am trying to interest them both in the cottage, making it home. Andrew is easier – he likes the fields and the walk along the lanes to the village shop for eggs and ham, and I feel he trusts me. Paul is harder. He likes me I think, but he behaves as though he's shipwrecked – he doesn't want to be difficult or uncooperative, but he is never spontaneous. I know this must be painful for you to read, but I'm hoping you may be able to give me some advice. Also, let me know what you think about the furniture, if you think it's a bad idea, just say, I haven't said anything about it to the boys yet.

I don't want to open old wounds, but can only say that there's nothing I wouldn't do to help you and the boys. Rightly or wrongly, I feel more than a little responsible for what happened to Zoë.

Felix sends his regards and asks me to say that he'll be in touch soon and has been working hard on your case. I am certainly witness to that! At weekends he promises not to, but shuts himself up in his study and works.

Remember I'll bring the boys any time you want to see them.

Warmest love,
Laura

Felix might be right about Laura being an angel. I have written back explaining that Paul has always been a wounded soul and needs to be given simple tasks – order and method appeal to him. And I've told her about the cooking. Also, that I don't think the furniture's a good idea. Let them forget. It has to be for the best. I've written to each child, individually. For the record, copies:

Dear Andrew,

I hear from Laura that you are being a good boy, and taking an interest in your new life. I can't tell you how glad I am to hear that. The attic sounds a wonderful room to have. You must paint the view from its window for me. My thoughts are always with you.

All my love,
Daddy

Dear Paul,

Thank you for your letter, darling, and I am sorry not to have written back sooner. It has been snowing here, and I hear from the weather report is also cold and frosty with you. I hope you are walking in the lanes with Laura and cooking her some of your delicious dinners. Try your vinegar chicken – I know she'll be impressed. I hope you are doing your best not to worry and that you will come and see me before Christmas. If there is anything on your mind, please tell Laura about it, or write to me. How is Seymour settling in?

All my love,
Daddy

Writing these letters has worn me out. I think it's something to do with coming to terms with life going on outside – as it inevitably must. Imagining the boys surrounded by yellow and green paintwork (yuk!) and Laura's cheerfulness. I have to believe that her love won't fail them as mine and Zoë's did. I have to believe in their new beginning, the gradual lessening of their shock and grief. I know that they have a good chance with Laura and Felix – the 'dynamic duo', as Zoë would sometimes call them. Darling Zoë was so insecure that no matter what she achieved she'd still worry about her little

152

sister and her husband overtaking her. I wonder what she'd think about Laura having charge of her children. I wouldn't be surprised if it weren't very much.

Tuesday, December 10th (Private Journal)

This from Paul today:

Dear Daddy,
Seymour is a bit cross and keeps himself to himself at the minute. He sleeps on top of my feet and legs at night and on my camp bed during the day. He ignores Laura and Andrew, but likes Felix when he comes down. He hides from the builders. I made Shepherds Pie last night. I think Laura liked it. I have asked her to bring me to see you next visiting day.
Lots of love from
Paul

PS I dream about Mummy every night – she is happy in my dreams. When I wake up, I think she is still alive.

Thursday, 12th (Private Journal)

Long afternoon with Felix. We didn't discuss the boys or anything personal. That seems to be Laura's department and is just as well. He has been researching the last months of Zoë's life, checking with Abbey and Nanny that all stories corroborate my description of events. He hasn't got on to the private detective yet.

He saw Lillian a few weeks back, but now she has called to

say that she plans to visit me – tells him she has something to discuss with me face to face. I am sure she only wants to gloat. I am tempted to refuse to see her, but Felix argues that murder trials can often throw up last-minute changes of heart, that those who were close to victim or accused can vacillate, and that if Lillian wants to see me it's likely to be because she wants to settle something in her own mind. The trouble with my case is that if I didn't murder Zoë there's rather a shortage of suspects, and accidental death is only believable in the context of Zoë's weakness and depression. Lillian would never accept such an explanation, because for her it means failure and guilt. It is hard for me to imagine that Lillian would ever choose to believe a version of events from which she did not emerge covered in glory – but that said, and despite my hatred of her, I have accepted Felix's advice and will see her. It would be an act of stupidity – and worse, moral cowardice – to refuse.

Friday, 13th (Private Journal)

Dreamt of Zoë and Beth lying in the long grass near the poplar trees at the end of the garden. Summer day. Zoë in a checked cotton shirt and jeans, Beth on a blanket on her front – she was older, nearly crawling. A few toys scattered around. Zoë also on her front, her head in her hand, looking now at Beth, now – her other hand sheltering her eyes from the sun – towards the house, looking for me? Andrew? Paul? 'I can't understand why he doesn't come, Beth,' she said to the baby. Out of myself, I saw my own figure on the lawn, giant size, towering above them and calling down – but Zoë, oblivious to me, still looking.

How easy to interpret my dreams are becoming.

Lillian wore black. This surprised me as the times I've seen her she's looked so gaudy. She had on a purple brooch though, and what looked like a thick layer of make-up, strong colours, and a pongy synthetic scent, which I remembered, and diamond rings and an amethyst one, on her wedding finger. She looked larger than life, as I also remember.

I only nodded when she greeted me, unable to speak properly, to follow the forms of politeness. She said, 'How are you feeling?'

I said, 'As well as can be expected,' which was childish I know. Then I said, 'Why are you here?' feeling sick-anxious in an unexpected wave.

'I'm here because I need to tell you face to face that your solicitor has been in touch with me, rather insistently, and has asked me to testify on your behalf at your trial.'

'I know that. I told him you would be unwilling. But, as he says, there's no property in a witness.'

She ignored my interruption and went on with her speech, as if prepared. 'He recommends I say that Zoë was disturbed, at the end, even possibly suicidal, for at least two weeks before her death. He wants me to say that your crime was only that of neglecting her. That's the story he wants me to tell, and I'm going to tell you what I'm going to do about it.'

'It's not a story,' I said, 'it's the truth.'

Lillian paused before replying, and then said slowly, as if

she were communicating a profound and subtle insight, 'It is your truth, Michael. I will testify to it as being your truth.' She looked so swollen with pride that again I could have laughed at her if I hadn't been so choked with hating her, hating in a gut-level, physical way. 'Every person has their own vision. Imagine a cake with us each having a slice, and each slice being different. It has to be someone's job to show the whole cake, the whole picture.'

'I think you'll find that that "job", as you put it, is God's.'

She smiled. 'I forgot you were religious.' I managed not to say anything, so she goaded me further, 'I don't think it is in your interest to deliberately misunderstand me, Michael. I am here, to tell you in person, that not only will I testify to your neglect of your wife, but also to your rages against her and against me, and your threats.'

'What threats?' I couldn't remember the threats – I felt overcome suddenly with sickness and heat.

'You remember,' she said, pretending to coax me. 'You threatened Zoë, on more than one occasion, to take her children away from her – you told her she was going crazy because she didn't happen to agree with you or want to live her life according to your idea of the way she should live it, you tried to control her, and when that didn't work, you came to my office in Devonshire Place and threatened me.' It was true that I had done all these things, but they were not the way she had made them sound. I couldn't recognise them the way she had made them sound.

I thought a little and fought back. 'How do you know what condition she was in two weeks before her death? You didn't see her.' When she didn't reply to this, I felt wild and hot again and said, 'You must not say things which aren't true.'

This put an expression on her face like that of a child at school who puts her fingers in her ears and hums when you try to clarify some infant dispute. 'Are you begging me?' she said, after a long time, eyes shining with excitement.

'No. I won't beg you. I only ask you to imagine how angry you would be if the person you loved most in the world began to destroy themselves, and not only were you powerless to stop them, but you were also blamed for their destruction.' I don't know why it came to me to appeal to her like that, but it was painfully misguided. She blushed as if I had somehow plunged her into the middle of something vile, her expression altered, although I can't describe how.

'Such a thing did happen to me. But I'm stronger and wiser for it now.' She said the last thing as if it were an incantation. 'I survived something terrible, but that has nothing to do with you or what happened to you.' She was angry, much too angry for it to feel real. 'I don't know if you killed Zoë, it is probable that you killed her, I will never know for sure. What I do know is that you threatened her, you threatened me, and not once but twice. I am not forgetting that the second time was actually over her grave, and that this is exactly what I am going to tell the court.' She tossed her head a bit on that last line.

'You wrong me. Before God, you wrong me,' I said – why, I have absolutely no idea. It was true, but it was pointless to say so. I think I was afraid, which I am ashamed to admit.

'I loved Zoë,' she replied, in a triumphant, theatrical voice. 'I am not concerned about wronging you. I will not wrong her by staying silent.'

'Time to go then,' I think I said. 'No more conversation necessary.'

'No. Nothing more.' Green eyes glared at me, and delighted in the stare. Seeing her again was like a chasm opening under my feet, a chasm opening to the summer, that insane time, where Zoë was mad and I was cruel. I cried hot selfish tears after Lillian left, tears of rage and helplessness and longing.

I've written to Felix explaining that Lillian came to see me as an exercise for her own ego. Put more simply, she came to frighten me and to triumph. I am beginning to think that my punishment for killing Zoë – for helping to kill Zoë through my blindness and weakness and folly – is to know that I did this and think of it every day, carry it with me. Lillian herself is just a demon, a teasing torturing hell-demon, and she is only powerful in that she tells the truth. Perhaps there is no difference between actually drugging and smothering Zoë and the actions I did take, the words I did say.

Thursday, 19th (Private Journal)

'Don't mention that you're a Catholic at the trial,' Felix said today.

'Why?'

'Juries don't like it. They'll think you're a religious lunatic.'

'Because I believe in hell-fire?'

'Exactly because of that. Nobody believes in hell-fire any more, not even priests. I'm hoping the prosecution won't get hold of it. If they do, acknowledge it openly, don't look embarrassed.'

'This is ludicrous, Felix,' I said.

'I know.'

Sunday, December 22nd (Private Journal)

Paul came yesterday. I've been too distressed to write, or do anything much at all since. He had on a new woollen coat – grey – too big for him. He told me that Laura had given it to him and yes he had thanked her properly. I don't know why I am getting so obsessed with manners. He smiled at me quite a lot, which is a new thing – he's never smiled much, since he was born. I asked him what he wanted for Christmas and he said he didn't know.

'You must want something.'

'Books. I want books.'

'Any particular books?'

'About explorers. I want to read about voyages.' I thought this odd and didn't know whether or not to be pleased.

'Have you brought your stockings from home?'

'Laura's bought us new ones.' He didn't smile when he mentioned Laura. 'She is very kind.'

'And very pretty.'

'Yes – very pretty.' He smiled then.

'Is there something special that is hurting you – something you want to tell me?'

'No, I just wanted to see you.'

'Are you sure? I have the feeling something special is hurting you.' In his look I knew that I was right, also that he was not going to tell me what it was. 'How's your brother?'

'He's fine. He and Laura have found a pony for him on loan. Her old horse has come from pasture. She says she missed him and wonders why she hadn't thought of it before.'

'He must be old though, now.'

'Nineteen. She says he can only be hacked lightly, his legs

are slender and delicate she says, so no trotting on the road.'

'What's his name?'

'Tenacious.'

'What a wonderful name.'

'Yes.' A single tear began to glide down Paul's cheek. 'Daddy, Laura says she will take me to the graves next week. Have you any message?'

'No. I will send flowers on Christmas Day.' I did not shudder that he spoke as if they were still alive. It is not so strange for a child. 'Your mother and sister are watching over us from heaven.'

'Andrew doesn't think so.'

'That's a shame. Now, how is your cooking?'

'I am cooking, Daddy. And I read. In January we can start at the school – new term. Laura is going to take us to meet the teachers.'

'That's good. And how's the attic?'

'Big. Bright colours.'

'Not like home.'

'No.'

'You must keep your chin up, Paul. And if there's anything you want to talk to me about – if you change your mind – I'm here. Is Laura outside?' He nodded. 'Give her my love. I know she's taking good care of you.'

'And Seymour.'

'And Andrew.'

'Andrew doesn't need taking care of.'

'Of course he does. He's just different from you, that's all.' Paul did not speak to me any more after that, but tried to smile at me with all his might when we said goodbye. I told him he was a valiant little soul.

I gave him a letter for Andrew.

Paul again this afternoon. He showed me photographs, holding them up like trophies, of Seymour, of Tenacious and the new pony, Blackie, in their stables and with Laura and Andrew up – also of the attic, each boy's corner, their beds tucked up hugging the wall. There was also a photograph of Felix and Laura outside the cottage, holding hands.

'Laura's very thin, isn't she?'

'Yes, Daddy. Felix is always trying to make her eat more. She gets tired easily. He wants her to go to the doctor, but she just laughs at him and says there's nothing wrong.'

'I'm sure she's right. Felix is probably just worrying because he isn't with her very much.'

'She eats when I cook. She's always so busy, though. She doesn't sit down.' I was glad to hear him talk about Laura with such obvious love. He told me that she mucked out the horses after breakfast, then they all went to school, then home for lunch, usually a riding lesson for Andrew, and a hack for her if not, then she was busy in the house, then tea, then evening feeds for the horses, then ironing, then bed, and then she sewed a lot, in the evenings.

'I hope you're helping her as much as you can.'

'Yes – in the stables and garden. Not so much the house.'

'I'm sure you can learn to iron.'

'Yes Daddy. She and Andrew are very close. He draws her a lot.'

'Do you feel left out?'

'No.' This, determined.

'What about Felix?'

'He sends faxes with hearts and kisses and jokes on them. He rings up in the evening, after we are in bed. He comes down on Friday nights.'

'Do they go out without you?'

'Sometimes on Saturdays and we have a babysitter. She smells of cabbage.'

'Does Andrew ever talk to you about Mummy?'

'Sometimes.' A look of intense inward pain came over Paul's face.

'I'm sorry, darling, I shouldn't have just mentioned her like that, suddenly.'

'Laura does. Laura tells us stories of when she was growing up and Mummy was in London and so clever with her career and Laura was jealous. She told us about your wedding. You dancing to that old Fred Astaire song and Granny crying and Laura said she remembered thinking that she wanted to look just that happy and beautiful on her wedding day.'

'That's nice, darling. I'm glad she talks to you about Mummy.'

'She never saw Beth.'

'She and Felix were in New York.'

'Andrew says she and Mummy didn't like each other.'

'I don't think they did, particularly. But that doesn't mean they didn't love each other very much. I think Laura misses Mummy, as we all do.'

'I know that.'

'You seem in better spirits, darling.'

'A bit better, Daddy.'

'Slowly does it. I'll speak to you on Christmas Day.'

'Yes.' He smiled a real smile this time, when he left.

December 24th (Private Journal)

I sent white roses and lilies to Zoë's grave and pink tulips to Beth's for Christmas.

The estate agents have had an offer on the house, which is a good one, and I should accept it, but I won't decide finally until the New Year.

Perhaps because it's Christmas, I have been examining my conscience and cannot help thinking about Lillian. She is the only enemy I have ever had. I feel ashamed about that but nowhere nearer to feeling that I could forgive her. I can't help raging against her for her wickedness – and yet I know that she is only a piece of our summer jigsaw, only a part of the picture of our destruction, the wreck of our lives.

What terrible hyperbole I've started using. I should cross all that out.

Laura came by herself today. She does indeed have the face of an angel – I don't know why I never realised it – saw it – before. She wore a big coat and scarf which she did not take off even though the visitors' room is quite warm.

'I love having the boys – they're a delight,' she told me. 'I think Paul is improving, holding on to life a little harder. Perhaps we expect too much of him. I think he's fond of us.'

'He loves you, which is a great blessing for him. I am very grateful to you both – you especially.'

'It has been the least I could do, and I've enjoyed it. Practice for my own children.'

'Have you thought of what will happen if I am convicted?'

I hadn't meant to say anything like that to her at all but she made me feel as if I could, somehow.

'If you wish it, the boys will stay with us.' I told her it was asking too much, but that I had no other choice, and could see no other way. 'I don't think Felix thinks it will come to that.'

'It still may.'

She smiled. 'I believe in my husband, though, Michael.'

'I really am so grateful to you.'

'Stop it – you're being silly.' I told her how Zoë always said she hated Christmas, didn't want to leave the office, always went to work between Christmas and New Year, but that once she'd bought the presents and wrapped them, and bossed me about a lot and I'd told her to 'shut up and be quiet', as we called it, she'd relax and let me cook and get on with it. She art-directed the boys at decorating the tree and she loved it. On Christmas Eve we'd have friends for drinks, always Jeffrey and his family, and there'd be champagne and ludicrously extravagant canapés Zoë bought at Harvey Nichols' food halls. She could be so mean about a lot of things, but never Christmas. We both used to get quite tipsy and sit looking at the tree with tears in our eyes after everyone had gone, too tired to go to bed. We'd tell each other we were the best thing ever and how lucky we were, then fill the stockings hung up on the mantelpiece. She'd go up to bed and then I'd write a letter from Father Christmas to the boys, and take a bite out of the mince pie they'd leave for him, and the carrot they'd leave for Rudolph the reindeer, and distribute soot on the fire rug. Then I'd stumble up to bed feeling extremely sentimental. That was the best bit of Christmas for me. On the last Christmas Eve Zoë was pregnant with Beth and so only had one glass of champagne, and I got maudlin all by myself, and she laughed at me.

Laura is an excellent listener. I didn't so much forget she was there as feel she was the only person I wanted to communicate absolutely with – that it was to her and her alone that my memories were meant to be entrusted. Her gentle, almost transparent soul-emotion surrounded me and I felt I spoke directly into her heart and she accepted my words like a benediction.

I hope that doesn't sound too creepy. The truth is that in this bog, this Slough of Despond, nothing has very much meaning or significance and there has been so much excruciating pain, chaos, and suddenly Laura, my wife's sister, forgetting her own grief, or loss, or shock, has changed the course of her life to take my children – and willingly – and driven over icy roads on Christmas Eve to hear me tell an inconsequential part of my story.

'Zoë adored you,' she said. 'You were her touchstone. She said to me that her life depended on yours, that it only began when she met you.'

'What do you think happened to her, Laura? How did we lose her?'

'I have thought about this and thought about it.' When she concentrated, a vein in her forehead came closer to the surface. 'A part of her was torn out when Beth died that was so precious she couldn't function without it. She couldn't live after the loss of Beth. She was so much frailer than people realised.'

'I failed her. I made it worse.'

'If you think that and only that, you forget the things that are important.' I didn't ask her what those were because it would have been crass. We both knew. I kept thanking her and she blushed and drooped her head a little.

I have seen so few people come and go in the visiting room – each visit reminding me of something I had forgotten or hurting me in some new way. But when Laura left she left me with Zoë in front of the Christmas tree and it's a vision that is with me still.

Felix's Journal

I have never been in the habit of keeping a diary, so this is a new endeavour. Just to be pedantic, I should qualify that: I have never kept one as an adult. When I was thirteen or fourteen and new at boarding school I kept one for just over a year, because I was lonely, but it didn't last. I am out of the habit of the long private narrative, my own version of my own truth. I write a great deal though: letters, notes, speeches. So much of my work is centred upon the written, spoken and remembered word; the process of justice is word-play and the words and phrases I use in court have to be absolutely right, clear, allowing for only one interpretation. Phrases have to be short. I often use alliterative repetition, especially where a jury is concerned. You must never appear to talk down to a jury or exclude them, make them feel as if they are invisible spectators at a private ritual or club. Clarity, brevity, bullshit. That's my motto.

For some reason, the events of the last months compel me to set them down, not just as scribbles and case notes, but consecutively. In my conscious mind I believe that I am in full command of the facts, and the means of interpreting those facts in court. But in this case I have the distinct feeling that the facts I am arranging so carefully to my client's advantage are not what constitute the whole truth, and that unnerves me. This is not a new sensation. I think only a fool denies the possibility that he may be wrong. I try to avoid defending someone whom I know to be guilty, but it has happened. In this case, though, there is so much at stake. The outcome has come to be central to my wife's happiness and therefore to my own, and for that reason I can't leave it alone, I have to try to puzzle it out.

Just as a witness' statement often reveals events or attitudes which the witness himself is unaware of, so I think this might be true of this case with my own words. If I write down what has happened, and add each new event as it occurs, as dispassionately as I can, and as if to a third person, I am hoping I will come upon the answer to my own conundrum. The feeling of taking part in a drama which I have not engineered myself concerns me. Under different circumstances I would not take this so seriously. To say I am alarmed is to put it strongly, but I am not tranquil in my mind. I haven't said anything about any of this to Laura, and I don't plan to. I could not make her uneasy unless I could present her with a solution. In the hope of attaining peace of mind, I have to try to look at our lives from a greater distance, but through a magnifying glass nonetheless.

Facts about myself, which have a bearing on the case, before I begin: I am thirty-seven years old. I am considered to be a brilliant, and rising, legal talent, which means I am highly ambitious. My reputation precedes me, although my office is not at all grand. I am extremely high-handed and intolerant, but I'm also said to be charming, which helps. Personally, I distrust charm. I believe in justice. I also believe in the old saying, Dickens of course, I love Dickens, that the law's an ass. That said, it's the only medium we have. Until they invent a better one, I have to work with this. I think Jews are good at that, working within a system that is, not only adapting to it, but embracing it. My family are Jewish middle class, now English, but my grandfather came from Poland, in the war. He was an artist in Poland, but in England he became a dressmaker. He made a business out of it, which my father, a dutiful son, continued. It made good money. I grew up in a large Victorian house in North London. I went to Harrow and Oxford. For my year out I travelled as much of the world as I could. Against Grandfather's wishes my father gave me plenty of money as I was growing up; my grandfather thought this would make me a wastrel and a profligate. When he saw that this had not transpired he shocked us all by leaving me even more money in his will, which is ironic, and funny. I think he felt that as an only child I had attracted far too much good will, that he had to put me to the test, lead me to expect nothing. I will admit that I was spoiled. I made up for it I suppose by deciding to become a criminal solicitor rather than a barrister: you make far less money, have to do endless legal-aid cases, and there's no glamour. Luckily now the law's changed I can go to court with the best of them, and feel good about myself at the same time, which is excellent. Rumour has it that the Crown Prosecution Service wants to filch me, but I love defence work far too much to be tempted. I also have absolutely no interest in becoming a judge. Unimaginable. Moving from the ridiculous to the sublime: Laura.

I met Laura at a gallery opening in Mayfair, one of those where the crowd make it impossible to see the pictures and no one is expected to show any interest in them whatever; I don't know what either of us was doing there. For our honeymoon we went to Rome. Every year we have a good long holiday, this year New York. I find it hard to describe Laura because I love her so much. But I must try. Laura has a gentleness of manner and of look which belies a great and rather awe-inspiring strength. She is delicate, physically, she gets tired easily, and when her body is tired, her mind races and she gets a crimson flush which spreads from her chest up her neck, although her face always remains pale. She has very very pale skin, alabaster skin, and brown eyes, and a Renaissance Madonna's head and neck, 'too much of a bony skull', she calls it. She's extremely emotional, none of it self-indulgent, which is good for me. She does all the feeling for both of us. She's honourable, she's generous, she laughs at my jokes. She has extraordinary empathy, which I think is a burden to her, because she hardly ever has the freedom to be selfish. In the children she teaches she instils calm and a peculiar sense of order and decency. Unselfishly, she teaches them discipline rather than 'getting in there with them', as she calls it, and using her imagination. She says children have enough imagination of their own only to need it from her in very small doses. To me she really is an angel. If I think about her for any length of time I am filled with profound gratitude that I have her and no one else. 'Just in time,' as the old song goes, and I often say.

We were in New York when this story began. Laura is the youngest of a substantial English brood, the 'country brood', as I've always called it, one of the five children of a retired Navy officer and his wife. She has three elder brothers whom we both consider tedious, so no arguments there. Her elder sister, Zoë, was a career girl, married to a very sweet man, a bit younger than she was. She was a television personality, a celebrity I suppose, certainly a household name. She and Michael had two boys, who have never appealed to me especially, and then Zoë surprised us all by getting pregnant again, at forty-five I think it was, and a baby girl was born in March last year. Zoë had never been interested in babies, even as a young woman, but Michael says she adored this one. We never saw the baby, Beth, because we were in New York when she was born and still there when she died, a cot death, at only a few weeks old. We weren't given the news until we came home. Zoë didn't want us to interrupt our holiday for a funeral. We were all shattered about it, the whole family, and Zoë seemed to lose her mind over it. From what we heard from Beatrice, my mother-in-law, she became unbalanced, not just unhappy, it was a kind of mania of denial which seized her. She gave up her job, claiming the baby's death was a sign that she must devote herself to family life. Except she didn't. She became reclusive, then appallingly depressed, and then she died; the post-mortem reveals that she couldn't have committed suicide. The whole process, from her baby's death to her own lasted only five months. April to September. (NB All the above description of Zoë's state of mind is hearsay from Michael and from her mother, mostly Michael.)

The facts are that she gave up her job, which was truly the most important part of her life, she refused to go to the baby's funeral, which wounded Michael deeply as he's a devout Catholic, and then she withdrew from the world completely. None of us saw her at all over that summer. Beatrice and Laura both tried, and failed. They both feel painfully guilty for not trying harder. Michael was frequently away on business at the end, and I'm still not sure why he chose to do that. I know there was tremendous financial pressure because Zoë effectively bankrupted her business and then started spending money like there was no tomorrow, which of course turned out to be true. But there was always the house, which was worth a great deal, and was in Michael's name, to stave off just such a threat if the business ever went under.

From what I understand, Zoë took the youngest boy, Andrew, a very gifted, artistic child, into her confidence, but treated Paul, the eldest, like a stranger. It was very peculiar, like a spell working, no one seemed to be able to do anything about it. We were all paralysed. I understand why Michael talks about evil taking them over. I hate that kind of superstition, but I know exactly what he means.

To summarise:
1. Zoë regularly visited a psychiatrist, a kind of confidence trickster in truth, from two weeks after the baby's death to two weeks before her own.
2. That Michael employed a private detective to follow Zoë throughout the summer, but that this also stopped about two weeks before her death. (I must remember to check this.)
3. That Zoë and Michael rarely spent time together that summer but when they did they quarrelled and Michael threatened to take away her children. He also threatened Zoë's psychiatrist, twice, once at her office and once at Zoë's funeral. (Extremely unfortunate.)
4. That Zoë and her baby were both suffocated, with no signs of struggle. The baby on her back, Zoë face down. Both deaths could have been accidental. Zoë was drugged up on Temazepam (tranquilliser and sleeping

pill). No doctor would endorse a theory of self-suffocation, so suicide is out.

5. Lastly, that Michael has been arrested for murdering both Zoë and Beth, which is the most likely interpretation of these events, according to the police.

The point about public figures is that the collective unconscious, for lack of a better term, the thing which makes the inhabitants of a city the approximation of animals in a herd, forbids the inexplicable where the death of an important member of that herd is concerned. They want Michael convicted so that they can rest easy and buy the tabloids for some other reason. So it has become a matter of common knowledge that he is guilty. The present situation is that Michael is awaiting trial and that I am preparing his defence. He is in prison ostensibly because he failed to make bail, but out of his Catholic sense of guilt he wouldn't want the family to use money which otherwise could be saved for the children, for bail, even if it were possible. All this means that the boys are living with Laura in our cottage in the country. This last affects us far more than the legal side of things. I go down and stay at the cottage at weekends. I'm not sure if I've said this, but Laura teaches Montessori kindergarten in our nearby town, Marlow. I feel ambivalent about having the boys, a rare feeling for me, but I suppose, natural enough. After their grandmother, my mother-in-law, Beatrice found she couldn't cope with them, there was no alternative but for us to offer to look after them, we're family after all. It simply means that now we are utterly entangled with the case – there's never a waking hour away from it. I suppose that would have been true even if I had only defended Michael, with no further obligation to him, but the responsibility for his children is enormous. They just have us, we're their last stop before hell.

Talking of shelter, Michael is selling the family house so that he can pay our legal costs, providing he doesn't qualify for legal aid, but I'm determined to ask for a minimal fee whatever happens, and persuade him to invest its substantial value for an income for himself and the boys when he is acquitted. This, of course, means that Laura and I are in reality supporting all three of them. I know that must sound selfish and resentful, and I can't deny it, it is another part of the picture. The whole picture has to be presented. Because of the boys I have to be separated from Laura all week. There's no flexibility. I hate her being in the country and me being in town, but the original idea was that the flat, the one I had before we were married, filled with books and papers and grumpy chain-smoking me, is no place for her even if she works. She is much better off in the country air, riding, being able to see the sky, tranquil, and me to puncture it all only at weekends. But now the presence of the boys rules out the occasional night in town for us both. I should also add that I am very old-fashioned when it comes to marriage, and Laura humours me about it, which is a good thing. I feel that I am her protector, that it is up to me to keep her safe.

Laura loved Zoë but they didn't get on. Zoë's famous talent for communication, drawing people out, did not extend to her family. I was fond of Zoë, and I discovered the trick of treating her as a man. That worked, and mutual respect followed. I think Zoë felt inferior to Laura because Laura is so content within herself, and Laura couldn't understand that, because she was so in awe of Zoë. I think Zoë envied Laura her nature, and her gift with children. Zoë loved children but she treated them like employees, which says it all really. Paul always tried to please his mother, but he was passed over for promotion in favour of his more promising brother. I don't think Andrew cares what anyone thinks of him, which is attractive to a certain insecure sort of person, and Zoë was very insecure.

Zoë's death was a shock that sent us all reeling, and as it was so soon after her baby's death, we blamed ourselves. Laura was particularly hard on herself about it, and we visited Michael quite a few times over that first fortnight. She would have invited him to stay at the cottage had she not been sure he would refuse. When Michael was arrested, the first person he called was me, and I went straight to the police station to see him. Laura was distraught when we spoke on the telephone that evening, making me promise I would defend him if the case went to trial. When I told her that I didn't think that was necessarily a good idea, she wanted to know if it was because I thought Michael was guilty. I explained that that wasn't the reason; it was just that my objectivity would be affected and he might not get the best possible defence. Laura argued that my being part of the family was exactly why I should defend Michael, and that it would show the world that Zoë's own family thought her husband innocent. She wouldn't even let me say, 'We'll see.' I knew then that the decision had already been taken. Depending on the complexity of the case I may instruct a barrister closer to the trial: two minds are better than one. I haven't broached this with either Michael or Laura yet. For Laura I took the case. For Laura I must win it.

Now that I've had the chance to think about it, I believe strongly that there's a connection between Zoë's death and the death of her baby, which is not confined only to the method of their dying. Taken separately, each death is a tragedy, a murky and indistinct and messy human tragedy, but I always believe that more than one death suggests the element of design. By saying this I am not leaping to the immediate conclusion that Michael is responsible, I can't allow myself to think that almost, although logically he is the only man alive who could be. I feel it is the wrong solution. It must be wrong. For a start, he has no motive. Why would a man kill his wife and baby one summer, just like that, for no reason at all? I am defending him convinced of his innocence. If he had planned two murders he wouldn't have done so many things to implicate himself, and publicly, unless he were stupid, which he's not. So I know there is a whole avenue I have not yet explored. Could it have been a kind of suicide of the soul or spirit, an abandonment of the desire to live? Could Zoë have pined away, that method of dying no longer mentioned in our century? I don't know, but I do know that such a notion would be laughed out of court. She did not starve to death, or drown herself, she was suffocated, and as in every case, there is a right answer to all these questions. I only hope that writing this will do the trick.

It's two in the morning. My study, which is papered in red in best English tradition, is feeling distinctly cold. From the window I see winter tree tops and buildings, lurid city sky, an unremarkable view. I do like mansion blocks though, so quiet, and they give the strange impression of being composed of blocks of mansions, a hyper-reality catering to the Englishman's fantasy of himself. And who would care about being an Englishman more than the grandson of a Polish Jew? Almost due west as the crow flies is Laura in our big

Victorian upholstered bed (we had to knock two cottage rooms together to give us a master bedroom) her window seat looking out over the fields and the country-dark sky. Sleep well my treasure.

January 15th

Since taking this case my first duty has been to establish the facts as they have been given to me by Michael. He has been sending me an ongoing written account of the summer, which is very emotional, and I think has become a form of therapy for him, so I have not discouraged it. Although it's wordy and embarrassingly personal, it is also very revealing about his state of mind, and the detail it provides is invaluable. I feel extremely sorry for him when I read it, but it's an ordeal I willingly undertake. If he had to go through it, the least I can do for him is read it. To corroborate his story I have interviewed Nanny, who was Nanny to both Zoë and Laura as children; Abigail the au pair and Lillian Taylor, Zoë's psychiatrist, whom I finally managed to see at the end of November. Lillian amazed me. She tried to overwhelm me, but she failed, and she knew that she had failed. This did not puncture her composure, but I think it surprised her. I went to visit her at her Devonshire Place office, and without going into detail (I have notes in the file at the office), she tried a number of tactics. First, she was professional and subdued, giving a quiet account of meeting Zoë when she agreed to appear on her show, her instant feeling of sympathy and identification with her, and her telephone call the next day during which she offered her help. She told me that in her opinion Zoë's treatment had gone well, she was beginning to 'discover herself and stretch her wings', was the phrase I think she used. She described how baffled she had been when Zoë's visits ended abruptly, but that she had been neither hurt nor offended, concluding that Michael had successfully interfered. This frightened her, because she knew Zoë was determined and accustomed to getting her own way. But it didn't frighten her enough to force her to act immediately. After more than a fortnight, she telephoned Zoë's home and spoke to Michael, later discovering that that had been the actual day of Zoë's death. She said she had also not been surprised to learn this: she has psychic powers and had sensed that Zoë's soul was in distress. I couldn't stop myself from commenting that if her powers had chosen a time to make themselves felt earlier in the day, Zoë might still be alive.

'It is not for us to pit ourselves against the Universal Plan,' was her reply. I don't think she knows how to blame herself. ('What does the Universal Plan look like?' I wanted to say. 'Can it be photocopied?') We went over the old ground about Michael's threats to Lillian and also those that Zoë had reported he had made to her. I asked her if she, Lillian, had taken those threats seriously. She conceded that at the time she had not. I asked her if Zoë herself had taken them seriously, and she replied that yes, indeed, she had. She cried several tears, none sufficient to disarrange her face or to stop her brain from working.

'I understand that Zoë's children are now under your care,' she said.

'What could be your interest in Zoë's children?' I asked, genuinely taken aback by the speed of this question.

'As you must know, I saw Paul over a number of weeks. I'm concerned about him.' I didn't say anything more to her about the boys, neither confirming nor denying that they were with us. When I asked her to give an accurate description of Zoë's state of mind and of the treatment she had been giving her, Lillian said that apart from being able to swear that Zoë was responding well and making good progress, it was confidential. She added, unprompted though, that she thought Michael a dangerous man. 'You know about the way he threatened me?' I acknowledged that this was all in the police report, which I had studied. 'As a witness for the prosecution I want to make it clear that I have only agreed to meet you out of respect for Zoë's memory,' she said. I thanked her, but explained that I was at liberty to call her for the defence also, whether she wanted to appear or not, if I so wished, to which she said nothing. Only later did she put forward her plan to visit Michael in prison, refusing to explain why she wanted to see him. I didn't push her about it because it would have got me nowhere. I didn't even try very hard to persuade her to be a witness sympathetic to our case. In the end, her visit to Michael came to nothing, I never imagined that it would not, though I couldn't say that to him. I had to encourage him about it, just in case. She wanted to see him in prison and gloat which, accomplished, confirmed her to me as the nasty piece of work she is.

Throughout the entire interview I found it very difficult to maintain my composure and politeness. I wanted to sneer at her, or laugh out loud. She is the kind of person who encourages the theatrical in those who meet her. She herself was emotional, but in an obvious, false way. So many crocodile tears and half smiles, bowing and lifting of the head, even wringing of the hands, made me impatient. She was a ham. If it were as simple as that, though, I would have felt quite smug, instead of which I had the strong impression that these amateur dramatics were just the outer casings of a quite formidable will. I don't think she cared if I believed her, and was taken in by her, or remained unmoved. She put on the show for her own gratification, it was a masturbatory act, from someone narcissistic enough to indulge in one publicly. Her professed love for Zoë, her dedication to her job, these were all manifestations of her ego. Michael knows this, and until I met Lillian, I was unfairly dismissive when he talked about her with such venom. Her lack of self-censorship showed her to me as a person undoubtedly clever, but horribly swollen with vanity and I hope that this may be her Achilles' heel when we need it. I feel that she has set her sights on being a star witness, a loving heroine whose attempt to save Zoë was foiled by her wicked husband, insane with jealousy. I'm going to encourage her in the witness box, give her enough rope to hang herself, but I'll have to be cunning and think, think, think. She's going to adore the photo opportunity, running from her car wearing dark glasses, pretending to detest the limelight. I can see all of it.

'Tell me, Felix,' she said, as I was leaving, 'did you love Zoë?' I declined to answer the question, but nonetheless it was followed by the inevitable: 'If you did, how could you defend her killer?'

Late Thursday, 16th

Tomorrow to the country, and Laura. I think I've updated everything in this story. It remains for me to interview Jeffrey McIver, Zoë's business partner, and the private detective, and then I will have to do some serious thinking.

Monday, 20th

Strange weekend. More and more it seems we have a ready-made family. While Christmas was a somewhat surreal novelty, January has the unavoidable air of normality. These children are here to stay. I have been given a riding demonstration by Andrew and Blackie, who are improving due to Laura's excellent teaching. The pony is very reliable and by all accounts could be quite fast. Laura and Andrew went for a hack and I was left with Paul; hard work, he answered my questions in monosyllables while he pretended to read. The cottage is coming on, kitchen floor now tiled and walls painted. Laura loves the Aga. Drawing room to be papered and carpeted. We're having two new radiators and they are to be boxed in, carpenters coming this week. Laura looking tired but lovely. She hugs and kisses the children all the time, is endlessly praising them, and endlessly patient. They both take her too much for granted already, in my opinion.

Tuesday, January 21st

Finally got to see the private detective today. I hate those kind of people. He's nervous about any kind of legal procedure and does not want to testify in court, though he did come to my office. I got the measure of him quite quickly: an efficient, ordinary man, as far as people in his profession can be ordinary. He said he was fond of Zoë, which I suppose isn't so odd. Wherever she went she was polite to people, he said, though often impatient. She suffered from vagueness, at times appearing confused about where she was, or why she had gone to a place. I was glad he said this with no prompting and obvious sincerity, her unbalanced mental state supports the accidental death theory, even if the physical evidence is less clear cut. I made one disconcerting discovery, which is that he did not stop following Zoë two weeks before she died, but was actually outside the house in a parked car at the time of her death. I don't know why Michael lied to me about these dates. What is he concealing – stupidly and ineffectually – and why has he lied? It is so unlike him.

Wednesday

Went to see Michael today. He looks more haggard every time I go. Not ill, just worn out with suffering. I don't think I've ever seen anyone suffer so transparently.

I asked him why he'd lied to me about the detective and I tried to be as gentle about it as I could. Everything you look at in that meeting room is ugly: the plastic cups, battered waste bins, stained carpet, dirt in the corners. Looking at ugliness withers people, I think. He told me that he had not intended to keep the detective on after he came back to London, and did not know himself why he did. The security of knowing he was watching, he said, drove all the practicalities out of his head, i.e., that it was unnecessary.

'It made me feel safe, knowing he was there.' I said that this was perfectly understandable, so again, why lie? He replied that he knew it was wrong of him to start having Zoë watched, worse to carry on with it once he had returned to London, and he had been ashamed to tell me. I was quite hard on him about it, wanting to make it painfully clear that he must not lie to me under any circumstances, that I cannot defend him to the best of my ability unless I know everything he knows himself. Thinking about it now, I am more than disconcerted. I think it bizarre enough that he should hire this man in the first place, but to lie to me about such a detail still doesn't entirely make sense. Although I don't think he's lying to me about anything else, I can't be sure. Because I like him and he has my sympathy, I should not rule out the possibility of further lies. Also, I can see now that he was far more disturbed mentally at the time of Zoë's death than I have understood. I'll have to have him evaluated by a psychiatrist, but I don't really want to take that route. I'm uneasy about it.

Later

Spoke to Laura tonight and I felt tempted to tell her about Michael's lie. But that would mean talking to her about all the details of the case, when we agreed between ourselves at the beginning of all this, in exchange for my taking the case, that we wouldn't do that. It was our bargain. We would never discuss the trial. For Laura's sake, ignorance is bliss. She's worried about Paul, who appears to have taken a turn for the worse. Almost completely silent, headache, stabbing pains in his eyes, tummy-ache.

Thursday

Fax following today from Laura. No time to call her until tonight, I was in court.

Darling,

Strange woman came to the cottage today, claiming to be Zoë's psychiatrist. I had no idea. Wanted to see Paul and Andrew, who thankfully were at school. It would have been rude of me not to offer her a cup of tea, she'd driven from London and seemed concerned about the boys' welfare. I told her they were fine. She talked on and on about Zoë – I thought she was going to burst into tears. Call me as soon as you can.

Your,
Laura

When I spoke to her on the phone she was puzzled and upset. She didn't even know Zoë saw a psychiatrist and feels I have been far too protective by not telling her about it. I reminded her about what we'd agreed but she says she feels she's been foolish, shutting her eyes when it's her own sister's murder that's being tried. I was surprised to hear her use the word 'murder'. She said that Lillian gave her a bad feeling and that she didn't want her near the boys again, felt sick about it. It was such a crazy thing for Lillian to do, just arrive like that, and why was she so keen to see the boys? Her 'love' for Zoë must be entering the good old territory of obsession; she's obviously madder than either Michael or I realised. I think I'm going to drive down to be with Laura tonight. I can come back early in the morning. I think we should be together tonight.

Friday

She was asleep when I let myself in last night, the whole house dark and quiet. She sleeps heavily, Laura, when she does sleep, although sometimes she stays up for hours, reading. I didn't want to frighten her, so I put the light on and banged about a bit, wishing I'd called to warn her instead of rushing to the car to get to her as fast as I could. I've always found the mere idea of a mobile phone untenable. It's silly, but I just couldn't bear for us to endure even the semblance of a quarrel. She must have woken while I was in the bathroom, because when I came into the room she was awake and sitting up in bed. 'You shouldn't do this, you know it scares me.'

'I'm sorry.' She looked more adorable, hair tumbled, than anyone has ever looked. 'I'm an idiot, and I'm sorry. And I'm sorry about today.' She didn't have to say that she forgave me – she knows we are always allies.

'I'm glad you're here. I want to talk to you. I've been so distressed. Get into bed and we'll talk. It's as if I'm realising for the first time that Zoë is dead. My sister's dead and I'll never see her again. I loved her, but I don't think she knew that.'

'Of course she did. Just because you didn't see eye to eye –'

'Hardly ever spoke, you mean. You don't have to be tactful. You know how it upset Mummy, it must be horrible if your children aren't close.'

'None of this is your fault – that Zoë's dead.'

'I really only tried to see her once last summer. I let myself be put off very easily.'

'You had other things on your mind, builders and –'

'I don't want you to try and make me feel better. The point of all this isn't for me to blame myself and you to say it's all right.'

'I just don't want you to suffer.'

'Everybody suffers.' She was impatient with me then. 'I think the worst thing about grief, about Zoë dying, is how

185

selfish it is. We're sorry she died, we're upset she died so horribly, for her we're distressed, but for ourselves, we're devastated, for ourselves we grieve more deeply, that we're left missing her, dealing with all this mess.'

'And now more of a complication, suddenly a psychiatrist.'

'I didn't even know she saw a psychiatrist.'

'Her name is Lillian Taylor. She came on Zoë's programme.'

'We didn't always watch –'

'Just after Beth's death. And they became close – it sounds more like a love affair than a therapeutic relationship. Platonic, of course.'

'Of course, Felix.' She smiled at me, teasing.

'Zoë was vulnerable and she believed that the doctor could help her, but according to Michael she filled her full of a lot of quasi-religious rubbish about Beth's death being meant –'

'How could she say that to Zoë? It's horrible.'

'I'll stop if you like.'

'No. But it should have been us. We should have been there.'

'She didn't want us.'

'That's true.' With a sigh, she sat up straighter in bed, reaching for her pony-tail thing on the bedside table and gathering up her hair into what she calls her work hair.

'Are you getting up?'

'No, I'm thinking. I don't blame you, but you've let me behave ridiculously. I have to know all about this case, number whatever it is. It's my sister's death. How could I be so stupid and cowardly?'

'Laura, it's confidential.'

'I don't care. You're my husband, she's my sister, I want to know all of it, the whole story.' There was no point in arguing with her, trying to put her off. And in a way I was relieved that I no longer had to keep it all to myself.

'I have it all written down – I've been keeping a diary, which will tell you everything, if you really feel you need to know. There's a lot of soppy stuff about you in it too.'

'Fetch it for me.'

'It's in the car. Can't. Impossible now. Tomorrow. Go to sleep.'

'Try, or I'll get it myself.'

'You're pretending to be in charge again.' I went to the car and found her the diary and slept soundly beside her while she stayed up all night reading it. I couldn't have stopped her. We had no chance to talk in the morning because I had to leave too early, and I took this book with me. I didn't want her going over and over it and brooding.

Monday, January 27th

Weekend where we looked after the children – and whispered in our room at night in the dark about Zoë and her life and death.

'I never knew her,' Laura said.

'You didn't know who she became. But no one did.'

'No, it's not how she changed. I don't think I ever understood her.' We talked about how peculiar an understanding of another person is, how it was that we should meet and instantly know one another, while Laura is still struggling to comprehend her own flesh and blood.

Jeffrey McIver came to visit me in my office this afternoon; it was in the diary, but I'd forgotten. We have already met once, when I asked him to corroborate Michael's story about the day Zoë had shouted at him on the telephone when she'd decided to walk out on her own business. He struck me then as a sentimental man, one with little talent but that of attaching himself to somebody who did have it, and holding on. But if he's a sycophant, he's an honest one and I like him.

He said he wanted to know how the case was progressing, but I think he really only wanted the opportunity to talk to me about Zoë.

'After that phone call, I only saw her once more, though I called often enough. She had packed up the paperwork I needed from her office and I used collecting the boxes as an excuse to see her. I didn't warn her I was coming in case she decided to hide. I was still angrier with her about what I saw as her betrayal of me than I was worried about her state of mind – but when I saw her, actually saw her, white as a sheet, really very very thin and distracted, sort of looking through me, irritated by having to see me, or speak to me, I was more upset for her than about anything else. I loved Zoë. She was such a great girl. Tough. Fun. Clever. I loved her without having to fancy her or be in love with her – I just appreciated her for what she was. We had some good old times together. She was like a lucky charm.' I offered him a drink, which was probably foolish of me because only one whisky later there were tears in his eyes. 'You never know what's going to happen in this life, you just don't. One minute you're in partnership with the greatest girl in the world, the next, you've gone broke, you've lost a precious friend, and you have no idea how or why it happened.' I couldn't say anything in reply to this. 'Keep me informed, won't you?' he said as he left. 'I loved that girl. Give my regards to your wife.'

Thursday, 30th

In court today. Came out to find a long fax from Laura. She could have saved it for the phone this evening, but must be wanting to communicate with me, even if we can't speak.

Darling,
Both boys had letters in the post when they came back from school. Typed envelopes, postmarked NW6. Paul went pale when he read his, tearing it up and putting it in the fire. Andrew said nothing but folded his neatly and put it in his pocket. They didn't say anything to one another but I had the feeling that Andrew at least knew what Paul's contained. I asked them both to tell me what was in them – no answers. I worry about how badly the boys are getting on. I rarely hear them talking together when I'm in another room, and they don't play. Ever since reading your diary I'm looking at everything differently – this is probably nothing, forgive me, I'm just worried.
Call soonest,
Laura

Saturday night

Laura excited when I came home last night – sending me up to our bedroom where a new picture hangs above the chest of drawers. A crayon sketch of Tenacious, looking out over his stable door. Andrew had drawn it and given it to her as a surprise. It's actually extremely like the old horse, as Laura calls him, technically accurate, but also capturing the expression, the look in the eye.

'Andrew is always up in the attic,' she said. 'He's working on a whole series of pictures up there I think. And he's been doing some sketches of me.' I was glad for her. Every time one of the children expresses gratitude or love she is so grateful, as if each gesture contributes to lightening that burden of guilt she carries around so uncomplainingly.

February 6th

I've just re-read everything I've written about this case and most of the papers Michael's been sending me too. Still feel no nearer to working out for myself what really happened, except for one thing which struck me – I can't have taken it in properly before. It comes from Michael's description of going to see Lillian for the first time and threatening her at her office. At the end of it he says, 'The passage and the stairs and the journey home remain a blur.' At another point, I can't remember where, he says that he ceased to be 'myself' over that summer, just as Zoë ceased to be herself. Strong stuff. Is it a possibility that Michael may have entered into some kind of dissociative state, and have committed this appalling act against his wife while not conscious of it? He constantly refers to the strain he was under, and the feeling of evil taking them all over. Have I been stubbornly set against coming to any such conclusion – committed an error of judgement because I am determined to think well of Michael? I must look at it from the beginning, and I must approach it slowly.

In the beginning there was the baby's death. Present in the house: her mother, now dead, her father, now imprisoned (and whose written account I have), her brothers, now under my care, and her nanny. Nanny. I must go and see Nanny again.

February 7th

Drove down to see Nanny this morning. She was kind on the telephone about my giving her no notice at all.

'I think about that baby all day long, so I won't mind you asking me to talk to you about her.' Nanny lives in a low red-brick block of flats on the outskirts of Hungerford. It has some gardens around it, flower-beds planted, and a concrete ramp which leads up to the main entrance and runs parallel to the stairs, with a hand-rail made out of bright green shiny plastic. The passage to her door is narrow with exposed red brick, and full of that institutional smell. Her door has a chain on it and a peep-hole. She has a small square box of a sitting room, with thin walls, a low ceiling, a sliding glass door which opens on to the gardens and a paved terrace. The room was tidy and dirty, or at least it smelled as if it were dirty. I wanted to open the window but it would have been rude to ask. I couldn't help thinking how wrong she looked there in the flat, not as if it were her home. I always imagine her home as being the big house Laura grew up in.

We had cups of tea and she put on the electric fire and fussed about where to put the flowers I had brought her. Above the fire on the shelf was a large black-and-white framed photograph of herself with Zoë, the boys and Laura as a baby. It looked like a photograph from another century, each face so solemn and sure of itself, with that innocence that belongs only to the past. I did not know how to begin.

'How is Laura?' she said. 'And how are the boys?'

'Fine. Very well – as well as possible.'

'I am glad that they are with you. I sent a Christmas card.'

'Yes. Thank you.' I couldn't remember if we had sent her one in return. I hoped fervently that we had, but she offered no clue.

'It's been a sad time,' she said.

'I know, and I'm sorry, but I have to ask you again about that day. The day Beth died. As much as you can remember, from the beginning.'

'Well, the beginning would have been four thirty in the morning, getting up to give her her bottle.'

'Didn't Zoë do that?'

'Yes, but I liked to be there too, to see that everything was all right. She never wanted me to get up at that hour, but she couldn't stop me. It wasn't for very much longer anyway, because we were going to have her sleeping through the night the week after. She had another feed at about eight thirty, and Mr Michael cooked us all breakfast in the kitchen, the boys as well, and then Miss Zoë went to her desk. Before she went I remember she said how pretty and sunny it was for April, but she wasn't really thinking about that, her mind was on her work, and I said yes it was, but blustery, and off she went. I went upstairs to the laundry room to do the ironing. I heard Mr Michael come up to his study a bit later – his study was next door to the laundry room.'

'Did you check on Beth as you went up?'

'Yes, I did, and she was fine, sleeping like an angel. She was such an easy baby.'

'What about the boys?'

'They were in their room or playroom, one of the two. I didn't look in on them.'

'But it was their playroom which had a door to Beth's room?'

'No, it was their bedroom.'

'Yes, of course. That makes it less likely that they would have been right next door.'

'They could have been. They weren't always together. Paul would read on his bed quite often and Andrew would draw in the playroom. They were good at amusing themselves, not always after television and things to eat. Not spoilt.'

'When you were upstairs ironing, how could you tell that Beth was all right?'

'We had a listener in the laundry room as well as the kitchen.'

'Are you sure it was turned on?'

'We never turned either of them off. We didn't want to risk forgetting.'

'I'm sorry to keep questioning you about this. I just want to make sure. Do you remember anything strange or out of the ordinary happening in any part of the morning?'

'No. It was an ordered, sensible day, like all the days in that house. I knew the baby was sleeping peacefully while I ironed. At about twelve I came downstairs for a cup of tea, I probably sat at the table for a bit and had a biscuit, then got up and sterilised some bottles, did a bit of tidying up.'

'When did Michael come downstairs to go to the dentist?'

'About quarter past twelve, I think, I don't remember exactly but he came in to see me and said he'd buy some ham for lunch and we could have it with mushrooms on toast. I was waiting for Beth to wake up at about twelve thirty, and when she didn't I didn't worry. She was a good sleeper, and sometimes she slept a little longer, there was no harm in that. Miss Zoë came in at about quarter to one and then she went up to check on her.'

'You have a remarkably good memory, but do you think you could have left anything out?'

'When a day becomes as important as that day is to us all now, it's not likely any of us would forget it. We all loved that little girl so. She was such a precious, such a good little thing.'

'Yes.'

'How is Mr Michael?'

'He is as well as he can be, Nanny.' We sat in silence for a while. Nanny had a crucifix, small and austere, on her wall, which I hadn't noticed before. 'Forgive me for asking this, but I have to. In your opinion, and this conversation is a private one and will remain just between ourselves, were Michael and Zoë happy?'

'They were happy as long as no one interfered with Miss Zoë while she was working.'

'How do you think Michael felt about the baby?'

'He didn't have very much to do with her, that I could see. He looked after the boys.'

'Because he didn't want them to be jealous?'

'That could be a reason.'

'In your opinion, could Michael have committed such a terrible crime?'

'I couldn't say yes, and I couldn't say no. All I can say is that if you've been a nanny for as long as I have, not very much can come as a surprise to you, in the end.'

'What do you mean by that?' I leaned forward.

'What I've said. I mean what I've just said. How can any of us know what is in another's heart? Only God knows that.'

I didn't know what to answer, so we sat in silence for a while. And then I said, 'Are you getting on all right here?' knowing I was intruding to ask again, once had been enough, but wanting to show her some consideration, some respect.

'I am lonely, but I think all old people are lonely.'

'We must bring the boys to visit.'

'Yes – and give darling Laura a kiss from me. She was a dear baby, very like Beth, very like Beth. Miss Zoë often said so.'

I had read Nanny's first statement earlier that morning, and I thought about it in the car on the way home. It had been identical to what she had just told me, but for one single fact: that there had been a baby listener in the laundry room. I knew it would be important as soon as she told me about it, but couldn't think about it properly while I was still with her. What it means is that the only time she would have been unable to hear the baby was on her way down the stairs from the top of the house to the kitchen, and for part of that time she would have been outside Beth's door. The implication of this is to pinpoint the time of Beth's death to the five minutes – at the most – it took Nanny to go down the stairs. What makes me feel sick is what it implies about the manner of the baby's death. If it had been accidental – a cot death – the likelihood would be that out of all the minutes that were in that day she would have started to struggle for breath at a moment when she could be heard. It seems far too much of a coincidence that she should die within the only time frame in which no one could hear her. It has to suggest a plan, a design, something timed and executed. Michael could indeed have executed such a plan. He would have had to get to

Beth's room just after Nanny passed it, without her hearing him behind her on the stairs, kill her before she reached the kitchen, swift and silent. Difficult, unlikely, but not impossible.

I called Nanny as soon as I reached my office, thanking her for seeing me.

'I cried after you left,' she said.

'I'm sorry, and I'm sorry to have to ask you one more thing. Every day, every morning, did you always go upstairs to the laundry room and come back down to the kitchen at about the same time?'

'Exactly the same time. Routine. I always stick to my routine. It was how I was trained.'

I'm going to have to talk to those boys next.

February 10th, Monday

I'd discussed it with Laura and we agreed that I had no choice but to talk to the children in detail about that day Nanny described so clearly. They might be the only ones who could provide a new fact such as Nanny's, which might be crucial. Laura prepared them, saying that on Saturday morning I was going to have to ask them some questions about their mother and sister. She told me that Andrew said that the police had questioned them when their mother died, but Laura explained that I was asking them because I needed to help their father, and so it was important. She apologised, she said, for causing them pain.

I felt guilty about broaching the subject with the boys. I wanted to be clear, so I wrote key questions down on index cards which I shuffled up and down on my desk in my study where the 'interview' took place. I had coffee, and Paul brought Seymour, and the children sat side by side on the sofa bed as if they were puppets, their legs dangling down.

'When your sister – the day your sister died, what were you doing?'

'We were in the playroom, all morning,' said Andrew.

'Yes,' said Paul.

'The playroom at the front of the house?'

'Yes,' said Paul.

'There was no time when one of you was in your bedroom next to Beth's room, reading? Nanny had asked you to be quiet, so I'm wondering whether you might have occupied yourselves separately.'

Paul looked at Andrew briefly before they both said, 'No,' in unison, again like puppets.

'What were you playing?'

'Dominoes,' said Andrew. 'We were playing dominoes.'

'And who was winning?'

'I was,' he said, 'I always win.'

'While you were playing, did either of you hear any sounds coming from the landing or from your sister's room?'

'No, it was too far away,' said Andrew.

'You didn't hear any footsteps, not anyone going down-stairs?'

'If we did hear,' said Paul, 'we did not notice that we heard. We were playing.'

'When Mummy went into the nursery and found Beth, what happened then?'

'She screamed,' said Paul, 'and we ran into the room.'

'Through the bathroom and bedroom, through the door that joined your room to Beth's?'

'Yes.'

'So you weren't already in the room, or standing in the doorway, when she came in?'

'No. We wouldn't have gone in because the baby was sleeping. We ran to the room when we heard her scream,' said Andrew.

'Are you absolutely sure?'

'Absolutely sure,' said both boys together, in their flat voices.

'Where was Daddy?'

'I don't remember,' said Andrew. 'He was out, at the dentist's. He came back before the ambulance arrived.' I asked the children especially about the doorway because Zoë's inquest account is unclear about when she noticed that the boys were standing in the doorway. It is possible that she might have jumbled it a bit, because it is far more likely that the children were alerted by her screams and then came running. If they had found the body first, her account would have been substantially different. As it was, they had had no reason to go into the room.

It makes me wonder, though, whether the children did in fact see the body, and were not hurried out of the room as quickly as Zoë describes. It would explain why they are both so disturbed. Zoë was so distraught that I don't think her sequential account should be taken as gospel. At the same time I feel wary about discounting her story. As Nanny said, a day of such horror is not easily forgotten, and Zoë had to give her statement at the inquest within only a short time. What is certain is that it would take someone far more trusted by those children to squeeze anything further out of them.

'What was Mummy like after that?'

'She was very happy,' said Paul. 'And she was busy and I didn't see her very much.'

'We looked for a pony,' said Andrew.

'Is there anything else you want to tell me about that time – about Daddy?'

'No.'

'What about Mummy, the day that Mummy died? What happened that day?'

'I was outside the door,' said Paul, 'when Daddy and the nurse went in.'

'You know that I was in my studio room,' said Andrew. 'They didn't come for me until after she'd been taken away.' I felt their minds closing like steel traps. The more I see of those children, the more peculiar they seem to be. I don't know how to begin to find out anything from them. I feel I've set myself back, if anything, by trying. Now I think I should never have talked to them formally, but should have tried to find out, with *faux* spontaneity, what is in their minds about the past. I dislike feeling so powerless: so outwitted.

February 16th, Sunday

Awoke very early this morning to the sound of crying as if from a long way off. Laura sound asleep. Went down to my study, now Paul's room. He was crying in his sleep, and I thought it might frighten him too much if I woke him up, so I just stood there in the doorway, helpless and watching.

February 19th

More and more I think those children are the key to the case, and upbraid myself continually for being so stupid as not to realise it sooner and for not being able to get a syllable out of either of them which might help. Could it be possible that they were somehow involved in those deaths, witnessed some unimaginable crime?

February 20th

Trial date now set – June 28th – earlier than I thought.

Time marches on and I've decided to talk to Michael about the boys. But I won't say anything to him about my visit to Nanny.

February 21st

Michael has developed the habit of talking softly, as if afraid of being overheard.

'Anything new?' he asked me.

'Nothing new.'

'How are the boys? Andrew still hasn't come to see me since that first time. It's his birthday next month.'

'I know. Perhaps we should just bring him anyway, next time. What do you think?'

'I wouldn't want to force him, but I'm anxious, I want to see his face.'

'Laura will bring him. How are Paul's visits?'

'We both make an amazing effort – talk about nothing, conceal what we feel.'

'When you say conceal, do you mean you think he is hiding something specific, about Zoë?'

'It could be imagination but I just feel that he's keeping secrets. I don't know why, or whose. Whether they have anything to do with what we might like to know, what we would consider valuable, I don't know, they are just part of his own anguish, his own memories of the summer.'

'Have you tried to make him talk to you?'

'I used to – but it's no use. And I don't want him to stop coming to see me because it comforts us both, so now I pretend I don't notice him struggling, and that's how it is. How is he with you and Laura?'

'Very guarded. I don't know if he's told you this, but he won't sleep in the attic any more, seems not to want to be with his brother, keeps himself apart. They don't talk to one another at all.'

'They've never been close.' We sat in silence for a while, contemplating our own ineptitude.

'What about that psychiatrist, Lillian? Do you think he would confide in her?'

He rubbed his thumbs over closed eyes and sighed. 'No. He hated her. I'm surprised you should ask such a question, Felix. You know what a charlatan she is. In fact, I've just remembered something that – I can't believe I'd forgotten this – Paul told me that she'd once told him something she told him he wasn't allowed to tell anyone. He'd promised her not to. Don't you remember? It's in my written account.'

'No. I can't have thought it significant. I'm sorry. Why didn't you remind me?'

'Because I forgot about it. Too painful I suppose. I remember things and forget, remember and forget. Some things are always on my mind, others go away. I try not to hate her too much, think bad thoughts about her, stir things up. She's made it bad enough for me already.'

'I'm going to find out about her – do a proper investigation – but I'll make sure she won't know about it – is that all right?'

'That's all right.'

'Are you sure Paul didn't give you any more detail? Is that all that happened?'

'That is all that happened.' Whether I can believe him, or he's still lying, I don't know. I wonder why Michael still lies to me. Concealment is only a form of lying, after all.

I've made sure my team has detailed research on Lillian's background as a priority. This investigation should have been put in train weeks ago, I should have seen to it after her peculiar visit, and that letter, which could so easily have come from her to Paul as a warning, 'Don't say anything, keep my secret.' Laura's promised to try to get the boy to confide in her if she can.

I'm exhausted and want only a glass of whisky and bed.

February 25th

Laura called tonight, she tells me that Andrew appears to be blooming. He rides out whenever he can and occupies himself hour on hour upstairs in the attic drawing, and writing too, he tells her, oblivious to Paul's misery.

'Because of his tragic circumstances I feel as if he should be as unhappy as Paul but it's not in his nature. He has blocked it out or surmounted it, I don't know, but he is not haunted by it. He is coming out the other side and we should be pleased about it. And he can be such fun to be with. I can't explain it, but he's very sensitive to mood, tactful. He doesn't intrude, but I always want to join in with his games and schemes when he lets me. There's something irresistible about him.'

'How's Paul?'

'Tonight I took him hot milk and a chocolate biscuit in bed and sat beside him while he ate and drank. When his eyes rest on me, follow my gestures, there's so much emotion in his look that I feel – I can't describe it – burdened. I tucked him in, and kissed him and asked him if he ever said his prayers, I don't know why. He told me he used to, and I asked him if he thought his daddy would like it if he did. He said yes, so we said the Lord's Prayer, and then he said, "Laura, do you think it is possible to forgive all trespasses?" I said I didn't know, but we must try, and I asked him if there was something he was thinking about specially, and he said no and curled up, turning over to face the wall. But I think he did hesitate, just for a fraction of a second, and I thought he might speak.' I told her she was doing well and she said, 'I'm doing my best. But I'm not sure I want to know what it was he might have told me.'

February 27th, Thursday

Had this fax from Laura today:

Darling,
You probably haven't noticed this, but February is nearly over.

I had a long ride this afternoon, and it's done me great

good – Tenacious stepping out and pointing his toes on the wet lane, water running fast in the thaw. Not very much breeze, clouds passing over a high sky, watery sunlight. The world is beginning to smell – damp ground, firm underfoot in the woods, hooves making that glorious hollow sound, thudding, and twigs snapping and birds flying up showing off. Tenacious arched his neck and snorted and pretended he was only five and might shy, though of course he didn't. We had a happy canter by the side of that field near the stream which flows down to the ford, a real surging forward restrained-power canter, and the wind in my face was soft and damp. We saw a lot of new rabbit holes, and crocuses, and snowdrops. Everything in sight beginning to change so I had to look at it and notice. So much of me is always buried in the winter, and this winter has been so unexpectedly hard. I love my old horse for making me forget about all of it, for giving me such a present of a ride. It was a private thing in a way, but I wanted to tell you about it instead of always giving you doom and gloom from home and more worry. I made a ginger cake for tea – it was a really good one. Andrew and I ate so much of it we were nearly sick. Paul took his on a plate to his room but seemed contented enough. Perhaps better days are here at last.

I'll have to start digging the flower-beds soon.

All my love,

Laura

Laura is remaking the garden. There is a small cottagey garden to the side of the house, which our new french doors open on to – she hates it because there is a rockery and she plans to pull it out and plant only roses, lavender and climbers. Then behind the house, where our bedroom and the kitchen window faces, is the bigger garden, with a rather sloping faded lawn and narrow flower-beds. It's prettily walled, but apart from that, untended. Laura wants to put in splendid borders and a terrace, and that's the spring project. Behind the garden is the field, divided by a fence along which are pretty fruit trees, some so old we will have to replace them, but we are very lucky, our view is wonderful and very private.

I miss Laura like a physical pain so much of the time. I don't know what I'm doing working here, being so far away, it's a stupidity. If we have a baby she'll be like a lone parent during the week. Why didn't we think of all this when we decided to put this distance between us? But of course, I've forgotten: we didn't have the boys then.

Friday, February 28th

Have the report on Lillian in front of me at my desk. It's eleven thirty. I've already read it over and over, but want to write about it as well. What an eventful life she seems to have led. Born to northern working-class respectable poverty. Both parents now dead. Only child – and a late child. Very loved, I would imagine, although that is conjecture. Married young, at nineteen, and married a doctor, who by what I can see encouraged her to train as a doctor also. He seems to have been a good, if unexciting man. After she had qualified they went to live abroad, in South America, where she gained a substantial reputation for dedication to the poor, results, and courage – there were various famines and wars that she distinguished herself in. She also made a devoted following for herself, something she has maintained ever since. She and her husband had two children, and a third who died in infancy. (This I have already underlined so hard the pencil lead broke.) This nearly destroyed her, she gave up her practice, probably had a breakdown. The marriage failed.

Here is where it becomes interesting. She leaves her husband and children, six and eight I think they were, and comes back to England. She begins to train as a psychiatrist. Her husband is generous financially so she can concentrate on qualifying. She is appointed to a private psychiatric clinic in Reading. The city is too small to hold her for long, she is head-hunted, moving to London to take up a position in a private hospital. She also begins to establish her own practice. She divorces her husband; she does not ask for custody of the children. There is no indication from the report that she has ever seen them since she left South America. A few more years of success, and she falls in love, this time with a patient. This patient is a man with a history of depression and alcoholism. They begin an affair while she is still treating him; this is against every medical ethic. The affair is discovered, Lillian's case is referred to committee. At the hearing she is quoted as saying, 'I reserve the right to fall in love with whomever I choose.' She is not struck off, she survives by a whisker, but there are rumours of corruption, and the establishment turns its back on her. She and her former patient get married quietly and begin living together in her very large house in the suburbs. Nine months later, he commits suicide. The facts surrounding the case are these: although he has a recognised psychiatric illness for which anti-depressant med-ication is recommended, no such medication is discovered to have been in use at the time of his death. When questioned, Lillian declines to comment. She is not responsible for this, she is his wife, no longer his doctor. There is no negligence to prove. It is each individual's right in any event to decide whether or not to take their medication. But Lillian's growing interest in the healing arts is well documented: visualisation techniques, hypnosis, diet, affirmations, essential oils, massage, even crystals. She begins to treat all her patients without drug therapy. She calls herself a healer. There are hints that this will rebound on her, but before it can, she resigns from her hospital, with no warning, and concentrates on building her career in private practice. Three years later she appears on Zoë's programme. She treats Zoë. Zoë dies.

It is not difficult to reach the conclusion that Lillian's secret is the suicide of her husband. No doctor could possibly want that fact to be in the public domain. She did her best to bury it, and she succeeded. But why should she tell Paul about it – if tell him she did? Human actions are rarely logical. Perhaps, like the ancient mariner, she feels compelled to tell her tale from time to time to an innocent stranger, and that stranger at that time happened to be Paul. She was safe within the confines of her own office, talking to a timid little boy, hardly a threat. Now the death of the innocent has a connection to them both, it seems, and she is under the spotlight again. Did she tell him in the hope of helping him with his own conscience, intending to make him free of the guilt he felt about his sister's death? I don't think her motives have ever been that unselfish, but it's a possibility.

It's perfect fodder with which to discredit Lillian in court though, and I'm going to delight in making use of it. I've run out of cigarettes. It's 3 a.m. I feel sick about it all, about dear Zoë and her tiny baby, and that horrible woman and her presence in our lives. There's no reason to feel afraid for myself, for us: Lillian won't know I know these things about her until the trial, and there's no reason to see her until then. She wouldn't retaliate anyway, I know that. I just feel so angry about it, that such a woman, such a disturbed woman, should have so great an influence over so many lives in the name of healing but really in the name of money and of power. Incidentally, it is two hundred pounds an hour she charges now, the report said, and how many souls has she claimed? In a way, there's hardly any point in any of us knowing, discovering these things now. It's too late for Zoë. I must remember, though, it's not too late for Michael, or for Paul.

I feel alone, and afraid, as if encountering something – I don't know – almost inescapable. Better sleep now and save the melodrama for court.

March 4th

Spoke to Laura first thing this morning, I didn't wake her, she was up to supervise the truck coming to dig up the garden for the terrace. She sounded excited about it, and I felt better just hearing her voice.

March 9th, late Sunday night – London

A busy week. I've had little time to think about Michael's case – or Zoë's case, as Laura now calls it. Very busy on other stuff, which is no bad thing. But when I came down on Friday, had a good talk to Laura quite late in front of the fire, brandies before bed. I think she's taken it all in much better now, and seems to understand that there's a great deal about

Zoë's life and death still to be discovered. We must be patient, strong, and avoid weakening ourselves by self-punishment. We're together and steadfast now, which is the most important thing.

This afternoon at home something happened which distressed us all, that I am now struggling to see as understandable, if frightening. It was Andrew's birthday today, he's twelve. Laura made a chocolate cake and decorated it with spangles. She'd warned me that we had to celebrate the day properly, that it was important. We gave him some drawing materials and a sweatshirt. From Michael a card and a letter which he did not show us. A book from Paul. I don't know if I've already mentioned this, but a while ago Paul asked Laura if he could go back to sleeping in my study on the sofa bed, and even though she offered him the spare room, he insisted that that was where he wanted to be, on the ground, where he felt safe. It's a small dark room, but snug. Paul hardly ever wants anything, and she would have accomplished nothing by saying no, so she said yes. He feels the attic is Andrew's territory, she says, and half of it has already become the boy's studio. Despite all the time he's spent up there, we haven't been allowed to go up at all. Laura has had a very frosty reception every time she's asked. It's odd, because Zoë and Michael are both such open people, that their children should be so secretive. They almost don't seem like children sometimes, with their measured politeness and their silences, and their lack of play. I remember when I was their sort of age having endless imaginary games to keep myself occupied and from feeling lonely. But I digress.

Before lunch, when Andrew had come back from his ride, he announced that he would like to give us an exhibition of his paintings, this afternoon after his birthday tea, as a special treat. We were surprised, Laura blushing with pleasure at this sign of trust. I'm sure he had planned it all, and his single-mindedness reminded me of Zoë. I was curious. I liked Zoë, and I must admit Andrew definitely has her short-nosed, small-featured face, and those rather beautiful dark blue eyes, but it's a less readable face. All Zoë's emotions used to cross her face in rapid succession and, according to Jeffrey, that didn't make her any less successful in business because her relish of her own power used to show too, to intimidating effect. I can't help thinking about Andrew now – he's in my head in a visual kind of way after the events of this afternoon. I see continual images one after another: that closed, watchful expression, that deliberately thought-out manner of speech.

It is bright up there, even in the March sun, and we had to wait for our eyes to become accustomed to the light. It was a minute or two before we began to look at the pictures, which were all carefully arranged, everything he has been working on since he came here. Dark charcoal sketches and lurid crayon studies were propped up against the walls or lay on the floor like stepping stones or the pieces of a vast jigsaw puzzle. At first we were confused, and could not work out why. We were overwhelmed by images of Zoë, except that the images were all taken from life, and had obviously been done since Andrew had moved to the cottage. There was Zoë, pulling her T-shirt over her head, her arm caught in a sleeve; leaning over the bath she was running; sitting up in bed with the radio beside her, sipping a cup of tea; planting; weeding; at her desk working, on the phone; stroking Seymour's domed head. But they were not memories. If they had any context, it was our own. We could see our kitchen, its Aga, the half stable door which leads to the terrace, our inglenook fireplace in the sitting room, even the window seat in our own bedroom. And yet it was plainly Zoë who inhabited our house, Zoë who appeared in the pictures.

'I don't understand. Why is Zoë here?' said Laura, the colour beginning to climb up her neck, blotches, standing out, angry. 'These sketches are from life, they look like me.'

'Mummy's head, your body. I can remember her face, but I needed you to pose for her body, for posture, to make her lifelike.' Andrew said this standing very close to Laura, looking up at her and smiling. I wanted to push him away from her, but was distracted by murmuring sounds that were coming from Paul. In succession he approached each picture, examining it closely, muttering and murmuring to himself like a little old man, things like, 'Pretty Mummy', and 'Mummy thinking ...' 'Mummy clever ...' and then, 'Mummy alone.' He put out his hand to touch her face, but he didn't, his fingers stopped a few inches away. Andrew ignored Paul, and continued to stare up at Laura, smiling almost playfully.

'Are you surprised?' he said.

'You're a very clever artist, Andrew,' I said. 'But this is upsetting your brother. I think we should look at your pictures more carefully another day.' Laura and I took the dazed Paul out of the room, almost wedged him between us both. Andrew did not follow us downstairs. Laura went quickly into our room and shut the door, and I took Paul down to the kitchen, where I started to clear up the remains of the birthday cake and put the kettle on for more tea. I wanted to have something to occupy myself with, to help us both feel calmer. Paul was very white. 'The pictures were upsetting, weren't they?' I said.

'Yes.' The child picked up the cat, who was lying stretched out in front of the Aga, and held him tightly to his chest. The animal dangled uncomfortably but remained limp and did not protest.

'Bit of a shock.'

'Yes.'

'I'm sorry, Laura and I didn't know.'

'He did it on purpose.' He didn't look at me when he said this, but down, at the top of Seymour's head.

'I expect so. He wanted to make the pictures look really like her. He loved your mother very much.'

'She loved him.' He remained standing alone in the middle of the kitchen, shifting the cat's position, gathering him up over his shoulder like a baby being burped. He began stroking him, in steady monotonous strokes, and the cat patiently endured. When I put his tea down on the kitchen table in front of him he took it quickly and, still holding Seymour, left the room. I heard my study door close. I took Laura up some tea and sat on our window seat, looking at her propped up on the bed, blowing her nose and wiping her eyes. She reminded me of one of the pictures, except that her own head was on her shoulders.

'I wish I didn't cry. It's so weak. How's Paul?'

I told her how he was, quiet as ever.

'I don't know why Andrew did that. It was cruel.'

'To make his memories of his mother more lifelike.'

'I don't think so. They weren't memories – that's a lie – they were me – drawn here. I was so flattered he was drawing me, don't you remember? I felt he was settling in, embracing his life here. But then adding Zoë's head – how could he even have thought of such a thing?'

'He's disturbed by her death. He wants to remember, he doesn't want her to die.'

'That's psycho-babble. It's not how you really feel – that's rubbish. This is an aggressive gesture to us all – aimed purposely to scare us.'

'He's only a child, Laura.'

'He's a sick child. I don't like him.'

'He's hurt you, that's why you're overreacting. We have to stand back, take an overview. We never thought that this was going to be easy. We can't think about our own feelings. It's not up to us to like him or not like him. We just promised his father to look after him.'

'I know that,' she said. 'I'm going to go and wash my face and then I'll calm down and see the logic of what you're saying.' When she came back she came close to me and put her arms around me.

'He's still honoured us by showing us his mother as he remembers her,' I said.

'Yes. I'm not going to think about it any more. I'm going to stay up here and read a magazine.'

'Fine. I'll muck out.'

'Paul will help you. It'll be good for him.' She smiled at me.

I didn't say this to Laura but if anything else even slightly strange happens I think we should discuss with Michael the possibility of taking Andrew to see a proper child psychiatrist. And Paul too, for that matter.

March 11th

Drove Andrew to see his father today. Silent drive over there. Cold landscape – bleak. I waited for him in the car, not wanting to go into the prison at all, and showing, I admit freely, a lamentable lack of courage.

For some reason he was quite chatty on the way home, not on the subject of his father, of course, but asking me about the law: how long it took to qualify, the intricacies of how the system worked, why they had juries and if judges were always good men. He is very quick, his mind skips from one thought to another fast and he likes analysing and drawing conclusions as if the information were not interesting enough in itself but only for what he can make out of it, a theory or an observation that is clever. He shows off. There's nothing wrong with showing off. Of all people, I should know that. I asked him if he were interested in becoming a lawyer. He said that he wasn't, so I asked him what he was thinking about doing when he grew up.

'I don't ever think about growing up,' he said. That was such an odd thing to say, it silenced me.

Michael reported that during his visit Andrew seemed very much happier, calmer and more settled than even he could have hoped, talking fondly of Laura and of Blackie and the attic and gardens. Talking fondly – what on earth will that child do next?

March 13th

Such a terrible thing has happened that I hardly know how to write it down. Yesterday, Paul fell from the attic window, we don't know how it could have happened, but he is not dead. He did not die. He has broken his neck and he is unconscious. They think the coma has come from the body's shock, but as far as they can tell, the spine is unharmed. His legs and arms are broken. They had been shovelling the earth from where the terrace is going to be laid and so it was heaped up and broke his fall. If he had hit the piles of paving stones which were littered around he would be dead. Laura has been to see Michael and has told him. I just feel stupid stupid stupid. The window is dangerous, because the sill is only a few inches above the floor – but we thought the children were old enough – we never dreamed. If he had intended it – but we cannot think that. We have tried to ease his suffering, cure all with the intelligent superiority of our care. We thought he was getting better. We thought. We were idiots. We – responsible for the boy – have endangered him. We have not kept him safe. We are to blame. They say he won't die. They do not think he will have sustained brain damage, but they are not sure, they think 'trauma only' – this is what they say, trauma only.

Laura sits by the bed and holds his hand and talks to him or reads aloud and I visit and sit with her, and she says fiercely, 'It is not our fault,' and I said once, at the beginning, 'Next you'll be telling me it was God's will.' She does not blame me for being so angry. Laura the sudden, patient fatalist, does not blame me, but I blame her for lacking the courage to blame herself as I blame myself. Of course I see that she has not avoided suffering: she suffers for Paul, she suffers unselfishly from the heart, not from the ego. I am useless, storming about what might have been; she is useful, sitting there as I could not, seeing the silence, the closed eyes, the bruised face, the broken fingernails, the hands grazed from the fall, and the covers pulled so straight over the shallow-breathing form.

I stay at the cottage with Andrew – compassionate leave has been enforced. How much better it would be for me if I could be working, in London, at my desk, in court, surrounded by the paraphernalia of action and success, without this paralysis. Instead, I am in the cottage with Andrew, but we are not in the same room. Laura has found a piece of paper – in the mêlée, the storm of panic and distress, no one thought to look up there, but she did, finding it sellotaped to the floor by the window, the words, in his childish print, 'A mother knows.' God knows what that means – what does it mean? Is it a suicide note? We can't, don't know – we can't know – the child cannot tell us, probably will not tell us when he can but will close his stubborn little mouth and keep it to himself, like all the other secrets that damned family have kept. I don't say 'damned' to swear, I say damned to describe. They are damned, they have no guardian angel, as Laura would say, no lucky star, nothing to guide them and save them.

I thought they had us, but that was selfishness. Last night, I asked Andrew if he thought his brother had fallen by accident, or had wanted to fall, and he looked me in the eye and said, 'I don't know,' with such coolness and lack of compassion, interest even, that all my other questions, all my determination to question dissolved as if it had never been there – as if it had not possessed me in so urgent a way ever since Laura had called me with the news. He had fallen at five o'clock, before tea, when the light was fading, when he could not see clearly where he was falling, his destination, the ground, twilit below him. It is inconceivable, and I know this scrawl is a childish self-pitying panic, but I can't stop it, can't stop scrawling in this awful speedy race to write just one phrase, word even, that might have any meaning. 'A mother knows.' What is it? A quote, a phrase overheard, a line of poetry, an explanation? There can be no true explanation – there is none.

I wake early, as Laura leaves for the hospital. I sit with Andrew and I feel afraid. At breakfast he eats eggs and bacon, and stares into space. I take him to school. I come home and muck out the horses, I make the beds and I clear up the kitchen and I call the office and hold everybody up, stop them all from doing their jobs. Sometimes I go to the supermarket. Then I read, sit and read airport novels all day, crouched in front of the Aga like an idiot, sometimes Seymour beside me, sometimes alone. At four, I collect Andrew from school, we sit in silence in the car. We get home, Andrew takes a carton of juice and some crisps up to the attic, where he doesn't make a sound. He does not go to see the horses or help me feed them. He does not stroke Seymour, who ignores him. He does not ask me anything, and I do not try to make him talk to me beyond the odd sentence. Laura comes home, we have a drink together, I cook. The child comes down for an early supper, fish fingers or baked beans, then he has his bath and goes to bed without a murmur or protest. Laura is too drained to do anything but kiss him goodnight, and she doesn't notice his silence – why should she? In her mind she is at Paul's bedside; when her eyes come into focus and come to rest on me, it is with such love, such relief, but as if she has not been with me, as if she has only just noticed that I am there. I feel calmer now, less angry about the child, but all the time the words go round my head, 'a mother knows', 'a mother knows', 'a mother knows', and I know that I am standing in the middle of an unknown landscape which should be utterly familiar to me except that I am blind. What will it take to bring me that click in the head when everything falls into place and I can look back and say, This is why this happened, this is what it means, this is who is responsible? Because I no longer have any doubt that someone is entirely responsible for all this. Michael. Lillian. Andrew. Paul. It could not be a child. No child could kill, kill his family. A child might be implicated, intimidated, even blackmailed. Perhaps – Michael after all. No. Lillian, witch-doctor, goddess. I don't even know where she was when Zoë died. Where was she?

March 17th

I've been calling that bloody private detective all morning, and no answer, no machine. When I spoke to him originally, I assumed that if he had seen anybody go into or out of the house on the day, the day that Zoë died, he would have told me. But I made no note of asking him the specific question, concentrating as I was simply on Michael, and why he had lied. That seems so much less important now. If Michael had been vague or distracted, or had lied, seems now to be so small a detail, when there was this woman, a woman who had lost a baby of her own, who was disturbed, who had an appetite for influence, who thrived on illness – but no – this is madness. I am brooding in a madness because I want an explanation, where there is none to be found. No reason. 'A mother knows.' What is it that a mother knows? I must think, coolly. I must make a list. She knows love, protective-ness, understanding, forgiveness, fear, boredom, I suppose, sometimes cruelty, sometimes failure, a mother knows all these things. But specifics. What did Zoë know? Would a mother know who it was who had killed her baby, and why, could she sense it in her soul? These are circles. 'Circles of hell', I'm sure Michael would call them. Tomorrow I must go and see him.

Michael is thinner and more hushed than ever. His face dissolves into tears, and re-forms, dissolves and re-forms, almost with every utterance, like a reflection in the water – in a puddle when you stir it with a stick or jump into it, stamping, laughing, as we all did as children, when we were innocent and did not know. To save him from asking I told him everything they say at the hospital about Paul, that he is stable, that there is no sign of brain damage, that the coma will lift, but they don't know when, can't say. He cried and told me how much he loved his son, and how Laura and I must not blame ourselves.

'Thank God he is not dead,' he says, smiling and crying with his dissolving, tear-streaked face, and I am like a stuffed dummy, an imitation of life, sitting opposite him and looking at him as if he were on television. 'Will you ask Laura to come again, if she can? I'll understand if she can't, but if she can ...'

'Yes. Andrew – would you like to see Andrew?'

'No. The child is – he's –' and he held his breath unnaturally, to stop himself from speaking.

'He is bearing up well, he is fine.'

'His family is annihilated, and he is fine,' said Michael, trying now to smile at me, almost jaunty, trying to show me his old irony, his humour. I didn't understand why, I don't finally now.

'He is resilient,' I said. 'I think children –'

'No.' He interrupted me. 'Don't try to explain it to me.' More tears streamed down his face, his face was wet and he pressed the heels of his hands against his eyes. I had meant to tell him how the case was going, even about Lillian and all that we had found out, but I could not, I could see that it would have been wrong of me.

'Thank God Zoë is not alive to know about this,' he said. 'Our children. I'm sorry, you'll have to go now because I won't be able to stop crying.' I got up slowly, patting his shoulder with one pat, one brisk pat only, before I left him.

Driving home, I wanted, with all my heart, just to go to the hospital, collect Laura, bundle my most precious thing into the car with me – and just go – go to the airport and get on a plane and run away. I felt as if there should be some court of appeal we could apply to, where I would plead and explain that we were a happy pair, we were filled with joy and promise, and that it was wrong that this should be happening to us, we wanted it changed. We were intended to be fortunate, always, and remain unchanged: me dark, she fair, both of us clever and kind and lucky and safe. Until all this happened I had no idea that I was such an incredible coward.

I looked at Michael today and I thought – How could I even have considered for a moment that he could have – I'm glad I never spoke of it to Laura. For that I must be grateful.

Later

My office called. They have found the private detective – he was on holiday in Spain. We've just spoken, he was expecting my call. I asked him whether he saw anyone go into or out of the house that day, the afternoon that Zoë had died. He has said that he doesn't know because he had fallen asleep. 'Occupational hazard,' he said. 'A beer at lunch time does it sometimes. One drink, and away you go.' He had seen only

Michael come and go in the morning, but that was all that he had seen, until lunch time, when he had eaten his sandwiches and drunk from his flask of tea. Nothing then until the ambulance and the police, the chaos surrounding her death. He saw her body being taken to the ambulance and after it had gone he had driven away.

Friday, 21st

Thank God the week is over. I think we are both in less shock, and are beginning to pull ourselves together. We are both going back to work on Monday, and so Laura will only be able to visit Paul in the afternoons. He still has not woken up, and although the doctors refuse to put any time to it, I have the feeling they are surprised it has taken so long. We tell ourselves we must not be alarmed. We hold on to each other for dear life at night. I am going to try to get down for at least one night this week, as I don't want to leave her by herself. There's Andrew of course, but I don't consider him company. I battle feelings of revulsion almost amounting to fear about that child, ever since Paul's fall. Laura is amazingly strong. She is white as white most of the time, but she goes about her business, her endless vigils, with so great a calm, almost a serenity, that I feel more in awe of her than ever.

Saturday, 22nd

A letter this morning from the last person I would have expected to hear from, but perhaps it is not so strange.

Dear Felix and Laura,

Forgive me if I cause you pain by writing to you, and reviving memories of Zoë and of her tragic death which I know will be painful.

I have heard about Paul's accident, and it came as a powerful message to me that I need to look again at my convictions about Zoë's death, and its meaning. I have made a discovery which I know will be valuable to you and it is expedient that I discuss what I know with you both personally.

This letter will anger you, I don't doubt, but please allow me to help you, don't refuse to see me. Think about what I've said.

With love and sincere best wishes,
Lillian Taylor

'She has said nothing,' said Laura, furious immediately. 'She just can't keep herself away from anything to do with Zoë.' All this as we sat at breakfast, Andrew upstairs.

'I wonder how she found out,' I said.

'Doctors gossip the same as everyone else – and it is Zoë's son, after all.'

'I'm surprised there haven't been any journalists,' I said, coming to this conclusion slowly.

'She's never had anything to say – she's a parasite – worse, she's unbalanced. She contributed to if not caused the death of my sister – I'm not having her in the house.' Laura is absolutely right, we must not have her in the house, but I also know I have to see her. I am just hoping that something she will say will help me. I'd do anything if she could help us all now.

I've sent her a fax saying I will come to her Devonshire Place office at eight thirty on Monday morning. She has power over us all now, but I don't care about that.

Monday evening – 24th

I had a sleepless night last night because I decided to stay in the country with Laura and get up at five to drive into town. Knowing I was going to be up so early and desperate not to oversleep, and thinking thinking thinking, all added up to almost a fever in my brain. Laura slept. I could not see her face distinctly, we both like a very dark room to sleep in, and besides, I always feel it an intrusion to gaze at someone while they're sleeping, even someone you know very well, who trusts you. Sleep is private, a refuge, and it is almost like robbing someone, I think, to look at them as they sleep for longer than a few seconds. She slept soundly, curled away from me on her side, hardly moving, and I sat up in bed because it helped me to breathe better, and stared straight into darkness, and thought of Andrew above my head.

I must stop this rambling and get to the point. Lillian looked plumper than when I last saw her. The same strong scent and full make-up, with the most disgusting shade of salmon-pink lipstick I think I've ever seen in my life. She wore a navy blue dress with a cameo brooch in about the same place on her dress that matrons used to wear watches – all contributing to the feeling I had of wandering into a nineteen-fifties Technicolor melodrama, where she was head matron or head mistress. She also behaves exactly like a film star, insisting on ordering tea and begging me to sit down as if I were an influential journalist visiting her in her dressing room. 'Rings on her fingers and bells on her toes' went through my mind for some reason. The room was hot.

'I have a confession to make,' she said solemnly, once the preliminaries were over. I was being extremely polite. 'I have to admit to having a very powerful interest in the welfare of Zoë's family, because I loved Zoë very much. For my own reasons, and I won't bore you with them – our lives have been – were, in fact, very alike.' I felt confident that I was as familiar with these reasons as she was, but I pushed, just a fraction, to see how far I could go.

'Zoë, like yourself, was a very successful woman. She headed her field in the way, I imagine, you head yours.'

'Yes, that is perfectly true,' she said, nodding slightly in an almost queenly way. The room smelled of cleaning fluid and furniture polish as well as of her scent, but I saw that there was an ashtray on her desk.

'Would you mind very much if I smoked?' I asked her, breaking the promise I had made to myself.

'I am afraid I do mind,' she said, without a smile.

'I'm a hopeless addict,' I said, in an attempt to be charming. 'I had to ask.'

'You are as entitled to ask as I am to refuse,' she said again, without a smile.

'Would you mind telling me what it is that you want to see me about?' I hadn't meant to sound so peremptory, but I had such a sensation of claustrophobia in that hot room, with that large woman, who seemed to take up so much more room than just the physical space she occupied.

'I've offended you, and I apologise, and that is not the only thing I have to apologise for. I'm afraid I have been dishonest with you, and behaved badly.' I tried to look surprised. 'After Zoë's death, her husband made the most terrible scene when I came to her funeral. You must remember.'

'Yes.'

'That's right, of course. It was hurtful, speaking personally, and not as her doctor or psychiatrist, because I felt bereaved, was grieving terribly, and the day of the funeral I had meetings to go to and patients I had to see, and so I missed the service and could only come to the interment, which I know is usually a very private ceremony. But Zoë, I know, would have felt it was right for me to have been there, we were so close in her last months – I think I understood her better than her husband did – but –' She hesitated. 'That does not matter now. I simply knew that I had to be there, at her grave, that it would be a beautiful as well as a tragic experience. As I walked up the hill – her grave, as you must know, is under a tree, on a slope, a really beautiful spot.' (When she said 'beautiful spot', I instantly thought of a picnic in a children's book, I don't know why.) 'And as I came up the hill, I recognised not only Paul, who I knew, but Andrew, her younger son, the only member of her family I hadn't yet met. He looked at me, and I had such a sensation, through him, of Zoë's presence, it was like a thrill coming over me – and I just fixed my eyes on his face, only after a little while, as I came closer, realising that Zoë's husband had recognised me. He started shouting, truly the most vicious words, slanders, saying I had no place there and I must leave. I have forgiven him now, but then it was just so cruel. All the time he was shouting at me, Andrew, the child, was smiling, it seemed more and more warmly, as if he were welcoming me, somehow. And that comforted me. Even after I was forced to turn away, anxious not to cause any more distress, I felt as if what I had come for had been accomplished: a connection had been made. Life is so often like that. You go somewhere expecting something and what you eventually receive is completely different, but always proves to be what you needed at the time. That's the way the universe works.' At this point she did honour me with a smile.

'You caused a great deal of pain that day.'

'I am not responsible for that,' she almost snapped.

'What is it that you do allow yourself to be responsible for?'

'I heal people,' she said, in a low but deeply self-important voice.

'What about the people you don't heal – like Zoë?' I hadn't meant to say that, but it is so ingrained in me to question people, attack them even, if I think they are lying either to me or to themselves.

'Really, Mr Bracewell, I'm not God,' she said, and she was so confident, she was teasing me. 'Let's not quarrel. I have much more than all that to tell you.' She sighed. 'I had a feeling for weeks after that that it was vital I maintain a connection with the boy, Zoë's son, Andrew. It took me a while to find out that he was with you and your wife – what a beautiful woman she is, Mr Bracewell, not like Zoë, but beautiful in her own way.'

'Yes. Thank you,' I managed, instead of an outburst like, 'How dare you comment on my wife's appearance, you vulgar cow?'

'I was also deeply concerned about Paul, who was clearly in the grip of a suffering more profound than grief.' At this point I was beginning to feel very tired. She so loved the sound of her own voice. 'Bear with me, please. Just wait a little.' I blushed, against my will again. She certainly has the power to divide even the strongest person from their intentions. 'I know how much of a companion Andrew had been to Zoë before she died. I had imagined he would feel as if part of himself had been ripped away, and what surprised me was how whole he appeared to be – tranquil, open, unscathed. I decided to pay the boys a visit, purely on the off chance – I had some cancellations and my afternoon was free. Foolishly, I had forgotten that, of course, the children would be at school, but I was delighted to meet Laura, she was protective about the boys which, again, is admirable. How was she to know that I was their mother's dearest friend? I'm sure her husband would never had told her that. Now I am coming to the part of what I have to tell you that I am sure will anger you, but that I can only say were actions I felt compelled to take. I wrote to both boys. To Paul, I offered my sincerest sympathies about his mother's death, and enclosed my private address and telephone number, promising him that I would be able to talk to him about his feelings at any time of the day or night. I heard nothing from him, which didn't surprise me. To Andrew I wrote more specifically and urgently, telling him that I felt we must meet, or rather renew a friendship that I believed had begun from the moment his mother first told me about how much she loved him and how very gifted and special he was. As I knew he would, he called me the next day. We agreed that we should keep our meeting secret, as it was bound to upset you and Laura, and you would never understand how necessary it was.'

I had to interrupt her. 'Do you mean to say that you and Andrew met – secretly – without us knowing?'

'Yes, yes – quite a few times. I know you will be angry –' here she was almost impatient '– met, have been meeting, on Saturday afternoons.'

'When he goes for his ride, every Saturday afternoon –'
'All the Saturdays I can.'

'But this is appalling! How dare you summon me here and tell me that you –' I can't remember if I said anything else, I think I was too stunned to continue.

'It was expedient.'

'It was wrong of you.'

'No.'

'It was wrong.' A horrible silence fell – where I struggled between rage and curiosity. 'Why was it expedient?'

'Because I feel that – know that – am convinced that Andrew is the only one who knows how his mother died.'

'Do you have any evidence which supports this claim?'

'Of course I haven't.'

'What happens – what happens when you meet?'

'Usually at the gate into the wood, there's a stile and a bridlepath – a few minutes' drive out of the village. The lane is quiet, we talk, only for half an hour at a time, then he rides away.'

'You drive all that distance for half an hour?'

'Of course.'

'Why? What has he told you? Has he told you anything?'

'He doesn't have to. It's what he doesn't tell me. He will chat quite happily about his mother, that summer, how they were looking for a pony that he and she would share, how she encouraged him in his drawing, how they played together, how he was a friend to her. But he won't talk about how Paul was that summer. I know only that she neglected him, even appeared to dislike him. She told me that, and Andrew confirms it. He was his father's companion, much more his father's child, and his father was away, so he was forced inwards upon himself. Zoë felt overwhelmed by him, sometimes afraid. I always had to prompt her to speak about him. Did you know they shared a bed? She was almost in his thrall – afraid to turn him away. He had nightmares, fears. Zoë couldn't help exacerbating this state when she rejected him, and his soul became diseased I think. I thought it was only grief. I should have seen that it was more.'

'Are you leading up to the disgusting idea that Paul may have murdered his mother?'

'And then tried to kill himself, out of guilt. He felt supplanted you see, he felt driven to it. Yes, I believe he killed her.' I wanted to stand up and go to the window and fling it open and shout into the street, 'I am here, closeted with a mad woman, help me!' Then I wanted to shake her and spit at her and shout at her I was so angry. My sane mind kept telling me that I was defending at a murder trial and that I had to remember my purpose was to exonerate Michael and to protect his family, and that if I attacked the mad woman who was a key witness, it would be an act of self-destruction. Thank God I remembered those things.

'Paul is the most gentle child I've ever known.'

'Appearances can be deceptive. He's very disturbed.'

'Has Andrew said in so many words that –'

'No. No words have been used. It is just that I now believe Michael to be innocent. I believe Paul is disturbed to the point of pathology, and I feel I must warn you. I am prepared to testify to all this.'

'Paul is not on trial.'

'There are ways of intimating to the jury – I've been in court before, I know.'

'I understand completely what you are trying to say,' I said, as if I thought she had a point, that she was being reasonable. When she looked at me, she wasn't fooled.

'You don't believe anything I've said and you think I'm crazy. I knew this meeting would be hard and that it was unlikely we would look at all this in the same way, but at least I have fulfilled the duty to myself – to Zoë – to tell you what I know, that the child is dangerous and capable of murder, and must be treated with the utmost caution.'

'He is in a coma, we don't know –'

'He will recover, and he will be under your roof again. I know that.'

'From now on, Andrew won't be riding out alone.'

'Yes. We knew you'd stop that. We have already said our goodbyes.'

'That only leaves us to say ours then.' I couldn't say anything further to her, so desperate was I to get out of that room.

This has taken hours to write, I started almost as soon as I came back to the flat. It only occurs to me now, now that I am calmer, to wonder why she has chosen this moment to put forward a new and elaborate theory. Has it truly only just struck her with full force, or is there another reason? One that necessitates my feeling so revolted by her that I never want to see or speak to her again. I must get my team on to where she was the day that Zoë died. I can't believe I've been so slow about this. I have become a tortoise where I used to be a hare.

I'm going to have to start rationing the whisky. I used to wait until after dinner – only wine or water before, but here I am, glugging it down now, trying to work out why first Lillian and now Andrew has been deceiving us. My head reels. I am more convinced than ever that Michael is innocent and the children – any such notion is aberrant, disgusting. I don't know how I am going to tell any of this to Laura.

Tuesday 11pm

I called Laura to tell her about the visit – but not about any possible interpretation of it – late last night, before going to bed. She agrees that Lillian's ideas are preposterous, but she didn't seem to be nearly as distressed by the whole thing as I was. Perhaps she has more perspective than I have, and she's further removed from Lillian's madness – after all, she's only met her once. But I was surprised that she didn't even mention that she'd been right, after all, about the boys' letters. Still no change in Paul – of course that must be what is uppermost in her mind. She didn't seem to take on board how deceitful Andrew has been, and didn't want to discuss how it should be dealt with. She just said she wasn't surprised, that nothing Andrew did surprised her. I told her that that's what Michael had said.

'He likes games,' she said. 'I think he met Lillian secretly because it's a good game. I don't think he's thought about deceit, or distressing anybody. Sometimes I don't think he has very much feeling for anybody but himself, which is why I am so surprised that I love him as much as I do.' I asked her if he's started drawing again, and she said that he says he's still writing – some kind of story, but that when he's finished he wants to go back to his artwork. She says the horses are getting fat on spring grass. She seemed so distant, I was almost worried. She wants to teach Andrew to jump logs in the woods. Plans. Laura loves plans.

Friday

In chambers today a huge bunch of yellow roses came – their cups are still closed. The card read:

Your wife is too shy to tell you herself, but she's pregnant. Come home soon. Love love love Laura.

I don't know what it is but the more that happens in my life, the more compelled I feel to write it down, as if only this book makes it all real. To think that I began this as an intellectual experiment, an attempt to find reasons, interpretations, and now I surrender to confusion, to my own failure – I have to. I am no nearer to understanding Beth's death and Zoë's death – no nearer to a culprit. But I am convinced of my client's innocence – utterly convinced, and I am sure of my defence, my thorough preparation. That fear and pain, the way I felt, so hampered by the nightmare of those deaths, unsure of how to approach them, that's gone.

My wife is going to have a baby, and I am overjoyed. All my doubts, even fears, have vanished. It is only a very few weeks, the baby will not be born until November, and it is too early to tell anyone, but that is fine – and I think it will probably be the only secret I'll ever enjoy keeping. Laura's in the garden having an inspection of her measurements for the new flower-beds. I've peeled the potatoes for lunch for her, and now I'm in my study, in Paul's room, and I'm trying not to cry I'm so happy. So happy, I want Paul to wake up so that I can tell him. I'd like to tell him that I love him, because I never did that while he was here. Laura thought I would be cross because we hadn't planned the baby, it just happened. Cross. Imagine. Silly girl.

Andrew's Papers

April 2nd

I am not home yet, I have not won. Paul lives and Laura lives, Laura's baby lives inside her. No one knows, and as Mummy once told me, the essence of attack is surprise. She said she wasn't sure she had the quote right, but it was the truth of it which mattered. She said surprise was the essence of attack and attack was the essence of success, attack first, before they attack you. She was clever. She attacked at work and she was a success. She won. At home though, she was defenceless. She never thought at all.

Baby Beth baby Beth baby Beth. With baby Beth she was all feeling. How many times did I find her with tears streaming down her face as much when Beth was alive as when she died? She said to me, 'Beth is the greatest achievement of my life,' which of course was a lie. Everyone lies, and everyone thinks they are telling the truth, just as everyone who says I love you means only I want you to love me. If you are still in your heart and quick in your brain you will discover these things and they will become clear. Paul lives, but I have conquered him, and so I should not be worried that he is still alive. When I showed him Mother's diary, that whole passage where she clearly states how much she hates him, when I showed him that, I could show him the window and the place to jump and it was not difficult. I did not have to say, 'Jump now, jump from here,' because it was obvious to him that he must die. He only ever lived in the hope of her love and praise and once she was dead he could begin to tell himself that he might be wrong to believe that she had hated him, and that perhaps she had loved him after all. She did not love him. She did not like him. She did not admire him. She despised him and she dreaded him. Paul has always lived with the knowledge that the people he loves dread him, but it has always been unspoken, nobody has dared say that they dread him because nobody wants to think of themselves as cruel. He knows this, but pretends he does not know it. When I showed him the diary, then he knew, because the words were simple and clear, he knew how she felt, felt without lying. He also knew that I had stolen the diary. I think he has always feared that I killed Mother and Beth, and I think the fact that he does not know for sure, at least for the time being, has worked in my favour because it has made him more frightened than if he knew, yes or no. The diary terrified him, and it told him the truth, and he did not want to live knowing how much she had hated him.

I still have the diary. My father was baffled at its disappearance, but because he could not think, cannot think, has never thought, he did not take the next step in the deduction process which begins, it could not have vanished, and continues, therefore someone has taken it. The only two people who could have taken it were Paul or myself. Paul is too stupid, I on the other hand am not. Because I am a child of twelve, nobody thinks I could ever do anything bad. That is very peculiar. I would like to find out whether they think there is a magical moment when a child, innocent, suddenly

234

becomes human, and so like them – capable of bad and evil thoughts, feelings, actions. Is the magical moment something to do with puberty, that mysterious phenomenon, sexuality, which still baffles adults as if all of a sudden they had been presented with a hump they must wear on their backs, or a tail, or were asked to walk on all fours?

My father and Laura think that they love me. Paul has never loved me. Felix, however, fears me, but it will become more obvious to him – there is no avoiding that. I want to get it over: all the killing I have to do. Only two more, at the moment two in one body. They are looked on almost as holy, as if they are two-thirds of the way to being the Holy Trinity my father believes in and taught us about. The only time men stop fearing and despising women seems to be when they are pregnant. But I'm generalising. Mother always said that to generalise was lazy and led to few rewards. And she was right of course. If I could get Laura on to her horse, I could engineer a fall. But Felix won't let her ride out in case of an accident, which is sensible for her but makes it more difficult for me. Perhaps it would be more fun to wait until the baby was born and to do them one after the other, the only drawback being that I might be caught before I could accomplish the whole plan. People cannot go on being stubbornly stupid for ever, and sooner or later they will stop refusing to see what is happening and what has happened and realise that Andrew, Andrew the child, is a murderer. I have a feeling that it will be Felix, because he is the cleverest. Part of him knows already, but he does not need to know, so he pushes the knowledge away. When Laura and her baby die, he will have to know and then if I'm lucky there might be a duel. He might not just call for someone to take me away to prison, he might try to kill me himself which would be more satisfactory. I do not want to live to know all they know, the hump on the back, the confusion of maturity. I'd like to die knowing I had accomplished the one plan of my life – the destruction of the women and children of my family. I don't know why I have never wanted to kill my father or Felix, perhaps it is something to do with being content with the fact that they will live knowing they have failed in the aim of their lives: to make a family and protect it and watch over it while it flourishes.

A child can destroy a man. I have proved that: my father is destroyed – I only had to see him once in prison to discover that, and after that I didn't need to see him again and tried to avoid it. How pathetic he was, and weak. I did not feel as much triumph as I will when he knows for certain that it was me, Andrew, who destroyed them. Andrew, who is gifted, and peculiar, and who has never needed him as my mother and Paul and baby Beth have done.

Felix's Journal

April 6th

Last night we went out to dinner to celebrate and to talk. More and more I feel that I can't really talk to Laura unless we are away from the house. She looks wonderful, has become extremely greedy and rather bad-tempered. All hormones, she says. When we're together it's as if she is only half listening to our conversation while the other part is listening outside an invisible inward door, engaged in some private dialogue which excludes me. I don't mind it, but it is rather an odd feeling. She's not really drinking but she did have a glass of champagne. We talked of the future, and as if by agreement avoided past and present, except for Laura's one remark, 'I wish Paul would wake up so we could tell him.' She says that Andrew is very excited, wants to help decorate the spare room, which is to become the baby room. It's just along the passage, so it's ideal, though at first we plan to have the baby sleep with us. 'Such a tiny thing won't need its own room,' she said. There's a great deal of equipment to be bought, she said, more than I can imagine. We might have to have a nanny who will live in, because I won't be there during the week. We didn't talk about that either. It all feels like a dream. No more holidays for two. I'm selfish, I know. She says she feels it's probably wrong of her to be so happy when everything is so bad for Michael and his family, but that this is a good thing for all of us, a beginning instead of an end. 'And I think I'm going to get fat,' she said.

My team have discovered that Lillian was out of her office on the afternoon of Zoë's death. As Laura's now *hors de combat*, I feel I must talk to Andrew about his meetings with Lillian.

Later

I made a great deal of noise on his stairs and knocked loudly at the attic door. There was a sound of rustling like dead leaves or expensive paper, and a long wait while he came to the door.

'Andrew, I want to talk to you.'

'The attic is private.' I couldn't see his face because there was no light behind him.

'Then downstairs. I'll wait for you.' He seemed to spend an age wrapping something up and putting it away – it sounded like – and then there was the sound of heavy books or boxes perhaps, piled up one on top of the other. We went into my study, a procession – Laura has left Paul's few things out: a photograph of his parents and Beth taken just after she was born, a Narnia book, some shells he collected with us at the seaside just before Christmas. Clothes hang in the cupboard; we couldn't see them but I felt as if we could. Andrew sat on the sofa, I sat on the chair, the rainy garden behind his head, trees swaying in the March wind.

'I went to see Lillian Taylor in her office in London this week. You know who I mean by Lillian Taylor?'

'Yes. She's been coming to see me on Saturdays.' Did I

imagine the challenging look in the child's eyes when he said this – the full knowledge that he'd wrong-footed me? I had thought it would take ages to get that much out of him.

'Why didn't you tell us about the visits, Andrew?'

'Because I knew you wouldn't want me to see her and I didn't want you to stop her coming.' I don't think he has ever spoken so directly to me before. I did not know how to answer.

'Why did you think we would try to stop you?'

'Because Daddy hates her and blames her for Mummy's death. We all know that.'

'What do you think of her?'

'She is interested in me.'

'Why is she interested in you?'

'Because I don't need her help.' I don't think I had realised before how clever he is, clever in a sharp, observant, analytic way, and without the distorting emotions of a child. 'She is interested in me in the way Mummy was, at the end.'

'What did Mummy think?'

'That I was talented, and that I could tell things, what she was thinking, how she felt.'

'Could you?'

'Not specially, I don't think, no.' It was hard because I did not have control of the conversation, I did not know how to embarrass him.

'Can you see that it is wrong to meet Lillian without our knowledge or permission?'

'I can see that you think it is wrong.'

'Why do I think that?'

'Because you want to be in charge. Everybody wants to be in charge. Adults usually are because they are bigger and stronger, but not always.'

'When are they "not always"?' I was too eager with this

question because I knew a candid answer might reveal something.

'You don't need me to tell you that.' He stood up and went to the window, pressing his nose against the pane and breathing against it, the way children always do. 'I'm not supposed to do that either, am I?' He did not turn to look at me when he said this. I felt as if I had never been in a room with the boy before at all, never talked to him, never concentrated on him, that I knew nothing about him, and that he had deliberately made sure that this was the case until this particular afternoon, when he had changed his mind.

'You may have your own reasons for thinking I only want to have control of you. The reasons are much more practical than that. Laura and I are responsible to your father for your safety and well-being. After what has happened to Paul, we are particularly anxious that you should be looked after carefully. While under our roof as a minor we have to protect you, we have to be responsible.'

'There's no need to protect me,' he said, still breathing against the pane, the palms of his hands and his forehead resting on the glass. 'I'm not in any danger.'

'It is also important that you learn obedience, it is part of being in a family, which is also part of society –' I stopped talking because I knew I sounded like a bad lecturer in sociology at an obscure university. I sounded stupid, and I sounded dishonest. 'Don't breathe on the panes.' I snapped this, and he turned to face me, saying, 'Lillian is lonely. She misses my mother. She liked coming to see me and giving sugar lumps to Blackie. She told me last weekend that she was going to tell you about her visits and you would stop them. I don't know why she told you, but it was what she wanted. I don't know why she made it all so difficult for herself, but perhaps she didn't want to come any more.'

'Did anyone ever tell you that you don't talk like a child?'

'Yes. My mother did.'

'But then I have never really talked to you before – why do you think that is?'

'Because I didn't want you to.' Andrew's face had the concentrated look that an animal's has when fulfilling a part of its life ritual without artifice. I felt truly disconcerted.

'You're an odd one, aren't you?' I tried to tease and to smile.

'Can I go now?'

'Of course you can. But please, try to think of us before you have secret meetings with anyone else.'

'I never didn't think of you,' he said, and then left the room, shutting the door behind him. He is not just a peculiar child, he is one who thinks and thinks. He has chosen to show himself to me today, and I don't know why. I do know that I feel actually frightened of him.

I've decided to go up to the attic and look through all Andrew's things. I don't know why, but I just have to.

Saturday, April 12th

I write now on Saturday night, Laura is asleep and I am downstairs in Paul's room, not wanting to disturb her with a light. I insisted that she take Andrew to see Michael this afternoon. They went with no argument. It's at least a fifty-minute drive to the prison and they always spend about half an hour with him once they are there, so I had plenty of time. For some reason Seymour came up the stairs with me, I don't know why, because he hasn't been near the attic since Paul moved into my study. It's cold up there, I think the child has turned all the radiators off, and with no carpet, it's draughty. All the artwork is stacked facing the walls except for one portrait of Zoë: she's on the window seat in the London house, done in oils in a very distinctive and sophisticated style. He has it propped up in the window so that it blocks the light, and I didn't want to move it in case I didn't put it back in the right place. He's taken the bulbs out of the two overhead lights, which hang from the rafters, so I was left with just the two bedside lights, which only illuminate the small circle directly below them. Why he wants to sit up there in the dark I can't imagine. Apart from the canvases against the wall, the floor is bare. There are no books on the bedside tables. On the work bench the drawing instruments and paints and palette knives are stacked tidily. I looked in the suitcases underneath the beds. Nothing. I looked in the clothes cupboards. Nothing. I felt stupid. I knew I wanted to find the story Laura says he has been writing, and there was no sign of it, anywhere. I looked for a box, for paper that might rustle, but there was really nothing. He has hidden it. I sat on his bed for a while with Seymour watching me, and blinking.

After I came downstairs, the cat behind me, I did something I haven't done for a very long time, longer than I can remember. I ran a very hot bath, staring at the water as it came out of the tap. I got into the bath, and lay back, sweating, under the water, and then I began to cry. I cried because I felt helpless and afraid. I still feel helpless and afraid. What had I been expecting to find? I don't know – I just know that here I am in my own house, with all my own things around me, all the tangibles which connect me, a floating soul, to the life I have created for myself, but I am helpless and afraid. What is it that distresses me so deeply about Andrew, more than anything he's said to me, more than anything that has happened? I don't know, I can't think about it, I just have a gradual but growing belief that he is to be feared.

Sunday night, April 13th

Paul has woken up. It happened this morning and Laura has already rushed over to see him. I was left with Andrew. He was not keen to renew any conversation with me, but went up to the attic, where he remained until she came back. Paul said he was happy to see her. He didn't seem to remember how he had hurt himself, and he didn't seem to be ashamed the way some suicides are. She held his hand and told him he would be well soon. She said nothing about coming home in case it upset him. I told her she was an angel.

Monday

Fax from my darling this afternoon:

I gave Andrew the day off school in honour of his brother's waking up. We hired a wallpaper stripper machine thing. He said it would be such fun to decorate the baby room ourselves. It was exhausting and so messy! I love you. Laura.

I'm worried. I don't want her doing anything strenuous, anything at all, not at such an early stage. I called her and scolded her about it, but she just laughed.

'It's such fun, you should be here with us.' I scolded her

some more and she gave in. 'You're probably right,' she said, and promised to stop all DIY. But I am now officially a spoilsport.

Andrew's Papers

April 18th

Felix is beginning to sense that all is not as it should be in his part of the forest. I want him to sense danger, but I want him to be too late, of course. Laura, Laura, Laura, Laura and baby, Laura and baby, Laura and baby. They can't go galloping across the fields into a ditch and die, die in a ditch. They can't die because Laura cuts herself on a knife or strains herself carrying a ladder. Would she rescue a cat up a tree, a child up a tree, me up a tree, me in a ditch? I can't think about it.

With Beth it was easy. I was in the playroom and Paul was reading in his room, on his bed reading was Paul. I could wait for Nanny to come down the stairs. I could wrap a cushion in a towel and I could go out on to the landing and into her room as soon as I heard Nanny go down the stairs and I could tiptoe across the landing and into her room, quiet, and lean over the cot, it was low, and smother her little self. She took longer to die than I had imagined, but really not that long and she was silent. After she had died I sat down on the floor under the window and stayed there with her for a while. It felt so peaceful with her, but knowing she wasn't alive any more. All that fuss over a tiny thing who could perish so easily if I willed it. I had spent a long time watching her in the days before. She never woke when I came into the room and I had known to do it when no one would be able to hear and I only had to wait for the right time. My mother came into the room and found her almost before I had had time to go out and close the door behind me. When she started screaming, I opened it again, so she saw me only after she'd discovered Beth, she hadn't realised that I was right there, behind the door, listening, with Paul on his bed with his book. When I opened the door he was behind me. The way she screamed and screamed was unexpected, perhaps I had dozed off for a bit in there, because I remember feeling very sleepy, in a daze really.

My Mummy, Mummy, Mother, Mummy was easier still. Oh, easy peasy was Mummy. She liked me to sit by her when she was ill. I sat by her that day, and I stroked her when she was asleep. I gave her the pills which calmed her down, so she was dozy, like Beth. I didn't have to turn her over. She was on her front with only half her face showing. She opened her eyes when I put the pillow over her face, and she wanted to put her hands up to struggle, but she couldn't. I smiled at her, and said, 'It's all right, Mummy Mother Mummy, go to sleep.' I stayed with her a long time, two or three hours it could have been, and I think I went to sleep. When I heard my father coming upstairs with the nurse I ran through Mummy's bathroom and Beth's room, into my own room and then into my studio. I locked the door and lay on the floor and laughed. I was really quite pleased with myself. It wasn't until later, in her study, after the doctor had told me she was dead, and I had cried, and we had sat there together, me, my father and Paul, that I remembered to get her diary from her desk and I kept it under my mattress for a long time where it was safe enough. I read it when I was by myself and I found out about her, when she was stupid and when she was clever and I felt she was close beside me, which I liked. All that was so exciting, but it feels so long ago now. With Paul it was not the same because I did not see him die. And now there is always the chance that he'll tell. That won't matter as long as Laura and her baby are dead by then. Then Paul can tell everyone what he wants to tell them. I didn't ask him to lie for me about our playing dominoes the day Beth died, it was lucky really that he just seemed to know he had to. So perhaps he won't want to tell after all.

Felix's Papers

Dear Felix,

Last night I was awake for long hours, at last falling asleep at first light to the comforting sound of the birds beginning the dawn chorus. It made me feel better because it meant I could be sure that the new day was here and that I was not living the beginning of an eternal night. I thought about the times when Paul used to have his night fears, when he believed that it would never be morning, and the night would go on for ever and ever and he would never see a bright sky again.

Thank God, now, we know that he will see days and their colours again, that we haven't lost him as we lost our girls. I have waited for days to write you this letter. Days when I have waited patiently, and in agony, for the conviction I now have to go away and leave me, to plague some other poor fool. But the conviction, the thoughts wheeling around my head, have not gone away. The instinct – the knowledge I have just grows – filling my head with screaming and my eyes with hot tears. In the nights – after the hot tears and the aching heart have left me, the knowledge – the voice inside me – is still there. Whatever I do, it remains. I have to write words down which describe it, and I have to write them to you.

I think that my son, Andrew, is a murderer. I think he killed his baby sister and his mother and I think he did it because he enjoyed it, and I think he is the reason that we are all still afraid. Felix, before you throw this letter away – disgusted, sure I am insane – consider the facts, and tell me, if you can, that it is not possible.

In our house, Andrew's and Paul's bedroom connected to Beth's room. And there is also the landing. Andrew is quiet, and he is determined. He knows the habits of the house. He has opportunity. It only takes a minute and a half to kill a baby, it is mercifully quick. He goes back to his room and waits for his mother's screams to summon him as they did Nanny and Paul. Only because he is a child have we not connected him, before this, to the killing. Only because he is a child.

With Zoë – about Zoë it is even harder to write, but we both know that she and Andrew would sit together while she was ill, sit together in the dark, they probably sat together that day. Easy for him to give her the pills, easy for him to lean over her dear face, and she would not be afraid. She would be weak, and she would trust him, and I hope she did not take long to die, knowing who her murderer was. When she was dead he would have left the room either by crossing the landing to his playroom, or by sneaking through all the interconnecting rooms before reaching his own. He was so still in there, so still that we all forgot about him, forgot until long after she had been taken away.

I have established that it was practicable, Felix, I have established that it could have happened. How do I know that it did? I know because I know they were murdered – I know I am innocent, and dear Paul is innocent, and that there has never been anything innocent about Andrew. We have always known that he is not like any other child, and because he was our child we loved him with all our hearts, while everything he did and said was cold and unnatural, we loved him with all our hearts. I can't explain how I did not used to know and how I came to know, how or when it was, but what I now know is IT IS NOT OVER. We must be afraid not for ourselves, but for Laura we must be afraid. We must be afraid for Laura.

Decide that I am mad to accuse my own child, or desperate, or crazed. It does not matter about that, but I beg you to look after your wife, make sure she is safe, don't let her live alone with him as she has done – for God's sake, protect her.

With love,
Michael

Andrew's Papers

April 24th

Last night I began to carry out my plan. I had known what it would be, what I was going to do but not how I was going to do it. As my last killing and my most exciting, my most brave, I did not want to rush at it until I was ready. Mummy always said that you must learn your plan of attack when it came to war, it was not enough just to have a vague outline in your head. You must plan it, down to the tiniest detail, know it so well that you could recite it in your sleep. She said that you must not allow yourself to become rigid, either, because your enemy might do something you didn't expect or hadn't calculated, so you must be flexible, and always think before you act.

Laura has never done anything I haven't expected in all the time I've known her. Like when she mucks out, for instance. She always does Tenacious's box first. She ties him up outside it and grooms him thoroughly, first with a dandy brush, then with a body brush and then she brushes out his mane and his tail, cooing to him. She scratches his head under his forelock where the coat grows in a swirl, and she rubs her face up against the softest part of him around his nostrils and across his muzzle. She picks out his feet and oils his hooves and she gives him a carrot. She replaces his rugs. She bolts the top door of Blackie's box so that he can't lean out and bite Tenacious and start a fight, and she moves Tenacious away from the entrance to his stable to give herself more room. She empties the water buckets into the yard, and takes away his manger and his hay net. She wheels the wheelbarrow up to the open stable door and begins. First she picks up the dung-covered straw with the pitchfork, and also the straw that is wet. She sifts the remaining straw to the side of the stable and piles it high in banks, until she is left with the debris, a pile of dark-stained straw, dung, and wet, in the middle. She leans the pitchfork up against the wall, and she scrapes up the mess with the stable shovel, a large unwieldy but lightweight instrument, which makes a horrible scraping sound along the ridged concrete floor. Very occasionally she leaves the floor to dry out properly for several hours before replacing it – that is if Tenacious is going to be turned out in his field or she is going for a long ride. But usually she puts the shovel on top of the dirty straw in the wheelbarrow to keep it from blowing away, squeezes past it on the other side, takes the handles – rubber-covered – and pushes the mound over to the muck heap on the other side of the yard. The wheelbarrow is tipped up, the muck trampled down under her feet – encased in thick stable boots – and she crosses the yard with the barrow ready for Blackie's stable. She carries a bale and a half of clean straw from the hay and straw barn, wearing gloves because the baling string can hurt the palm of a hand, and cutting the strings with her stable scissors, scatters the clean straw over the bed, Tenacious looking on. She uses the pitchfork to pile the straw up high in banks, refills the hay net and water buckets, and puts Tenacious back in his stable. Always the same order, always the same actions, always the same time – twenty minutes per box.

Watching her and occasionally helping out, I noticed what an excellent weapon the shovel is. It is light, but has a broad flat blade, with a surprisingly narrow, almost sharp edge. The wooden handle is D-shaped, so you can put it down, pick it up and wield it easily. To kill Laura, I knew, would be very difficult if I began while she was fully conscious. She is taller than I am, and much stronger. She would need to be caught off guard, and it doesn't take a genius to work out that to start my attack while she was sleeping would provide all the elements of surprise Mummy once lectured me about. Felix in London and Paul in hospital – not that he would have presented much of an obstacle if he had been at the cottage – gave me plenty of opportunity.

Laura continued sweet and outwardly affectionate to me after Paul's fall, but I knew from the time of my showing her the pictures of Laura-Mummy, that she had ceased to feel genuine warmth for me. It was really a silly piece of showing off for me to show them the drawings, but I felt it futile to go to all the trouble of doing them only to have no one appreciate their artistry. I think Felix and Laura felt ashamed of how much they disliked me after that, and they tried hard to overcome their own feelings, which was useful to me because it made them confused and so easier to manipulate. It was the mucking-out shovel which gave me my first surprise weapon, and I practised swinging it for hours in the privacy of Blackie's stable, using his hay net as a target. I wanted to strike a glancing blow, just enough to immobilise her, perhaps make her unconscious, but not for very long. I wanted her to be able to see me and see what I was doing.

I chose Wednesday night. Wednesday is such a boring sort of day. I didn't wait very long after she had gone to bed, probably only until just before twelve. I didn't want to fall asleep myself, and had calculated that if I used my alarm clock to wake myself up at two or something, that the sound of it might just wake Laura below me, and my plan would fail. At nearly midnight on a country night, the sky is black, it's not like London with its pink sky and constant traffic and moving lights. To save having to get dressed in the dark I went to bed in my clothes, but barefoot. I had to pass Laura's room to go downstairs and across the yard to the hay store, which is an open half barn stone building, to fetch the shovel. I couldn't have taken it upstairs earlier and kept it in my room in case she noticed it was missing at evening feed or her final check on the horses before going to bed. So I had to sneak out of the back door and across the gravel of the yard with bare feet, waiting outside the back door for a while, looking up at the stars, to get my eyes accustomed to the night. Everything I did, no matter how hard I tried, seemed to make the most awful amount of noise. The horses heard me and Tenacious came to the front of his box, curious. By the time I got back into the house, locking the door behind me, I had to wait ten minutes in the kitchen so that if she'd stirred in her sleep she could settle down a bit. I wasn't nervous or afraid, I was only excited, but so excited I could hardly control my breathing, and my heart felt as if it was leaping about in my chest. Such a murder – and the idea of seeing Laura die – it made me want to cry I was so impatient, crouched by the Aga in the dark trying to take deep breaths.

Laura and Felix's bed is quite close to the door, behind it almost, so that it faces the window on the opposite side of the room with its lovely view. Felix sleeps on the side nearest the door, so I had to go into the room, slowly, slowly, and walk around the bed to Laura's side. I didn't look at Laura, but concentrated on dragging the shovel across the carpet so that it would make as little sound as possible. She slept on her side, turned towards me. The curtains were drawn, so there was only an ambient light from the landing to guide me. After a few minutes I could just tell that she was wearing a white cotton nightdress with short sleeves (useful for me) and a high-buttoned neck. She had left the top button undone. The bedside table with lamp stood between me and Laura's head, and I didn't want to move anything in case she woke up. I had to lift the shovel slowly into position, over my head and behind it, holding the handle with both hands, tilting it so that the side and not the flat of the shovel would hit her skull. I remember wishing it was not quite so dark. Counting three and taking a breath, I swung the shovel down, coming at her from the front rather than directly above her head, which would have been better. The shovel made the most delicious thud and when I moved it away I could feel her hair on the side of her head warm with blood. She had stirred, but only very slightly. I went to the window and opened the curtains. There was no chance of being seen because the window overlooks the garden and open fields beyond. There was only a little bit of a moon, but it didn't matter because I could turn on the bedside light and get a better look. It looked as though I had managed to cut into the side of her head about three inches across, the bleeding was not heavy, but the wound was messy and dark. It was wonderful. It was what I had hoped for.

I took two pillows from Felix's side of the bed and put them behind her, lifting her up by putting my hands under her armpits so that she was more upright in the bed, although her head lolled to one side and she looked like a drunk. I wasn't sure how long she would take to wake up, I didn't want to have to wait too long to start the second part of the plan. It was lovely though, looking at her bleeding. I sat on the window seat opposite the bed and watched her for what seemed like twenty minutes, but I think may have been as long as an hour. I got fidgety. She was breathing heavily, but was still insensible, so I remembered my mother's instructions about staying flexible and began to think of a remedy. Brandy. Brandy might bring her to her senses. I thought again and realised how silly I was being. She would wake up anyway when I started the next part of the plan because of the pain. I climbed onto the bed and sat beside her, laying the shovel down carefully where Felix sleeps, beside my right hand, in case I should need it again. Out came my trusty penknife from my pocket. I had been holding on to it so hard that it was a bit sweaty. I had sharpened it the day before on the old-fashioned knife sharpener Felix keeps in the larder drawer. Even so, the blade is small and the knife not really an ideal weapon. I wanted to use it, though, and not the Stanley knife I use for my artwork or a boring everyday knife from the kitchen. I wanted to use the knife that reminded me of being little and playing at the end of the garden at home. I started with her right wrist, first picking up her arm and holding her hand in my left hand, palm up, I dug the top of the knife deep into her wrist and then attempted to carve a substantial horizontal gash. I drew blood the first time, but the knife wasn't as sharp as it should have been. I had to saw it to and fro a bit before a satisfactory gash was achieved. The blood did not gush from the mouth of the wound as I had expected, but it bled all right. Laura groaned, an ugly guttural sound, and her eyelids fluttered. Still barely conscious, she drew her hand, masked in blood, out of my hand, and lifted it to her head, blood spotted her sheets and the front of her nightdress. Stirring again, she lifted her head back and opened her eyes properly. They rested on me, close to her, for a few seconds before she actually saw me.

'Andrew?' she whispered. 'My head hurts.' With her hand, wrist bleeding, she was feeling along the side of her head and amongst her hair for the wound. Finding it, she flinched, and moving her head awkwardly, began to notice the blood which was staining her sheets because it was beginning to run down her arm. She appeared half asleep and puzzled. 'Andrew, I'm hurt,' she said, letting her hand drop down, and then dropping her head to examine it. 'My wrist,' she said, looking up at me slowly. She was in pain.

'Yes,' I said firmly, taking hold of her other hand with my right hand and cutting it clumsily but hard with the knife held in my left.

She flinched, trying to draw her hand away from me, but I held on. I made another cut, just to make sure. She flinched again and I released her, getting off the bed and resuming my place on the window seat where I could see the whole picture. She was slumped, her head down again, although I think she was trying to raise it so she could look at me again. This took her some minutes. Her hair fell over her face but I could see her eyes, and she said, 'Help me.'

'No,' I said. I don't think she fully understood until that moment that I had hurt her and that I had hurt her on purpose, because I wanted to, and for no other reason.

She looked at me for a second longer and then closed her eyes, saying distinctly, 'Felix.' At this point I wasn't sure whether the loss of blood and the blow to the head would weaken her further, until she bled to death, which I understand can take over an hour, or if she would continue to regain consciousness and try to move or get out of bed. I wanted to watch her die, and enjoy it without fearing she might recover, so I decided to wait only a few more minutes and then if she spoke or moved again, I would strike another blow with the shovel. I had had the pleasure of seeing her understand that I had not come to rescue her, but was in fact the one who wanted to harm her. I had watched her look me in the eye and begin to know, and I could enjoy the remainder of her death without feeling it necessary for her to remain conscious. Her head was still lolling forward and to one side and I moved forward again to kneel beside her and get a better look. Her eyelids were drooping but still open, she looked drowsy.

'Can you hear me, Laura?' I asked her. I took hold of a bit of her hair and tugged it. Her eyes remained the same, half open, filmy. I could relax. There would be no struggle. I took up my place on the window seat once again and prepared to wait it out. I remember sitting back, feeling the cold window pane against the back of my head, moving it so that it rested against the wall, and I think after that I must have slept a little, fitful sleep. I felt an amazing sense of serenity, calm and dreaming and happiness. Each detail of the room was clear to me, the beamed ceiling, the armchair with Laura's teddy bear on it and the clothes she had worn that day, her row of wooden cupboards with their china handles, Felix's side of the bed still made, his bedside table empty, the lamp turned off, and Laura's lamp on, with a glass of water and her rings, a book (which I think was about garden design) and a daffodil in a vase. The bed was made up with sheets and blankets, covered with a quilted eiderdown and a white bedspread. The carpet was deep, soft, rose pink, and Laura herself, bathed in blood, staining her pillowcases and her sheets, was dying slowly in front of my eyes. It was so safe and warm, cosy and secure in that room with Laura dying.

When I woke it was to the sound of a deep voice, Felix's voice. He was shouting.

'Laura! Wake up. Do you hear me, Laura? God God God!' I saw Felix sitting on the side of the bed where I had sat, shaking Laura violently. I couldn't speak or move, I felt as lifeless as she was, and numb. He got to his feet, and turned towards me, seeming both to see me and not to see me, he rushed past me and I heard him thunder down the stairs to the hall and the phone. I heard him dialling and asking for police and ambulance. I had no idea what time it was. I felt extremely cold and powerless to move. I wanted to go over to Laura and see if she were still alive and if so, if there was anything I could do to hasten her death but I just remained slumped against the wall, feeling my breathing begin to speed up. Back into the room came Felix, ignoring me again, holding the brandy bottle, he poured out a capful and, lifting her head, began to pour it against her lips. He couldn't work out how to hold her head and her mouth open at the same time. He kept saying, 'Oh God, Laura,' over and over. She didn't stir. He took one of the pillowcases off a pillow and began to rip it roughly into strips, which he used to bind her wrists, the blood beginning to seep through the white cotton and on to his hands and clothes. 'Laura, don't leave me,' he said.

Presently, I could hear the sounds of engines and sirens, which came closer very fast, and I could hear the wheels on the drive. He had left the front door open and they shouted for him from the hall and he called, 'Upstairs!' in his deep hoarse voice. I felt dizzy as what seemed to be a horde of strangers erupted into the room. A man who ran to Laura almost pushing Felix out of the way, placed his ear against her chest.

'She's breathing,' he said, and Felix made a peculiar animal sound. The man lifted Laura in his arms and carried her out of the room, leaving Felix and two policemen who stopped him from running out of the room after her.

'Can you tell us what happened here, sir?' said one, in a voice that was so loud, so firm, so foreign to me that I wanted to cry.

'Take the child,' said Felix. 'Take the child out of here, out of my sight – now before I try to kill him.'

'Do you mean, sir, that the child – the child is responsible for this?'

'Yes. The child. The child is responsible,' I said, feeling an exhausted disappointment and nausea because I knew that she would live and I had failed. After that there was a strange slow-motion feeling as they all stood and looked at me, and I, leaning back on the window seat still, looked at them and tried to smile.

All this I write down for the police and call it my confession. It is to be given to them with my other writings and my mother's diary, which I kept in the new baby's room.

I sign this confession, Andrew Warren, and I date it again, April 24th.

Felix's Journal

April 30th

I write this as the last entry in my Journal, which I am to turn over to the police as evidence in the trial of my nephew, Andrew Warren. He is accused of the murders of his mother, Zoë Alexander, and his sister, Elizabeth Warren, and the attempted murders of his brother, Paul Warren, and his aunt, Laura Bracewell.

I do not know if this is what Zoë meant when she said that a mother knows.

Our dear Paul is recovered and will be returned to his father shortly. My wife Laura has survived the child's vicious attack and our baby, miraculously, still grows inside her. If it is a boy we will call him Michael, after his uncle, whose brave letter, opened late at night after a long day, sent me to Laura just in time.

If it is a girl we will call the baby Zoë.